# A Cowboy on the Beach?

He moved closer. His faded, well-worn jeans had been ironed but scuffed; his unpolished boots were in puzzling contrast to the expensive leather vest and large, silver belt buckle. His sandy hair, silky clean and touched with gold in the twilight, fell thick and straight to below his collar, contrasting with his sideburns which were flecked with gray.

She guessed his age at about thirty-five, although his face was smooth and unlined—lacking the rough texture of years in the sun and wind.

He hesitated. "I'm Cody. Cody Williams."

Nice name—it fits as well as his boots, she thought. "My name is Jill. Jill Kerry. Glad to know you, Cody."

# I CAN WAIT

**Patricia Linn**

TOWER BOOKS   NEW YORK CITY

A TOWER BOOK

Published by

Tower Publications, Inc.
Two Park Avenue
New York, N.Y. 10016

Copyright ©1980 by Tower Publications, Inc.

The computerized recording commanded, "Deposit one dollar and thirty-five cents, please, for the first three minutes." Jill fumbled with the coins then waited in the lonely phone booth through several long rings.

"Auntie Mil?" The telephone had an annoying buzz. "Can you hear me?"

"Jill!" The voice was husky with sleep. While she listened to the fumbling for a light, she pictured the dark bedroom in the big house next door. The house she'd deserted three years before.

"Jill, yes, I can hear. Where are you?"

"I'm in New Mexico. Sorry I woke you. I forgot it was one in the morning in Ohio. . . Just was lonesome to hear your voice."

"Oh, I'm so glad to hear yours too. . . Is everything all right?"

"Yes. Sure. I'm going to California tomorrow. May as well try to track down that last letter to Mara."

She regretted the words instantly. The mention of Mara always upset the older woman.

"Jill, come home. Please. Come back and make a life for yourself. Mrs. Nelson and I miss you."

The fear was evident in the older woman's plea and she was sorry now she'd made the call. The static began against as she rushed to get the conversation over with.

"I can't." Her throat tightened. "Have to follow through to the end. . . You know, I think I keep up this Mara hunt. . .not so much to find her. . .but because I'm a gypsy. Any of that blood in the family?" She tried to laugh. "Got to go, Auntie Mil. Glad to talk to you."

"Jill," her aunt was awake now, more persistent, "Jill, Mara's not worth it. Not worth wasting your life over. . .I've thought about it so much. She probably did love your father. But she was young. . .too young. . .couldn't stand the ugliness of his illness. . .or face the fact of his dying."

"I was young too!" The old defiance roared through her. "No, you're wrong. She didn't love any of us. I've found out so much from those letters. She planned it all long before she left. From the very beginning. She talked Daddy into signing that power of attorney. Hired the best lawyer in Chicago to convert those securities into cash." Her head began to throb as it always did when she thought of the immensity of her stepmother's deceit. She was anxious to end the converation.

"It was wonderful to hear your voice, Auntie Mil. Got to go now."

Her substitute mother gave up, defeated by too many years of wasted pleas. "I'm so glad you called. . .Jill, I love you. Be careful."

"I love you too," she said to the deserted parking lot. The line was already dead as she put the receiver back on the hook, cutting off her past. Hello. Goodbye. It was always the same, a hopeless reaching back to a nebulous and outgrown security.

Although the Santa Fe evening was still quite warm, Jill shivered, then put the conversation aside and concentrated on tomorrow. What would she find in California? More blind alleys like the last three years?

It was a typical early June beach day. By midafternoon the sun finally broke through the low clouds and fog to warm the sand and, in turn, the bikini-clad bodies sprinkled in confetti-like disarray on its surface. Since school was still in session, except for a few truant types bodysurfing in the chilly 63° water, the beach was populated mostly by young mothers with toddlers; the permanently unemployed; and Speedo-garbed "gays," sweating motionless beneath a layer of oil to achieve the golden tan so important to their cult. As Jill passed by, one thin young lad raised himself from the hot sand sauna. The eight knot breeze pushing onshore towards the thermal low of the inland desert, surprised him. "Oh my, Bobby," he exclaimed to his older, more muscular companion, "that damned wind is making goose pimples *all* over me!"

Jill hurried to free her feet from the confinement of their high leather boots as the sun dropped nearer the watery horizon. Housewives from the neighboring San Fernando Valley, tugged at cranky offspring and loaded picnic baskets into their cars. They had to hurry through the canyon if they were going to get a shower before their commuter weary husbands arrived home. Oblivious to their presence or absence, Jill rolled her jeans above her knees, burrowed aching insteps into the deeper layers of cool sand and lay back, waiting for the rhythmic surf sounds to numb her. Instead, her doubts increased as each high tide breaker curled and thudded against the silky sand bottom.

What if? . . .Come on, say it. What if this is another dead end. *The last dead end*. Auntie Mil said come home, give it up. Three years of planning. Three years of tracing one lead, then another. Maybe she's right. The hate gnaws less. Today's long freeway drive; with semi-trucks sucking the radio's music away in their passing thunder; the sinus inflaming smog blasting your face. Finally, the Santa Monica turnoff and the first glimpse of the Pacific Ocean. But the smell of sea air could mean failure, with no more excuse to run. And you've never prepared for that alternative.

*Come on. Conjure it up. Your security blanket of hate*. She shivered as on cue, the face of Mara, her absent antagonist, projected itself across the back of her closed eyelids. The smooth olive skin crinkled at each side of the dark brown eyes. A toss of head and the mane of black hair danced. Then the smile changed. The lips mocked, laughed at her.

Jill missed her first ocean sunset. That last moment when the earth's heat source changes from the familiar sphere to a shimmering hourglass, then sinks into the farthest swell. She floated in half sleep, fevered probably. Why else would Mrs. Nelson be bathing her face with a warm washcloth? When the washing became uncomfortably persistant, she opened her eyes. A large German Shephard replaced the kindly housekeeper of her dream. His rough tongue attempted to wash away the tension and exhaustion of the day.

A voice behind her said, "Oh, I'm sorry, ma'am."

She reached instinctively for her purse. It contained little money but held a packet of letters Mara had forgotten in her haste to leave. Jill lifted the large canvas bag onto her lap and looked up.

From sand level the long lean jeans and western boots gave the impression of a tall man. But with the short torso, she reasoned, he was probably only a few inches taller than her own 5'6". He had stopped, mistaking her protectiveness for fear.

He threw up his hands in a gesture of mock surrender and backed away a few steps. "Don't worry, ma'am. I was just down givin' ol' Dude here a romp on the beach. We do this most every night." *Texas? Louisiana?* She decided the accent was probably Texan.

He moved closer. A cowboy strolling the beach? And a cowboy with inconsistancy, she thought. His faded, well-worn jeans had been ironed but

9

scuffed, unpolished boots were in puzzling contrast to the expensive leather vest and large, silver belt buckle. His sandy hair, silky clean and touched with gold in the twilight, fell thick and straight to below his collar, contrasting with slightly darker sideburns which were flecked with grey. She guessed his age at about thirty-five, although his face was smooth and unlined—lacking the rough texture of years in the sun and wind.

She rubbed the dog's ears, and asked, "Where did you get a name like Dude anyway?"

The cowboy answered for his canine.

"Oh, I was up in Jackson a few years back, punchin' dudes on a friend's ranch. . . .you know, takin' city folks on trail rides and like that. . .This one guest went back to Chicago and had a puppy sent out to me. Air express, yet. So I just had to name him Dude." At the mention of his name, the big dog loped back to his master's side.

"I'll bet that Chicago dude was a pretty lady."

The pale blue eyes had been wary, windows with the shades drawn. He laughed now, allowing a glimpse inside. "Well, she wasn't pretty. . .and she sure as Hell wasn't no lady. But I guess you could say she was female." He sobered again. "Anyway, that's how Dude got his name." He hesitated, "and I'm Cody. Cody Williams."

*Nice name. It fits as well as his boots.*

He stood with thumbs in pockets, waiting.

"I'm sorry. Not quite awake yet, I guess. My name is Jill. Jill Kerry. (She'd dropped the Schneider name when she'd left home) Glad to know you, Code. And you, Dude." The dog raced

10

to her side and sat down, scooting his rear close to her. He reminded her of a fat lady forcing her share of a bus stop bench. As she looked up and laughed, it came. The now familiar electric shock always began at the back of her neck and traveled with alarming speed through her skull, ending with a searing blast at her temple. It ripped her equilibrium like the first jolt of an earthquake. The horizon and the cowboy's face blurred together. Beads of sweat popped out on her upper lip while her heart race to recover the strength that drained out into the sand.

These assaults began shortly after Mara left. They hit her unexpectedly but always with the same frightening force. She'd kept them a secret, as if they were a punishment she was committed to bear alone. This like all the others left her limp and shaking. It must have been the straight through drive from Albuquerque without eating, she reasoned. Plus the smog. She lay back. The blur leaned over and a hand shoved the dog's wet tongue away, felt her forehead.

"Hey, what's the matter? You're so white! Are you all right?"

*Don't faint. Breathe deeply.*

"Listen, I better get you home. Where do you live? Close around here?"

A voice, strangely removed from her body, answered, "I don't live anywhere."

". .get you on your feet. . .damn pushers. . ."

Hands under her arms lifted but she sagged back, surprised at the laser light show going off in her head.

11

"Got to walk, move. . .come, on try." He dragged her across the sand, then back and forth across the blacktop parking lot.

"Stop!" She couldn't decide if she'd spoken the command or just thought it.

"It's OK, girl. I know all about drugs." he said as he continued to move her. "Don't freak out. It's gonna be okay. . . . .I'll take care of you."

He lifted her, then, into the front seat of a pickup truck. Breathe, she told herself. Stay awake.

The crazy man shoved her overboard in Antarctica, maybe, or under a Yosemite water fall. Her jeans and shirt were an icy shroud.

Finally, the last freezing water trickled between her toes and down the drain in the bathtub. Her last drop of strength followed. Goodnight, sleep tight don't let the. . . .Daddy, I loved you.


Love is warm! A down comforter and clean sheets. She closed her eyes to the burst of light as a door opened, then burrowed deeper, content to float in the security of duck fuzz.

He lifted her, propped the pillow, propped her on the pillow, tucked the blanket around her bare shoulders.

"Come on now. Don't go out on me again." A hot mug touched her lips. Gentle man, her foggy mind stated. Crazy, gentle man. What a combination! "You got to drink this soup. It's only instant but it will put some strength back in you." Chicken broth. Jewish penicilin they call it. Is he Jewish?

Her thoughts hopped about without logic or reason. Cody Williams. No! Jews don't live in Texas. The soup went down and stayed.

"Man. . .Woman, you had me scared."

He let her lie back again. His fingers were rough on her forehead. *Crazy, rough, gentle hands.* Then he left her again as quickly as he'd come.

In the comfort of warm darkness, she resented her brain's insistence that she review once again her reason for being in California.


She'd wanted to hate Mara. She didn't need a mother to replace the one who had died giving her birth. But if there was to be one, she had always hoped it would be Auntie Mil. Why hadn't her father married *her*, the girl next door, instead of an eccentric girl from California, just ten years older than his daughter.

But Jill hadn't hated Mara, hard as she'd tried.

Her 12-year old mind was ready and receptive to the electric character who breezed into their dull midwestern lives and gobbled them all up with her enthusiasm. Even Mrs. Nelson, their somber housekeeper, was enchanted with Mara's herb teas and disorganized cooking sprees in her spotless kitchen. And Jill's father was intrigued with his wife's surprise picnic lunches at his office, her uninhibited displays of affection.

Jill fell faster and deeper than the rest of them into Mara's pool of warmth—from the first night the taxi stopped in the driveway and her new step-mother blew in the door on the cold night air. She hated the hours she was forced to spend in school, away from the flashy clothes, conversation, and dark eyes. She rushed home each day to the ceramics studio her father had built for his new bride, anxious to share precious hours with the female who had become her best friend.

That's what Mara had said one day. *My best friend*. She had stopped in the middle of throwing a pot, grabbed Jill and held her close. Close enough to smell the Musk she always wore. "I'm so lucky, Jill. I feel like a princess living in a castle. . .and in of all places. . .Columbus, Ohio!"

"Oh, come on, Mara," she had answered, embarrassed, "this isn't a castle."

Jill knew they weren't poor, the other kids at school told her often enough, but she never thought of her family in the royal catagory or the mansion on the Scioto river as anything but home. Her father always reminded her that her great grandfather had just been a smart and lucky farmer. He had turned several of his farm machinery experiments into patented inventions that escalated the Schneider Implement Company into the chief competitor of John Deere. But they lived simply in the large rambling house that Mara was calling a castle. She went to public school in town, like her father had done, and their only help was Mrs. Nelson. . .and she was practically family.

Mara hugged her again. "I'm especially lucky since my Prince Charming's daughter also turns out to be my best friend." Mara had wrapped a wet towel around the clay then and said, "Come on, let's take walk down to the river."

14

The path along the slow moving water was one of their favorite spots. Here Mara, often forced into a false maturity by the presence of her husband, could revert to her childhood. They would wrestle in the tall grass, tickling each other and laughing, until both fell back breathless and panting. Mara made her aware of so much she'd taken for granted—the vivid green of an Ohio summer, the maple tree's cool deep shade, the perfection of the peonies blooming in the garden.

"Nothing like them in California," she'd said.

"Daddy said the bushes are very old. My grandma planted them when she was a young bride."

The river helped Jill's words flow. She told Mara of her embarrassment at being a head taller than the boys in dancing class.

"Kiddo, you're a gangly colt now—but with that gorgeous auburn hair—you're going to turn into the most beautiful filly anyone has ever seen. . . then watch out. . .the stallions will be snorting and stomping to get at you."

It was two years later when she confessed that Chuck, her first boyfriend, had put his hand on her sweater and she hadn't stopped him—had liked it.

Mara had gathered her into her arms and said quietly, "Jill, for God's sake, don't ever be ashamed of those feelings. Touching and caressing are part of loving. And love is everything."

*Love is everything.* Jill carried the three perfect words wherever she went. They starred in her day-

15

dreams at school; enhanced her bedtime fantasies. *Love is everything*.


"My bag, my purse." Jill sat up, frantic. "Where is it?" The overhead light blinded her with its cold brightness. His face was different now, not gentle at all, and harsh words replaced the soft drawl. They fought through lips and jaw clenched in disapproval.

"I have it, I got your bag. But you're not going to get it. Not until you leave here. If you want to kill yourself on dope you do it someplace else. Not here." He flicked the switch and slammed out the door.

Why did he make her feel guilty? She never even took an aspirin. She had ignored the drug cult at school. Wouldn't submit to their urging to try marijuana—grass as they called it—refused the red and yellow pills. Yet she felt guilty now. Like the time her father thought she broke his stopwatch. "Just admit it, Jill," he said, "I know you like to play with it. Just don't lie to me." The accused innocent. She had refused and was punished. For the lie, not the broken spring.

This man, Code, in the doorway again with the light off, his voice still flat and angry. *Just admit it, Jill*.

"I gotta' go to work now. You can stay or go. If you want your belongings though you'll have to come back in the mornin'. I'm not giving you anything to get you in more trouble. . .not in my house. Your clothes are still wet, hanging in the bathroom," he finished as he started out of the room again.

"Codey?" He stopped, didn't answer. *Forget explaining*. You're guilty until proven innocent. Just like in Mexico. "Cody. . .Thank you."

She thought she heard a "Yes, ma'am" as the door slammed again.

She lay stiff, held her breath, listening as her pulse pounded in her ears, blotting out sounds from the other side of the door. Then she eased out of bed and opened the door a crack. No doubt about being alone. She could see Cody's total living area: hall, bath to left, kitchen, dinette, living room. It unfolded before her, maybe thirty feet total. She was in a house trailer. A neat, clean, *small* trailer!

She stepped in the bathroom. Her wet jeans, shirt, and undies hung neatly next to his wet jeans, shirt, undies on the shower rod; a mute evidence that the doctor had received the same icy therapy as his patient. She studied her reflection, surprised that her New Mexico tan had assumed the color of California smog, and in just a few hours. The yellow tinge accentuated the sprinkle of freckles and added a sudden, and she hoped, temporary age to her twenty-one years. She picked up a comb from the counter and tried to unsnarl her hair. Still damp, it clung to her neck and back, gave her a chill. Weak still, sh held onto the wall and went back to the bedroom for a blanket. Wrapped Indian style, she felt better. But starving.

Snooping in someone else's refrigerator was like eavesdropping on privy information. She

17

discovered the owner was compulsively neat. All the Coors labels were lined up. No dried up cheese or worn out leftovers. No crumbs or drips. A quart of milk, a tub of butter, bacon and eggs stood neatly in the sparkling porcelain. No cooking tonight, she decided. She found a box of crackers and a jar of peanut butter in the cupboard above, and with Dude oblivious to her companionship, she eased into the vacant chair opposite him and devoured most of both. *Convicted. Death row. What would you like for your last supper? Steak? Chocolate ice cream? No thank you. Ritz and Skippy, please.* As they dropped the black hood over her eyes she would shout, I'm innocent! I didn't break the watch *or* take drugs. *Just tell the truth and you can go free*, the executioners said.

"Forget it, Jill. Guilty, innocent. Nobody really cares." Dude raised his head and looked at her from droopy eyelids. "Sorry Boy. Go back to sleep. Just a bad habit I have from being alone so much. Talking to myself so others can hear." She stood then and crossed the tiny room. The opposite wall was covered with photographs, mostly unframed, just snapshots. In one she recognized Cody standing in the midst of a group of leather-faced men in wide-brimmed, black hats. They were laughing together at a private joke. Probably taken by one of the dudes on the ranch in Jackson. There was a snapshot of a blonde on horseback. She had her head thrown back with the practiced style of a beautiful woman who knows her best camera angles. He lied, Jill thought. She's very pretty. The next was of Cody the way he

18

looked this afternoon. His arm was around a different blonde and the way he held her left no doubt about his feelings. She moved closer to get a better look at the girl. Tiny. Size six, maybe. She smiled at the camera but her eyes seemed vacant, as if she were daydreaming. Jill resented her. So nonchalant with him.

Watch it, she told herself. "Don't get involved." Dude ignored her conversation this time.

Jill curled up in the chair. The soft light from the lamp in the corner warmed the wood paneling, making the room cozy. It reminded her of her bedroom at home—and the candle.


Mara had come home with the white box soon after their talk. "For you," she'd said and plopped it in her lap.

"But it's not my birthday or anything?"

"Open it, Kiddo."

The tape peeled easily and when she lifted the lid, the rustle of white tissue excited her. The pale blue wax glistened as she ran her finger over the smooth surface, tracing the design. It was like reading braille. The four letter, thick cutouts, their wicks unused, spelled L-O-V-E.

The lump in her throat hurt as she forced her voice to remain normal, "I'll never burn it."

Mara had laughed.

Jill set the candle at the back of her desk next to the velvet pincushion Auntie Mil had brought her from Europe. She washed it carefully in warm water when dust settled on the tops of the letters. It started her playing the word game like the cartoon in the paper. Love is. Love is: Daddy, Auntie Mil, Mrs. Nelson, Mara, maybe Chuck. Love is talking under the maple trees, making a perfect pot, winning a sailboat race, Mrs. Nelson's fudge.

Then she experiemented, changed the main character. To Mara love is: listening when Auntie Mil talks about work, praising Mrs. Nelson's peach preserves, taking Jill to get her ears pierced.

When her father first got sick and was home in bed Mara's game changed to love is: horehound drops from the health food store, poetry readings, gentleness, encouragement, hope.

As months went by, the game went on. Love is: long hours at the hospital, reading a husband's favorite book aloud, massaging dry loose skin. Saying bald is beautiful.

Jill shivered, tired of the game but unable to stop. Love wasn't roaming the house like an approaching storm cloud, refusing to walk by the river, chilly silence—leaving and never coming back. Or the cruel backhand scrawl on a piece of typing paper, "Sorry, Kiddo. I just can't handle it."

Thanks to morphine her father never knew. His drugsoaked brain OD'd on a phony "Love is" high.

But Jill's healty grey matter hadn't been so lucky. It had reasoned first. Emotional shock. Mara will be back. She loves me. Then it sorrowed. Rose Bowl day, wading in the knee-deep snow. A rectangular cavern in the frozen earth that told her she was an orphan. It hated when it heard, "He signed a power of attorney over to Mara six months ago. She methodically disposed of stocks and securities, has a nice chunk of cash." And later ignored. "Don't worry, Jill. There is plenty of money left, to keep the house, and you for the rest of your life."

Finally, *it threatened*.

I'll find you, Mara.

And I'll force you to look me in the eye.

And tell me how "Love is everything."

Auntie Mil had asked her often, the same question she asked herself. Why? Why toss your life away chasing after that worthless bitch? What will it possibly accomplish, even if you find her?

She had never been able to give a satisfactory answer. She only knew that Mara's leaving had erected a barricade between herself and the rest of the world. She wouldn't allow herself the pleasure of an emotional involvement if it meant facing the scalpel later, and suffering the long recuperation from the gaping wound of disappointment. But perhaps if she could see Mara again, prove to herself that Mara was not worth the pain, then the devil of Mara would be exorcised once and for all. At least the chase gave her excuse to keep moving.

As her eyelids closed, Jill wondered if the candle and pincushion were still on the desk. Her trophies on the shelf above. Or if, like her father's room, they had hurried to clear out any evidence that she'd ever been. Jill is gone. Call the Salvation Army. Get rid of Jill.

No, Jill is alive and well and living. . .in a house trailer. She smiled at her own joke.

21

The pain grumbled down her neck and jarred her awake. Cody must have put a pillow under her head and added the quilt when he came home. The trailer was silent as she tiptoed through the kitchen and into the tiny hall. Dude was stretched out on the floor at the foot of the bed. He thumped his tail in greeting when he saw her.

"Shh," she commanded. "Don't wake your master."

Cody sat up, smoothed back his hair. "It's all right. I'm awake." She found herself admiring the bare, broad chest and shoulders. *Stop it. Jill. If you like him, leave him alone, for God's sake.*

He picked up an alarm clock from the small table beside the bed and turned it towards himself, without looking at her. "Nine o'clock already. Time to be up. You get first shot at the bathroom. Your clothes should be dry by now. There's a new toothbrush on the bottom shelf in the medicine cabinet. . . .Always keep one handy for unexpected guests."

The events of the day before still had her puzzled and unsure of herself.

She left without a word, followed his instructions to dress and brush her teeth. She borrowed his hairbrush and smoothed the rumpled clothes from the shower rod. When she came out of the bathroom, he was in the kitchen putting bread in the toaster. Coffee perked on the stove. He turned off the flame and poured two mugs, again without looking up.

22

"Cody?" She wants to explain about yesterday. *Innocent. Innocent.*

He turned, and in the small kitchen they were no more than a foot apart. She could feel his breath. He stepped back so she could pass, his eyes still a blank and the jaw tight and somber.

"Grab a cup of coffee and sit down at the table. Toast will be ready in a minute." He made every effort to avoid her eyes.

She sipped her coffee and stared at him while he concentrated on the butter and toast.

"I don't smoke." she began. "I drink very little. I've never shoplifted. Or snatched old ladies' purses. . . .And I *do not* take drugs."

She could see the doubt and wanted to tell him about "it," the pain. How it happened more often now, how it planted a nameless fear that lingered long after her strength returned. But she couldn't. She'd never told anyone, so she continued before he could respond. "I don't know what happened yesterday. I've never fainted in my life. But I had driven straight through from New Mexico. Hadn't eaten all day. I guess the heat on the beach, or the smog. . . .was too much for me."

He set the plate of toast and a jar of jelly on the table and leaned back in the chair opposite her. A slight twitch started in his right cheek and his voice was flat still, "Gal. . .I don't care what you do. . . or don't do. I just know dopers. They're all alike. They'll tell you anything." He raised his eyes to meet hers then and the cold blue continued to stare a steady accusation.

She slammed her cup on the table. The hot liquid

ran into her lap. She wiped at it with her arm while a lump began to form in her throat. How dare he? The anger at his mistake and the desire to make him believe her sent the blood rushing to her face. She willed the tears to stay in place and not dampen her already faltering dignity.

"If you don't believe me, go get my bag. Wherever you've hidden it. . . .Search it. . .You won't find anything."

The frost melted some as he studied the red blotchy cheeks.

His hand slid towards her, then retreated, as the drawl softened, "I wouldn't stoop to searchin' no one's belongings. And I'll get them for you anytime you want. . . . I believe you. Awright?. . . I believe you. Now tell me about a girl who says she don't live nowhere."

Jill wasn't fooled by his misuse of the English language. He was no dumb hillbilly. She'd met numerous people, some college graduates, who hung on proudly to their colloguial style of speech. They didn't feel like Texans, or West Virginians, or whatever, without it. Forgive me, Daddy. I remember your love for words, emphasis on correct grammar. But I find it charming.

He wanted to know who she was.

"Just a girl with gypsy blood, I guess. Been traveling three years now. I find a job and stay awhile, then move on. Have a change of clothes and an old Pinto I live in."

"You live in?"

"Yes. . . . .if it's still parked at the beach where I left it yesterday—before I was kidnaped and put

24

through an ice water torture."

They laughed then, together for the first time and she watched his features relax, the eyes drop their protective mask. Love is laughing together, she thought, then, God! you are impossible, Jill.

"It's a wonder I didn't kill you," he said and the warning flag dropped in her head again.


Jill concentrated on the widening puddle of coffee on the formica table top. Don't listen to your quickened pulse, feel the tightness in the center of your chest, the weakness in the palms of your hands. Love isn't laughing together, stupid. Love is death. Love is lonely. Love is pain.

The trailer door wrenched open with a jerk and she reacted to the interruption, but not before an involuntary instant of desire sparked the gap of the tiny dinette. It flickered and was gone as a minia- ture Paul Bunyan strode up the steps and into the room.

"Mornin'." The no more than five foot two frame stopped. Fists clenched and unclenched, flexed and unflexed the bulging biceps. The young man glowered at her through a thick black beard while a tiny gold earring winked from his left ear. She tried to smile as he fixed her with a ferocious stare.

Cody broke the silence. "Mornin', B.J. Look here at what the cat drug in. This is Jill. She had a problem at the beach yesterday and I gave her a place to sleep. . . .Jill, this is Billy Joe Miller."

Ignoring the introduction, the intruder threw

himself into the chair that had been her bed and sulked. When he finally spoke, the deliberate sharpness was obvious. "Come on, let's go, Cody. We got important business today, you know."

Cody stood up, his jaws tight. "Look buddy, I just introduced you to a lady. Where are your manners?"

The sour man spit out a "Hymph," and picked up a record album from the stack beside the chair, studied the cover.

She stood up. "Cody, if you'll just give me my bag now, I'll be on my way. Thanks for everything." She held out her hand to offer as dignified a handshake as she could manage with the surly man looking on. Then she remembered, "Oh, how do I find my car?"

The man in the chair slapped his forehead with the palm of his hand and exploded with a loud, "Oh, brother!"

Cody's chest seemed about to burst the seams of his shirt as he took a step forward and glared down at the lounging figure. "Billy Joe, you may be my best friend. . . .but sometimes I would love to whop you. It ain't what you think. This is a nice girl." His next words were a measured hiss. "Now, apologize."

Billy Joe looked up at her and mumbled an unconvincing, "Sorry, ma'am."

Cody started for the door. "I'm going to take Jill to her car. You wait. I'll be right back." He held the door open and she exited without a word of farewell. Billy Joe's parting look made her feel guilty again and unclean.

She stopped on the step, astounded by what she saw. The trailer was parked in a narrow driveway between two old garages. But had she opened the drape between the two chairs last night, she would have been treated to an panoramic view of the Pacific Ocean. Old beachhouses clung haphazardly to the cliffs and a wooden stairway made a meandering descent between them to the parking lot and beach below. Surfers, black specks in their wet suits, rested on their boards in the calm water, waiting for the next usable wave.

Cody spoke rapidly, perhaps to overcome the embarrassment of the scene inside. ". . .lot belongs to my friend. . .park here whenever I'm in town. . .just pull out and head north when I want to. . ."

Jill wasn't listening. She stared to the right. Was this her link to Mara? "Is that called Santa Monica Pier?"

He stopped his explanation, confused by the interruption. "Why yes, sure pretty view isn't it?"

Her heart increased its temp. "It certainly is. The most beautiful view I have ever seen."

"Come on. Hop in the pickup and I'll take you to your car. It's just about a mile down the beach."

She sat silent and impatient as they backed out and started down Ocean Avenue past the slightly run down motels, corner groceries and bars. Cody turned right one block and into a parking lot.

"There it is over there, the red Pinto." she said. She was so anxious now she opened the door and jumped out before the truck came to a complete stop. Then realizing she owed Cody a little more

27

than that, she turned to thank him, but he was already opening his door to get out too.

"That's a mighty nice car for its age. But what did you mean, you live in it?"

I've waited a long time, she thought, what's a few more minutes. With a sigh she started her explanation.

"I converted my car to a camper." She unlocked the passenger door. "You see, I removed the seat on this side and built a storage chest in its place." She showed Cody the two drawers and the plywood top that opened into a 3-foot storage space. "That's for my cooking utensils and other junk, the drawers are for my camera, books, radio. I have an ice chest, portable stove, and a bag of clothes over there behind the driver's seat, and" she climbed in, "this is where I sleep." The plywood met the back deck to form a full length bed. "I just unroll my sleeping bag and it's home," she continued as she sprawled out in the car.

She remembered the same explanation to Auntie Mil. The day after graduation she had cashed her monthly trust fund check—she was eighteen and no longer under the control of her trustee at the bank—bought camping gear and kissed them all goodbye. Mrs. Nelson had fled to the house in tears and for the first time, she gave Auntie Mil a clue to her real intentions. That she was not on an aimless ramble around the country.

Cody's voice jolted her back to the present.

"Clever girl, you are." He shuffled his feet, stared at the ground. Then in a rush he said, "You can stay with me for awhile until you get organized

28

if you want."

She forgot Mara and the pier for an instant, letting the warmth sweep through her unchecked. Why not succumb to the law of nature? Pair up. Male and female. He and she.

Cody misunderstood her hesitation. "I don't mean anything like you're thinking. But that chair you were huddled up in last night opens into a bed and you're welcome to use it. A lot safer than sleeping in a car. Around here anyway."

Jill remembered some of the scares she'd had. The gang of kids in Oklahoma. Sitting all over her car. The promises of what they would like to do if she'd just unlock the doors. And there was the car that followd her down the deserted road in Missouri. Yes, she would like a safe place to sleep.

She felt her breath quicken as a greater fear took over. The fear of risk. Risk of future pain. "I don't think so, Cody," she answered.

The curtain dropped once again behind the blue eyes. He stepped up into the pickup, slammed the door and started the motor. "Well, as they say back home . . . write if you find work." Then he was gone. She watched the red truck disappear around the corner, aware of a disturbing emptiness. She unlocked the other door, sat down on the seat and took the letter out of her pack.

The envelope was soiled now from so much handling but she knew every mark and word. It was one of six letters she found in Mara's room after she disappeared. This was the last. All the others had led to dead ends. The postmark date was August 12, 1970—the year after Mara married her father. Santa Monica, CA 90401. The envelope was addressed to Mara Smith and had been sent to a post office box in Columbus.

Her hands shook as she opened the single sheet of paper. The handwriting was childlike, part printing, part script, but the words were those of a man. It began,

"Hi lover,

So you went and did it! Found yourself an old dude with a lot of bread."

Anger boiled in her to think of her father as the "old dude", remembering Cody's distainful use of the word yesterday. The letter continued,

"You know you really fucked up. With my new connections it wouldn't have been long before I could have built you a castle too. And not in hicksville. How about the end of the pier? Ha, ha.

"If you ever get tired of the Geritol set, I'm here.

J.D."

She looked up as a small boy ran across the sand in front of her, sending hundreds of resting seagulls into slow circling flight above her head. Her thoughts swirled with them. Far down the beach to her right was the pier she'd missed seeing yesterday. Did the mysterious J.D. work there? What were his new connections? Did Mara accept his offer to come back?

She pulled her canvas bag from the back seat and walked across the parking lot to the public restrooms. The concrete floor was still wet and sandy from yesterday's bathers. She quickly changed from the rumpled clothes and boots. The metal mirror on the wall distorted her clean skirt and sandals but assured her she was beachy enough now not to attract attention.

The man startled her as she came out the door. He walked slowly towards her, grey pants and brown tweed sportcoat, limp and too large for his thin frame. A pair of pointed-toed shoes protruded from the top of his suitcase, a brown paper bag. Folds of skin hung like two deflated balloons under his eyes.

"Have a dime, pretty lady?" The question expected a negative response but she stopped, fumbled through her change purse, handed him a quarter. "Thank ya'." He shuffled on. No joy. Just survival. She felt guilty for a moment to have encouraged the alcoholic weakness with her money. Our choice for survival is very individual, she thought. His is alcohol. What is yours? Hate?

She drove back the way she'd come with Cody and parked in the lot below the pier. A steep stairway led from the sand to the carnival atmosphere of the pier itself. Carousel music thumped from the merry-go-round to her left and the early patrons, mostly small children, circled before her, waving excitedly at their waiting mothers. She walked along, suddenly unsure she would be able to find a J.D. in the jumble of snack shops, penny arcades, fish restaurants, and bait stores. The right side of the pier was lined with fishermen, mostly young boys and old men, gathered in small groups, more interested in their conversations than the idle rods leaning against the railing. Three Mexican teenagers, lounging against a storefront, nudged each other and grinned as she passed by. Whistles and several, "EE-ee's," followed her steps along the old rough boards. Germaine, the fortune teller, had a large closed sign in her window. No palm reading to help find Mara. Not today.

She continued out the end, stopped to look at the weather station on the Coast Guard building. Temperature, 68°; wind velocity, 4 knots. Perfect conditions for catching a thief. Buoyed by the thought, she followed a weathered sign down a stairway to a lower level restaurant. Maybe the waitress would have raven hair and serve herb tea.

The smell of grease battered at her shaky stomach when she walked through the cafe door and slid onto an empty stool at the long counter. The other customers were fishing types not so much interested in nourishment as diversion from the boredom of limp monofiliment.

"Hi, Sweetie! What'll you have? We got the best scrambled eggs and home fries this side of Tonapaw." The woman was fat and friendly. Her weighty jowls refused to compete with the upturned mouth and hearty laugh, the large bosum threatened to pop the middle button on her flowered shirt, and the bleached hair had won the battle long ago against comb or brush. It bristled on top and frizzed back from each ear like two batches of cotton candy.

"Just black coffee, please."

"Honey . . . . you ain't never gonna get strong and healthy like ol' Irma," the gregarious woman pointed to her own chest, "if you don't eat. Ain't

32

no vitamins (she said it with a short 'i' like in bit) in java."

Jill gave in. "Well, if you insist, I'll have two poached eggs on toast."

"That's more like it, gal." *Cody had called her that. Gal.* Irma turned and shouted the order to a thin man in the soiled chef's hat who stood at the grill not more than two feet behind her.

The man next to Jill laughed. "You're in rare form this morning, Irma," he said.

"Fine as the hair on a frog, Ernie. Fine as the hair on a frog."

The eggs were perfect and Jill finished everything on the plate, including the famous home fries, while she listened to the jolly woman banter with everyone up and down the counter. She came to take the empty plate away and refill her coffee cup.

"Haven't seen you around here before, have I? Been here thirty years and always remember every face."

"No, I just arrived in California yesterday. Thought I might find a job on the pier somewhere."

"What can you do?"

"Well, I've clerked, waitressed . . ."

"Can you cook?"

Jill glanced at the small man's back, wondering if she was being offered his position. Irma caught her expression and slapped her thighs. "Oh no. Oh, no," she roared. "I'm not givin' you Hugo's job. He's my ol' man. Me and him been together too long." She threw a massive arm around the small man's shoulders and planted a sloppy kiss on the back of his neck. He turned and smiled up at her. Women push themselves through beauty shops and fat farms, Jill thought, spend thousands to be curled, manicured, dieted, exercised and massaged to perfection—and they never get one look from their "ol' man" like that.

Irma turned her attention back to Jill, "Well, can you cook? Do you like boats?"

Mrs. Nelson had thought it was very important for a young lady to acquire "the homemaking skills" as she called it, and had taught her to make everything from bread to Hollandaise; and she *had* sailed her little boat every summer.

"Yes, to both," she answered.

"Hey, Rick." Jill jumped, startled again by the woman's incredible volume. "Come on down here."

She hadn't noticed the man at the far end of the counter and now wondered why. As he slowly turned and got up from his stool, she thought, this is what they mean when they say "California beach boy." Gold from the top of the sunsteaked head of hair, through the six feet of even tan, and the bleached fuzz that covered his legs to the bare feet. He smiled, exposing a dentist's dream.

Irma asked, "What's your name, gal?" then made the introductions.

"Rick, this gal needs a job. How about on the *Sea Maiden*?"

"We'll see, Irma."

The older woman shrugged and walked back to the sink as he slid onto the stool next to her, fingering a napkin before speaking.

"OK, here's what the job is that she's talking about. We run the sport fishing boats from the pier here. We use a half-day boat year 'round. But in the summer, we bring *Sea Maiden* down from Ventura and run her on all day trips too. We need a cook. The food is simple. Ham and egg sandwiches in the morning, then hamburgers from noon on. That's all besides coffee, pop, and beer. But it gets kind of hectic 'cause all the sixty passengers seem to get hungry at the same time. We have a kid that helps out taking the orders and collecting the money . . . And of course, the galley is pretty primitive. Probably not what you're used to."

Jill started to respond but he continued without a stop:

"Then also you have to be on board by 5:00 every morning to get the food ready and when the boat gets back at 4:30 there is still cleaning up to do. So it's a long day. And six days a week. We don't go out on Mondays. The pay is $4.00 an hour." He finally paused. "That is, if you work out."

This was no emptyheaded beach boy. "Could I see the boat and galley before I decide?"

"Sure, come on." He stood up and started for the door with her hurrying to keep up.

*Sea Maiden* strained at her heavy mooring lines in the surge at the dock.

"She's old, forty in fact, but she's sound." he said without looking back. "I replanked her myself this winter. And we put in a new diesel so she's really seaworthy now. We usually go out to the

35

12-mile bank and most of the time it's pretty smooth. But once in a while we get more wind than we bargained for. The *Maiden* here can take it and get us back without a lot of green faces hanging over the rail. Do you ever get seasick?"

Since she had never been on the ocean she didn't know. But she was sure she wanted the job. "No, I never have." An honest answer.

He didn't offer to help her aboard. A hired hand shouldn't expect any courtesies. She stepped onto a smooth, clean teak deck; the rails and cabin glistened with a coat of fresh white paint. A mass of fishing rods were stacked against the back rail, waiting for their eager angling partners. Inside, three booths lined the salon on the port side, the galley was opposite. It was simply a small version of a lunch counter.

He ordered her to come behind the counter as he pointed out the equipped. ". . . have 110 so we use electric griddle, to make toast and warm the buns . . . . fry ham in one skillet here on the hotplate, eggs in the other. Hamburgers in both. This is the beer and pop cooler but Jody, your helper, takes care of that . . . . that is, if you want the job?"

Perfect, she thought. A way to meet people on the pier. Ask questions. Find J.D. Then Mara . . . Be honest, Jill, this also looks exciting and fun. "I'll take it. I know I can do it."

"Good enough," he answered, again without expression. "Start Tuesday. Better get here a little early the first day so we can show you everything. Meet you at Irma's." He turned to leave. "Got to

36

get busy now. Have a bottom to do this morning."

"A bottom?"

"Yea. I run the yard out there on the end of the pier too? We haul boats out with that big hoist, give their undersides a new coat of antifouling paint. Also run the bait boat. Go out and get our anchovies at 4:00 every morning." He stopped, suddenly angry. "That is, we try. If they don't control those bastard commercial boats though, it won't be long before we don't have any anchovies . . . or any fish . . . in this whole damned area. Sometimes now we have to use frozen squid." He was gone.

She stood alone on the boat, listening to the pleasant squeak of the rubber protective bumpers between the hull and the pier. Her new employer was all business. No nonsense. He wouldn't have noticed if she had had two heads. Just needs a cook.

Jill walked slowly back the length of the pier, glancing into the stores and restaurants. Lots of black-haired girls but no Mara.

The first priority on her list was a good supply of seasick pills and as she drove out of the parking lot she was relieved to see the sign, NO PARKING BETWEEN 2 AND 6 AM. The people wandering around the area had made her uneasy about staying here in her car. She remembered Cody's warning. And his invitation. *Relax. Decide later.* After a stop at a pharmacy, she spent two hours running her meager wardrobe through the washers and dryers of a corner laundromat. By the time the jeans and shirts were rolled navy style and

37

restowed in her clothing bag, her watch read 5:15. The other patrons were hurrying to get home. To something. To someone.

He did offer, she thought. Well, maybe just one night. Only until she found a place to stay. She wouldn't get involved. Knew better. She ignored the warning; an impatience to get back to the silver trailer and the man who lived there.

The red pickup was gone, and although she gave a few perfunctory knocks on the door, she knew only Dude was inside. She walked to the front and spread a bandana from her pack out on the concrete drive and sat down to watch the changing colors of the sunset. She breathed deeply, hoping for the humid salty, fishy smell from today at the pier but it was too far away. A squadron of gulls soared high above her. They glided on the wind currents, flapping their wings only enough to stay aloft. As they reached their destination high above the sand, some made a smooth circling descent, while others—probably trained by Jonathan Livingston—changed to a spinning, flapping dive, much like a kite that has lost its wind. Each one pulled out at the last moment before impact to make a perfect on-the-feet landing. They settled onto one area of the sand, each a wing's span apart from his neighbor. From her vantage point, the area of the beach now looked like a well-planned, bird parking lot. The air became cool but she folded her bare arms together rather than go back to her car for a sweater. The lights began to blink on in the establishments of the pier just as she heard the truck pull in behind her.

Code had to have seen her in the headlights, but the door slammed and the footsteps crossed the drive and went up the steps. Wrong decision, coming back here. The key turned in the lock.

"Door's open." A light switched on and he was already inside.

It was entering the principal's office, a crowded restaurant alone, or the first performance in a school play. She wished she could disappear. He made a big fuss over Dude who left him to jump with delight when he saw her. After what he considered an ample greeting, the big dog charged out the door and they were alone.

"I guess I shouldn't have come back. But I was afraid to stay on the beach . . . . I'll go to a motel." She knew what she was doing. Fishing, her father called it. Fishing for what she wanted to hear.

He still didn't smile or look at her. "I told you this morning you could stay here didn't I? So take the load off your feet."

*It isn't a lunker catch, Daddy, but it will have to do.* This man obviously didn't hand out invitations easily, especially after being turned down before.

"I found a job." Nervousness makes her rattle on about her day, Irma, Rick. She wanted to stop but couldn't. Mirth finally played at the corners of Cody's solemn mouth and erupted in boisterous laughter when her machine gun narrative reached the afternoon's laundry.

"My God, Woman. You sure can talk. Relax!

Dude likes you. You can keep him company when I'm gone nights.''

*Hooked and landed*. It was settled. She would stay.

"Where do you work? I've been wondering what a cowboy does in the city, especially at night."

"Well, I'm not punchin' dudes no more, that's for sure. Except with my music. I sing to 'em now. We got a gig at the Ranch."

She glanced at the stack of records in the corner, crossed the room and picked up the top one. *Cody Country*.

She studied the album cover. Cody was leaning against a split rail fence while horses grazed in the background. Sidelighting emphasized the contour of rugged cheek and chin, drawing attractive shadows in forehead lines. "Here you are, someone famous, Cody Williams, and I didn't even know."

"It's better that way. Now I know you came back for a safe place to stay not because I can sing."

"That's true. I might not even stay here after I hear you sing. Will you play it for me?"

He took the record form its jacket and put it on the turntable. "You might be sorry . . . This is our last album, we're recording a new one right now." His rich baritone drifted from the speakers then, drawing a slow, dreamy picture of lost love. She felt it coming, the emotion that always began in the pit of her stomach. It happened when a brass band passed in a parade or children sang Christmas carols. The waves grew stronger and moved upward until tears threatened to seep from the corners of her eyes. She looked away, afraid he'd seen the unexpected flood of emotion. He did notice and tried to help her recover.

"Ths next one is for you." he said. The song began, "If you got the money, honey, I got the time . . ." She flushed a deep red, then to her surprise, so did he. He looked away, mumbled, "I was only kidding," and opened the refrigerator. "Guess it's gonna be bacon and eggs for dinner."

She jumped up anxious to help and for something to do. As their arms touched in the small kitchen they both backed away. She knew her reasons but wondered at his. Maybe the blonde in the snapshot. He popped bread in the toaster and with his back to her said, "Look, let's just keep it simple, OK?" Not knowing whether he meant the meal or their relationship, she gave him an affirmative reply. He sat opposite her at the small table and talked about the day's recording session while his other voice sang about broken hearts, honky tonk bars, and jail. When the record stopped, he turned off the stereo.

"Can't I hear the other side?"

"Naw," he said, "I hear enough of myself every night. You can play it after I go to work."

"Can I come along?" She saw him tense and was immediately sorry she had asked.

"I don't think you'd like it," he said quickly. "Western bars are no place for a lady alone."

She fought the urge to argue, glanced at the blonde in the snapshot. She'll probably be there. *Jill is jealous*.

Dude scratched at the door and Cody opened it, letting the dog break the tension. Then to her surprise, he suggested a walk on the beach. When she stumbled on the last step of the steep stairway, he grabbed her elbow to steady her, and, for an instant, neither of them moved. But the electric moment short circuited and they continued as if it had never happened. She stopped to remove her sandals and Cody flopped down on the cool sand beside her. A half moon lighted the sand and turned the churning foam of the breakers an irridescent green.

"Always remind me of my daddy's irregular heartbeat," he said.

"What?"

"The waves. The way they come in a pattern. Three gentle, then one crasher."

They watched a fourth one collide with the outgoing traffic, its spray shooting high in the air, befire it hit ground with a force that vibrated under them.

"Is your father sick? Where does he live?" *Sick fathers.* A body, emaciated, motionless. Trapped in a web of plastic tubing. She closed her eyes, trying to blot it out.

"Well, we're from Texas . . . Beaumont, over on the east side. My daddy and momma both came from musical families. They got married and sang together all over the state. As each of us kids got old enough . . . there was six of us, we joined the group. Then momma retired. But my dad had a bad heart. Irregular like I said. Didn't give him much trouble, just some pain. Until one night, when I was 15, he had a heart attack on stage, was at the Magnolia Club in Atlanta . . . . A real big job for us. He died right then.''

"My father died when I was fifteen too."

"No kidding." She could tell he didn't really hear her, was lost in his own painful memory. "We split up then. An' I come west. My brother still has the group—the Magnolia Boys they call themselves in honor of the ol' man. I picked up some rock sounds since and they all think I'm lousy, man. My momma calls me a long haired hippie. That's a joke isn't it? She should see some of the characters walking around here." She heard the hurt and wanted to comfort him.

"How long has it been since you've seen her?"

"Oh, long time now." He stood up, dropping the invisible barrier again. "Better be heading back. I got to get ready for work." The waves continued their irregular pounding, at her back now, matching the thud in her chest.

When Cody opened the door of the trailer, Billy Jo looked up from his sprawled position in one of the chairs. He scowled again when he saw her but Cody didn't seem to notice this time. His face lit up, "Hey, Buddy. I'll jump in the shower and be ready quick. Keep Jill company will you?"

The running water broke the silence and Jill decided to try and make friends. "Would you like a cup of coffee, Billy Joe?"

"Sure moved right in and made yourself at home, didn't you?" He threw a leg over the arm of the chair, spit out the words. "No . . . no coffee for me."

"Look . . ." she fired back, angry now.

"Just a minute. Hold on." He threw his arms up in mock self defense, his sarcasm obvious.

"Look." Her volume stopped him. "I don't know what your problem is. But Cody just offered me a temporary bed." *Correct that.* "I mean he said I could sleep here, on that chair you're lounging in, for a few days . . . until I get working and find a room."

"You telling me you are going to be working here? Where?"

"Yes, I am. At the pier." She was tired of the conversation and this man. But he didn't stop.

"Listen, girl. That guy in there has had enough trouble from a woman to last him a lifetime. He's comin' 'round now. Good things are happening for him . . ." He lowered his voice. "So why don't you just split out of his life. Before it gets all screwed up again."

"What kind of trouble?" The shower stopped then, cutting off the possibility of any more information. She didn't want Cody to hear them discussing him. She did see Billy Joe's quick glance in the direction of the snapshot on the wall, however.

"Don't worry, Billy Joe. I have no intention of getting involved with anyone."

"Good," he said, apparently softened by her emphatic denial. "But I wouldn't hang around too long." He looked up at as Cody came out of the bathroom. "Guess I will have that cup of coffee after all."

44

They left at eight, and she dragged the small packet of letters from her purse again. They lay unopened on her lap. The top one, addressed to Mr. Everett Reasoner, Attorney at Law, Chicago, had been the beginning, the starting point she'd decided on, long before she drove out of her driveway, away from Auntie Mil and Mrs. Nelson. But that morning she had crossed the river and pulled into the county park. The terrible urgency of the past few years suddenly left her. She sat in the thick new grass, stared back across the water at her home and thought about the night before. They had all been serious, marching to *Pomp and Circumstance,* sobered by the dark caps and gowns. After the ceremony they'd hugged each other, vowed to keep in touch. Chuck had whispered, "I really do love you, Jill." And she'd believed him, at least for the moment. But she would probably never see any of them again. They would be frozen in a high school time capsule. Strangers at a twenty year reunion. And she didn't care. The house stood still and strong and safe, high above the moving water. It didn't understand. But the willows and maples, toughened by their location at the water's edge, survivors of flood and drought, waved merrily in the breeze. Goodbye, Jill. Good Luck.

She headed north through the flat farmland. The neat rows of corn were ahead of schedule. They would be more than knee high by the Fourth of July. Soon Schneider harvesters would interrupt their life cycle, strip them of their yield. When the kernels were swollen with nutritious sugar and starch, before they hardened into seed.

She had parked in a suburban shopping center of Toledo and ignoring the portable stove in the back seat, treated herself to a double burger and fries at a fast food restaurant. She watched the last customers, and then the employes, drive away in their cars. Street lights blinked on and she unfurled her sleeping bag for her first of many nights alone. The bed was hard and unfamiliar. It wore at her hipbones, prodded her spine out of sound slumber. Sometime, in the midst of the tosses and turns, a Lake Erie squall ripped inland and changed the calm blacktop to an angry sea. Sheets of water flooded the windshield, blotting out the safe surroundings. Then the sky would light, and for an instant, change the trees and lamp poles into grotesque monsters. They discharged a thundered wrath that shook the helpless red Pinto. She hid in the sleeping bag, sweating in the steam of the closed up car, quivering with the terror of aloneness. Finally, when her nervous system could endure no more, it escaped in sleep.

"Look Mommy, someone is sleeping in that car."

"Come on, Danny. Don't look. It's just another hippie tramp. Why don't the police throw all those people in jail? That's what I'd like to know . . . scum . . ." The mother and son went into a store.

She had laughed then, at the mother's opinion of her, and at her own night terror. The sun glistened now on the red paint and other than a few puddles as evidence, the storm of last night could have been iimagined. *I'm here. I survived.* Alone.

She took the ticket from the tollkeeper and merged onto the turnpike. Destination Chicago.

The windy city was calm that afternoon; sail-boats lounged on Lake Michigan, too lazy to move in the heavy still air. The drivers were another matter. Cars and taxis darted and cut across the unlined outer drive, hostile that a newcomer should get in their way. She made three unsuccessful passes before she pulled up relieved, in front of the Michigan Avenue building she was seeking.

A horn blasted her short lived complacency.

"You dumb broad! Get your stupid red ass out of the taxi lane." The surly man held up his middle finger and shook it out the window where she would be sure to see it's message in her rear view mirror. Her hands shook as she turned the corner and drove into an underground parking lot. Seventy-five cents a half hour. She went into the building's public restroom, splashed cold water on her face and with trembling hands brushed her hair and smoothed her skirt and blouse. The mirror said she looked presentable. Clean cut young lady seeking employment. Anxious to get a look in Mr. Reasoner's files.

Why, she asked herself for the thousanth time, had Mara thought it necessary to get her father to sign a power of attorney over to her? Or to hire a Chicago lawyer to help her liquidate stocks and securities? Her father loved Mara. He provided for her in his will. Jill loved Mara. She wanted her to stay. So did Auntie Mil and Mrs. Nelson. The answer was obvious. Mara planned to get what she could and get out from the day she got married.

She never loved or cared about any of them. It was all an Academy Award Performance.

Mara didn't fool around, Jill thought as she stared at the gold leaf lettering on the heavy mahogany door—Reasoner, Mittingham, Webster, and Price, announced her choice was the senior partner. The office was as hushed as the hallway. Heavy carpeting muffled footsteps and voices. The receptionist looked as expensive as her surroundings.

"Yes, can I help you?"

"I'd like to see Mr. Reasoner please."

"Do you have an appointment?" The scarlet nails paused over the typewriter keys.

"Yes, ma'am."

The woman looked frantically for Jill's name on the book in front of her, then went through another door to the back office. It worked. She was back in just a minute, directed Jill down a long hall, past rooms of clacking typewriters and banks of filing cabinets.

Jill wanted to hate him, had, in fact, prepared herself for a slick big city attorney in a custom tailored suit.

"Jill Kerry is it?" The long anticipated Mr. Reasoner stood and offered his hand across the wide expanse of desk and paper. He was short and portly, probably seventy. His grey jacket hung unbuttoned, his tie was narrow maroon satin with crossed golfclubs embroidered in the center. Yellowed teeth extruded from his gums exposing a portion of their roots when he smiled. But the smile was relaxed and friendly. Senior partners can take it easy, she guessed. "We seem to have had some mixup about your appointment. What can I do for you, young lady?"

He didn't believe her, she knew. He had nothing to do with hiring and she would never have been given an appointment with him. But he admired her determination and did believe she had a burning desire to study law.

"Well, young lady, God helps them that help themselves, they say. I'll hire you as a file girl. The pay is terrible but you can work up. Let's go see Evelyn, she'll get you started."

Evelyn was a friendly girl who even offered to share her apartment until Jill found a place of her own, but she wouldn't be needing it. She waited until Evelyn went to the restroom, then hurried to the "S" file. There it was, Mara Schneider. All of the confidential material was sealed, but she found a copy of a form letter telling the client to get her records together for income tax preparation. It had been mailed to an address in Kansas City. Worse than Mara, she walked out of the office without even leaving a note. The tires of the Pinto sang their own song as they raced out of the windy city—"Goin' to Kansas City, Kansas City, here I come."

The letters fell from her lap to the floor. She let them lay, suddenly tired of the past, of holding back, pushing away, hurting, being hurt—killing. That shrink, the one Auntie Mil took her to, he had said it, to try and make her talk.

*You didn't kill your mother, Jill. Babies are born every day and the mother's survive . . . It was just a freak.*

*You didn't kill your father. He died of lung cancer.*

The doctor had been clever. She had almost broken her stubborn silence and answered him.

*Maybe you're right, Doc, but it sure killed something inside of me.*

The first sunlight sliced through the venetian blind, drawing prison stripes across her bed. It was Sunday. Her new job didn't start for two days. She turned on her side and went back to sleep, waking again to a crash in the kitchen.

"I'm sorry. Dropped the damn coffee pot . . . You can use the shower first while the coffee's perking." He kept his back to her.

The spray was hot and strong, made her want to sing. A fluffy white towel, folded neatly, waited on the counter. She dried and brushed her hair, decided to wear her green teeshirt and print skirt today. As she looked at herself with satisfaction, she admitted to the mirror that she was dressing to please the man in the kitchen. But when she came out, he handed her a steaming mug without looking up.

"What you going to do today?" he asked.

Play bloodhound, she told him silently. *Jill Kerry, private eye.* But aloud she answered, "I heard about some pottery shops in Venice . . . that's close to here isn't it? I like ceramics so I thought I'd go browse through a few of them." *Someone might know about Mara or her pots.*

He struggled with his words. "Want some company? I don't have to work today." Then he searched her face uncertain. Been hurt bad, Billie Joe said. *Don't do it again, Jill.*

"Maybe I better go alone," she answered. "You would probably be bored to death with bowls and jars . . . and I . . . well, I spend hours once I get into those places." The words made a metallic taste in her mouth.

His protective curtain shaded the blue eyes, only the mouth smiled with his reply. "Sure enough. Dude and me, we're gonna take a ride out to Bakersfield . . . visit some rancher buddies of mine. You probably wouldn't like the heat and dust anyway."

The subject was closed. They washed and dried the dishes and he told her how to find the shops.

As she followed his directions, she spotted The Ranch on the other side of the street. The large building was a replica of a clapboard ranchhouse, complete with hitching posts. A billboard towered over the club and read "Cody Williams. Held over by popular demand. Hear his hit record, 'I'm Not Afraid of Losing You,' nightly Tuesday through Saturday." A couple strolled down the street, their arms around each other's waists. A young man and woman rode their bicycles in front of her, side by side, laughing their affection. But Jill was alone—wishing she was in a truck going to Bakersfield. As she turned right and parked in front of the small shops under the arcade on Venice Boulevard, a familiar spurt of adrenolin speeded her pulse and dried her mouth—even as she wondered if the end

51

of her search would bring the satisfaction she hoped for—or if she was a hunter who discovers the hunt is the thing, not the kill. She shivered at the comparison.

The first building housed a sandal shop. Then a long patchwork and embroidered skirt in the next window reminded her of Mara's clothes. She felt a flutter of hope. Next door was the pottery.

*Maybe she even worked here.* The strong smell of incense and soft Indian music added to the artful arrangements inside. Bowls and vases stood at different levels around the room on rough cut boards and railroad ties. Some held dried flowers. A young girl looked up from her macrame board as Jill browsed.

"Welcome, sister." Her voice was soft and dreamy, in contrast to her natural hairdo which had the texture of a coarse grade of steel wool.

"Good morning," Jill answered. "You have lovely pots. Do you do them all yourself?" She knew the answer. The variety was too great; the styles too individual to come from one artist.

"Nooooo . . ." The word seemed to go on forever as if suspended in time. Finally in gear, the girl continued, "No. We buy from lots of different artists. Some 'crazy' from Redondo makes the blue stuff there in front of you. But only when he needs the bread. Hand him a twenty and you won't see him for weeks." The girl continued her knot tying then; Jill continued her sleuthing. She spotted the red clay pieces in the corner and moved in that direction. Only one was of interest. A small weed pot. She picked up and examined several others, then steadied her hand and reached for it. The bamboo design done with Japanese brushes, was one of Mara's favorites and the signature on the bottom was unmistakeable . . . A large scrawled 'M', followed by the tiny 'ARA'.

"Is this one made by someone around here?" she asked.

The girl put her twine aside and walked over. She examined the markings on the bottom. "I don't know. But Duane might. He's been around longer than me." She called to the back room, and after a few seconds the curtains over the door parted and Jill gasped. The man was thin to the point of appearing undernourished, with a mass of curly black beard and hair. But what caused her reaction was his grotesque black eye. The socket and right cheek were a mixture of black, yellow and purple; the eyeball was bright red. An irridescent pupil stared straight ahead. As he came toward them, the eye seemed to look through her, to know what she was thinking. He examined the pot and spoke in the same soft, sluggish way as the girl.

"Oh . . . yea . . . Mara. I remember her." *Maybe this is the guy Mara told about living with?* He dashed that hope as he continued, "Kinky type. She was a biker's chick for awhile. Used to bring her pots on the back of a chopper. Haven't seen her in a long time."

Jill tried to keep the tremor out of her voice as she said, "I love this one. And only six dollars." She handed the girl the money and turned to face evil eye again. "Do you know where I could find her, maybe? I'd like to have her make me some

53

bigger pots for my apartment.''

The eye made her look away as she felt her face flush. It seemed hours before he answered, "Well, I think her ol' man is one of the Fiends but I wouldn't recommend going to their pad. They bed down in some old warehouse and they're real mean dudes . . . They hang out in The Ranch sometimes . . ." He paused while the eye surveyed her, "I think you're wasting your time. Haven't seen her around in years . . . and I'd remember. She's one good-lookin' woman.''

Jill scooped up a large pot beside her without looking at it. "Well, it doesn't really matter. I'll take this one instead. Maybe I'll come back after payday and get a few others.'' She handed him another bill and hurried out. He stood in the doorway, watching. She would have liked to hear the conversation going on between he and his companion.

The girl asked immediately, "Think she's a narc?''

"Naw, not unless they use Ohio license plates now. But she sure was interested in that Mara chick. I'll ask around. She *was* nervous. Oh, forget it. Let's lock up and kick back with some good weed.''

Jill drove around the corner and pulled to the curb. Her hands shook as she took a deep breath to try and stop her internal pounding. This was the first person she'd met who actually knew Mara. What he said whirled through her head. Fiends. A motorcycle gang. Hang out at The Ranch. Cody might even have known her.

She stopped for groceries then hurried back to the trailer, hoping Cody changed his mind about going to Bakersfield. But the truck was gone.

A girl sat on the step of the trailer. Her head was on her knees and long blond hair dragged on the ground. Jill knew even before seeing her face that this was the girl in the photograph. Her head rolled, then slowly raised. The small mouth hung slack and the beauty in the picture was gone. Pale glazed eyes, framed in blue-black sockets, searched Jill's face obviously not able to catagorize what they saw. The mouth refused to cooperate when she tried to speak. "Who are you?" was slow and slurred with a hint of insolence.

"My name is Jill."

"What are you . . . doing here?" The girl fixed her attention on the pot and groceries she was carrying. Jill didn't know how to answer. The girl got slowly to her feet. Her arms were pencil slim; her tiny frame carried no fat. Yet her stomach was distended like the pictures she'd seen of starving children.

The skeletal frame tottered, then the girl caught herself on the side of the trailer, and took a step forward. "Cody is my ol' man." She swept her hair back behind her ears and raised her chin, the anger contorting her mouth and turning her eyes to beady bright dots.

"Cody is your husband?" Jill felt the flood of disappointment.

"Naw, naw," the girl moved closer, "I said my ol' man. He's my fuckin' ol man . . . Now get your little butt out of here."

Jill froze. She wanted to explain, to tell her she was only temporary, that the girl had nothing to worry about. *Tell yourself that Jill*. She took a deep breath, "Really . . . ," she began.

The girl lunged, screaming, "You damned groupies. Always hangin' around him. Won't leave us alone." She grabbed at Jill's hair, close to the scalp, and pulled. The pain set fire to the top of her head. She was shocked at the frail girl's tremendous strength, however falsely produced by some narcotic. The pot she was holding smashed to the ground, along with the groceries. Skin scraped away as hysterical fingernails gouged her neck. She swung her arms, desperate to escape the attack. Her ears rung with the foul shreiking and when a sharp heel bared her shin, she doubled over, unable to protect herself from the rain of hitting and clawing. Then she heard the slap, and looked up thankful for help. Billy Joe hit the girl on the side of the face again, hard, sent her crumbling to the ground. "Cocksucker, bastard," she continued to curse through her whimpers.

His words sliced, gouged, stabbed "Slut! You no-good doper slut!" The vicious rage showed in curled lips and clenched teeth. As he leaned over Jill was frigthened for the girl. "Trouble," he hissed. "Always been trouble." He grabbed the frail shoulders and jerked her to her feet. Her sobs were pathetic. He changed his grip to a handful of shirt between her shoulder blades, and as if she might get free, hung on and dragged her around the Pinto and up the alley.

Jill could still hear his ferocious threat, "Here's

56

a quarter for bus fare . . . And Marcia . . . if you ever come back here to bother Cody, I'm gonna kill you. Got that. I'll choke you 'til you're purple.''

Jill slumped on the step, dazed and weak, not wanting to hear anymore.

"Now get the hell out of here," Billy Joe finished.

His boots clicked on the pavement as he hurried back. She sat stunned, watching a stream of blue-white milk meander towards her from its ruptured carton. He knelt to retrieve a package of hamburger and a head of lettuce from under the car.

Then he lifted her chin, gentle now. "Are you all right?" He helped her inside, to a chair. "We better get you cleaned up and something on those scratches," he said. "Just like from the claws of a cat. Easy to get infected." She couldn't move or answer. The unexpected violence had numbed her. No tears came, or shaking, just a dull throb in her temple. He went to the bathroom and she could hear him rummaging in the medicine cabinet. He came back and without a word, poured alcohol on a wad of cotton and dabbed at her neck and scalp. The pain dug and spread. B.J. put his arm around her shoulder, and awkwardly patted her back. "It's OK. Go ahead and cry," he mumbled in her ear. But the tears didn't come. They never did.

When he stood up the anger returned. "God, I hate that bitch."

"Billy Joe," she was anxious now, "Billy Joe . . . don't tell Cody about this."

He frowned. "You better damn well believe I'm gonna tell Cody. That whore put him through livin' hell for two years."

"Please . . ." He ignored her begging.

"She started out a nice girl . . . But when she got on dope it was shit from then on. He'd get a call and leave right in the middle of a set. She OD'd and he took care of her . . . . Even after he caught her in bed with some other dude."

She wanted him to stop. Didn't want to hear it.

"You know what she did? After he'd had it. Couldn't take it no more? She got a can of spray paint, went down to the Ranch one night . . . . and wrote 'Fuck Cody' all over the building."

"Stop it," she screamed. Electric shocks ran to her wrists. "Don't tell him. Don't put him through anymore." She stood up, surprised that her legs would hold her and walked to the bathroom.

He called to her after a minute. "OK. Guess you're right. I won't say nothin' about it."

She stared at herself in the mirror. On each side of her center part, two spots the size of quarters were devoid of hair. They glistened as blood seeped slowly from the burning skin. Four ugly welts ran from her chin to above her left breast. Her right shin was raw to the bone and blood poured down her ankle and instep. She found a septic shaving pencil and although the pain made her limp she was able to stop the bleeding. She washed her face and changed into jeans and a clean blouse. She buttoned the top button and tied a red bandana around her neck. It hid the scratches. Wincing, she parted her hair on the left and combed it over the wounds, catching it with a barrette on the right. Maybe Cody wouldn't notice.

Billy Joe whistled when she came out. "Hey, good job. Sit down though. Here's some coffee."

"How did you get here so fast?" she asked.

"Oh, I just live next door. On the other side of the garage. I heard the commotion and thought it was Millie upstairs. She gets pretty drunk sometimes. But then I recognized Marcia's voice.

"Thanks, Billy Joe."

He looked embarrassed. "Listen . . . I been meanin' to tell you . . . . I'm sorry the way I been treatin' you. You're a nice gal an' . . .''

The door opened. Dude charged in, followed by Cody. He stopped, looked from one to the other of them. "What's going on around here? Something broken out there on the driveway . . . and a quart of milk?"

She commanded her voice to sound natural, "That *was* a flowerpot I bought for you. But unfortunately I slipped and fell when I was trying to carry too much. Billy Joe came around the corner just then and helped me gather up what remained of the groceries. I guess we missed the milk." She willed her body to stand without showing the pain that was pulsating through it. "But I did leave something in the car. Luckily I wasn't carrying it too." She hurried out and came back with Mara's pot.

"For you." She put it in his hand. "Thanks for letting me stay here." Another game began in her head. *Thanks for*. Thanks for believing the story. For the shy, little boy smile that brightens the

59

room. For coming home early from Bakersfield.

Billy Joe said he had to split, and slipped out the door. Afraid Cody could read her mind, she opened the hamburger and concentrated on making patties.

"How was your day at your friend's ranch?" He ignored the question.

"This mug is real pretty." He turned it around, examined the design, making her feel guilty that she didn't really buy it with him in mind. "Real nice of you to buy me a present. Think I'll have some coffee and bourbon in it right now." She didn't tell him it was made for flowers, not bourbon.

He walked the few steps to the kitchen, poured his drink, and gave her a platonic peck on the cheek. "Thanks for thinkin' about me . . . Now, Gal, I want to know. Did you hurt yourself when you fell out there?"

"Oh, not really. Just skinned my leg a little on the car bumper. Nothing to worry about." She tried for lightness. "I come from strong German stock, you know." He picked up her slip of tongue right away.

"German? Kerry sounds Irish to me?"

"My mother's side. She was German." The lies were so easy now. Easier than the first year, or even the second. They flowed from forked tongue, gathered momentum, repeated themselves until her brain began to believe them. It argued now though, worried by the increasing ease of deceit—and also disappointed with the casualness of Cody's kiss on the cheek. This is the way you want it, she told herself for the thousandth time since she'd met him. But it was just another lie, another lie to herself. She gave up the internal battle, asked instead, "Again, how was your trip to Bakersfield? Did you go riding?" It was as if he was reading her thoughts. She felt his closeness at her back. The same sensation when one's arm almost, but not quite touches the stranger's in the seat next to you, when the hairs brush, and you withdraw quickly. But she didn't pull away.

He wrapped his arms around her waist and nuzzled past her hair to kiss the back of her neck, saying simply, "I wished all day you'd a come along with me."

As he turned her around, she knew there was no more neutrality. The intensity of her response frightened her and coming on top of the other events of the day, she started to shake.

"It's OK, Babe . . . It's all right." He murmured, stroked her hair. He smelled of soap and ranch dust. Hard masculine scents. He misunderstood. "You must have really hurt yourself in the fall. Come on . . . come sit down. I'll fix us some dinner."

They ate in silence, both making an effort to concentrate on the food. She was afraid to meet his eyes, to explore meanings, feelings, emotions lest they evaporate. When he poured another shot of bourbon into his mug, a second dam of emotions broke. This time she began to giggle uncontrollably as she asked, "For the last time, how was your day in Bakersfield?"

He was relieved too, to laugh with her. Then he

sobered as he answered, "Damned dull. Dude couldn't find no rabbits to chase and I was without my woman." He took her hand then and led her toward the bedroom. She forgot about Mara and Marcia, the physical and emotional bruises and scrapes—and the vow not to get involved.

The callouses on his fingers, rough from the years of plucking guitar strings, danced across her nipples causing them to rise, and as he continued to touch her ever so gently, his hands moving slowly downward, her breath came in gasps along with more involuntary tremors.

"What's wrong?" Uncertainty flickered in his eyes.

"Nothing, Cody, nothing." She was remembering her first experience with sex, it had never been love. The night with Chuck after her father's funeral. He had fumbled with inexperienced teenage urgency, mumbling, "I love you, I love you," over and over while she lay motionless, telling herself *I'm alone, I'm alone.*

Cody's gentleness and the familiarity she felt for him in this short period of time erased the nightmares. She held and caressed him, enveloped his body, pressed closer and closer. Then they moved apart, savoring the slow, gentle coming together again. When they were finally locked in ultimate intimacy, she burrowed her head into the comfortable hollow of his neck, clinging to the security long after their mutual passions were satisfied.

He chuckled as he brushed her hair back from her face.

"What's so funny?"

"Know what a buddy of mine calls this?"

"No."

"A soak. Used to say he was gonna go home and give the ol' lady a good long soak. Said she liked at least two hours . . . Never did believe him 'til now."

"Well, I agree with her." She increased the pressure of her arms. "You have an hour and a half to go."


Jill raised her head in the unfamiliar dark of the bedroom, waited for her eyes to adjust, then read the time on the luminous dial of the clock. She leaned across Cody and pushed the button before the nerve shattering buzzer could wake him. But his breathing changed at her movement. His arm gathered her close and her head found again the crook between neck and shoulder; the secure refuge that seemed to have been waiting for her. *Does he know it's me?* Or could it be any warm body? Maybe Marcia. His breathing evened out again as she allowed herself another moment's pleasure at his closeness, one more minute of his pulse beat in her ear, his new growth of beard against her forehead.

Although it was only four A.M. and she had lain awake long after last night's lovemaking, she was not tired. The renewed feeling of trust in another person made her want to stay suspended in her warm environment forever. But she eased away from him out of the bed and tiptoed to the bath-

63

room, decided to wear her boots and heavy jacket. The ocean air would probably be chilly early in the morning, even in summer. The bald spots on her head burned as she ran the brush through her hair and fastened it again with the barrette. Cody had asked about her different hairstyle, said he liked it better the other way, but she'd begged a woman's right to always be changing.

The horizon was still in the brown out stage, waiting for the full voltage of the sun, as she descended the steep steps to the beach and started off across the sand to the pier and her first day of work.

A vagrant lay sleeping in the iceplant to the right of the steps, an empty Mogan David bottle at his side. As the first slice of sun peeped from the water, he curled fetus-like around his shoes, in a subconscious protection of his most treasured possession. She jogged across the sand, then slowed to enjoy the quiet of the pier. A few fishermen talked softly together on the benches or leaned in silence, watching their lines undulate in the swells below.

It was only a quarter of five when she reached the door of the still dark restaurant. She leaned against the building, hearing Irma's footsteps on the stairs seconds before she saw her. The heavy woman, breathing hard from the descent, still found the air to beller a greeting, "Top of the morning to you. Guess we made it through the bottom of the night, Huh?" Her great bosom and belly shook with good humor. "Hey, I can tell you're going to be all right. Anyone who can beat ol' Irma to work can't be all bad." She unlocked the door and switched on the lights. "Got to get the coffee going first thing," she continued, as she began filling and measuring. "Them fishermen will be flooding this place in a few minutes . . . . Now here . . ." She dragged two cardboard cartons from under the counter and began filling them with packages of bread and buns. "You take these out and put them away," she directed Jill, "then come back for the meat and eggs."

As Jill stepped aboard *Sea Maiden*, the slight movement of the deck reminded her of the pill in her jeans pocket. She had taken one before she went to bed and now swallowed another. She wanted to take no chances with seasickness. In a short time she had her food stored, the cooking equipment and procedures mentally reviewed, and was back into the restaurant for a cup of coffee with Irma.

"Rick's still out in the bait boat but he'll be in soon. Along with Captain Fat Ass . . ."

"Who?"

"That's right you wouldn't know. Rick's not the captain of the boat. He does all the work and knows more than any of these fair weather sailors around here will ever know, but Joe Green is the captain." The older woman wiped absently at the counter as disgust filled her voice. "And what a pile of crap he is . . . . Retired navy. Stands around in his gold braid looking important. Don't know his ass about nothin'." She continued, "It just ain't fair. Rick has been working around here since he was thirteen. Passed all his tests and got his license a couple of years ago. But old Mr. Ferguson—he owns all these concessions—he thinks Rick looks too young. That the tourists wouldn't have confidence in him. So he keeps him on as First Mate .... Rick gets disgusted but he can't do nothin' about it. He just has to cover all Fat Ass's mistakes."

As if on cue, the door opened and a middle-aged man lumbered under the weight of a rotund middle towards the counter. His blue jacket, slightly rumpled and too tight, was obviously a leftover from his last tour of duty. "Here's the Admiral now." The woman's sarcasm was obvious. She set a cup of coffee down, two stools away. "Mornin' El Capitan. You look like you run into some rough seas last night. Got your ship rocking a little this morning, I bet . . ." Irma suddenly slapped the counter in front of him with a flabby palm and raised her voice. "Wake up, wake up, old man. I want to introduce you to your new cook." She pointed her finger. "Jill, this is your skipper."

He turned slowly to stare at her through weepy eyes, dulled by too many years in officer's club bar stools. Blue veins traveled across his cheeks and fought for space on his rosy swollen nose. He acknowledged the introduction with a mumbled, "Hope you can cook better than that last kid. He burned everything in sight .... Then worse yet, fell off the damned bait boat and got himself drowned . . . Caused me all kinds of red tape." He tried to control the tremor in his hand as he turned back and picked up his cup. Irma rolled her eyes in disgust.

Jill excused herself and left. She wanted to get the galley organized and be ready for her first day.

As she started aboard, a smaller boat, dirty and unpainted, eased against the dock on the other side and farther out. A teenage boy tied her up, the diesel stopped its chugging and Rick stepped off. Just as she was about to shout a greeting, two Latin men, dressed in polyester flowered shirts, black pants, and platform shoes, stepped out from the other side of the bait shop wall and blocked Rick's path. The obvious anger on his face caught her between the curious desire to know what was going on and the discomfort at maybe being caught eavesdropping. She moved slowly across the deck, not looking in their direction, yet straining to hear the gist of the disagreement in progress. But other than Rick's, "unload at two," the rest of the words were lost in the morning breeze and surf. They must be bait buyers or sellers, haggling over price, she decided. She continued into the galley then, and turned as three cases of beer seemed to be following her. They came toward her on blue jean-clad legs. The cartons hit the floor with a thud and she was incredulous to see a small pigtailed blond of about fifteen. The girl raised up smiling.

"Hi . . . . I'm Jody. We're going to be galley buddies, I guess."

"You surprised me. I just assumed Jody was a boy. How do you carry all that weight at one time?" The young face bobbed up and down before her as the girl began loading cans into the cooler.

"Oh, Irma yells at me all the time. Says I'm

67

going to ruin my back, carrying a lazy man's load, she calls it . . . but I'm strong." Freckles danced across the tiny nose and grey eyes flecked with brown and bordered by surprising dark, thick lashes joined the face's jovial celebration. As the young girl left to get a load of soft drinks, Rick's two companions passed by the window.

"Do those men buy bait form Rick?" she asked.

The girl's face clouded, "I don't pay any attention to Rick's business." She retreated then and returned shortly with another heavy load and her high spirits. When the first passengers began to come aboard Jody whispered, "Watch them, Jill. They'll all fight for a place on the stern."

"But why?"

"Because they can fish either side. If you get on the windward side, your line drifts under the boat and tangles with the ones from the leeward." Jill watched the truth of Jody's words as a wiry little man, carrying a tackle box and his own pole, stepped onboard and hurried to the rear, followed by a steady stream of men, women, and kids. She could hear their arguments about who was first and who had which spot. Each fisherman was given a numbered gunny sack for his catch. "Saves more fights," Jody explained while Rick and the two baitboys, introduced as Tim and Scott, settled everyone into place and distributed rods to the passengers without their own. At exactly eight o'clock by the marine clock on the wall, the boys threw the heavy mooring lines ashore and the warmed diesel chugged away from the dock. They passed the breakwater and Jill was introduced to her first ocean swell. She grabbed the counter and Jody laughed, "I hope you get your sea legs before the mob scene hits. We start serving breakfasts at 8:30."

Jill started warming ham slices, and filled the griddle with slices of bread. Just as Jody warned, when the big hand reached the bottom of its circle, they began the race. She slapped ham and eggs between slices of toast while Jody poured coffee and made change. It became so automatic that she was amazed when the girl said, "That's it, folks. We stop breakfast at eleven. You can start getting hamburgers in an hour."

Other than being aware that the boat had stopped and moved again several times, and of hearing some cheering and a fairly regular, "Look out, I got a big one," she could have been cooking in Cody's trailer.

She sighed and poured herself her first cup of coffee aboard. Jody opened a Coke and hopped up to sit on the counter. She said, "Now we have to clean up and get the lettuce and tomatoes ready for the burgers."

Jill looked out the window for the first time since leaving the breakwater. The boat was making a slow circle and she couldn't see any sign of land, or even the horizon in the thick haze. Jody explained, "We're out at the twelve mile bank. We have a two thousand dollar fish finder up there in the pilot house. It's so good you can see the schools of fish on it. They look like the blips on a radar screen. Now we're circling and the boys are throwing out chum . . . that's lots of bait, to bring the fish up around the boat." The motor changed sound then and stopped. Rick's voice over the loudspeaker said, "OK everyone. Lines down. Let's bring up some big ones this time."

He came down the steps from the pilothouse and into the salon for the first time. Jody handed him a cup of coffee.

"Hi, buddy." The young girl threw her arms around his neck and gave him a hug. He held the cup away from him and squeezed Jody with his other arm.

"How's my best girl today? He pulled a pigtail and looked up at Jill then, "Well, what do you think of your first day so far?"

*I love it*. The honesty of her thought surprised her and when she voiced it, seemed to surprise him also. He gave her a quissical look before starting back up the steps. They began slicing tomatoes and she forgot everything but the chores.

The afternoon was a repeat of the morning except for the change of menu and an increased demand for cold drinks. And Jody's instruction to put on a kettle of water to heat.

"It's for Dirty Harry."

"Who is Dirty Harry?"

"He's one of our regulars. Comes everyday. But he has a problem . . . . Itches . . . . Rick suggested to him that he may need a bath but he says 'No', it's allergies.' He cut out milk first and cheese and eggs, then meat, won't eat vegetables or fruit . . . . So now all he eats is rice and cereal . . . pours boiling water over them and stirs the stuff into a yucky mush . . . here he comes now.

Jill had seen the old man when he came aboard. He pulled a wire laundry cart loaded with boxes, paper bags, and a varied supply of fishing gear. Now he came to the counter with one of the small brown bags and dumped the contents out on its top.

"How you doing, girlies? Got my water ready?" She watched the arthritic fingers, each one dressed in a dime store ring, mix up the oats, bran and barley and stir until he had a bowl full of brown paste.

"You're all right, woman. Sure know how to boil water." His laugh, between spoonsful of the sickening mush, was deep and steady, not that of an eighty or so year old man. His name was appropriate though, a once green sweater was mended amply with various colors of thread and embedded with grease and grime. His grey beard was not a beard, just four or five days growth. Yet the dark brown eyes were sharp and surrounded by clear whites. And the Greek seaman's cap looked new.

"Well, Jody, shall I get engaged again?" he asked.

"Sure, Harry, if you keep trying one of these days you'll find someone to marry."

"Hey, girl . . . . What's your name?"

She turned from the hotplate, ignoring the customers waiting in line. "Me? I'm Jill."

"Jill, huh? Nice name. OK everybody. You're all invited to an engagement party . . . . Jill, give me your left hand . . . . Oh, shut up back there. You can wait five minutes for your lousy hamburgers. Anyway, it'll just make you itch." He pulled up his pant leg then to show everyone the knarled white shin streaked with red from scratching.

"Just be quiet a minute. I'm about to get me a new fiance." He removed a cheap silver ring with a plastic, turquoise colored stone from his little finger and with a great flourish slipped it onto her ring finger.

"There we are." He leaned across and gave her a peck on the cheek. "It's official now. Miss Jill is my thirty-ninth fiance . . . . And they're all waitresses. Saves me a lot of tips."

Jody said, "You sure are ornery, Harry."

"Listen little girl, you know you're right. My daddy had two sons besides me . . . And he always told everyone—if he had one wish it would be for his three boys to all die just five minutes before he did . . . Know why? Cause he said we'd have Hell wiped out by the time he got there." He turned then on his pointed toed shoes, clicked his heels and went out the door. Jody winked and they continued serving. *Yes, I love it*. Love is working on a fishing boat. Love is the Dirty Harrys of the world!

By 4:00 the engine's constant rhythm lulled the weary fishermen and they sat quietly for the ride back to the marina. She washed skillets and Jody tied the huge bags of trash.

"We try to train 'em to bring their empty cans in here, but some of the slobs still throw everything overboard." She could hear the disgust in the girl's voice. "It all ends up on the beach."

The Captain's comments from this morning came back to her then and she asked, "What

72

happened to the cook before me?'' Jody continued smashing and tying.

"Oh, he couldn't fry an egg."

Jill couldn't see the girl's face and her voice revealed nothing.

"What was his name?"

Jody looked at her now, puzzled, "Ronnie, Ronnie Jamison. Why?"

"Just female curiosity." She was relieved to know he wasn't the mysterious J.D. in Mara's letter. And aware also that this was the first time all day she had even thought about finding Mara . . . what she came here to do. *Love is a fishing boat.*

*Sea Maiden* came to a gentle stop at the dock and the passengers hurried to get off and to their cars. Some were excited with their full gunny sacks while a few looked glum as they carried only their tackle and a limp bag.

"Just don't know how to hook 'em," Jody scoffed. "We cut fish open and find as many as six hunks of our bait in their stomachs. That means they've gotten away five times before someone gets them. And the dummies sometimes blame Rick for not taking them where the fish are."

"Take all the food back to the restaurant," she ordered. "We don't leave anything on board because of the varmints."

"The varmints?" Jill asked.

"Yea," she laughed, "The rats."

Jill shivered, stood back and opened the cupboard door cautiously.

Jody giggled, "Don't worry. They wait for us to get off before they show their shifty eyes and buck

73

teeth."

She shivered again. Love is *not* rodents . . . not even little mice.

They had everything in order by five and she said a quick goodbye, anxious to spend some time with Cody before he had to go to work. She wanted to tell him about her exciting day.

*A confusing day.* Except for the one question, she hadn't asked anyone about J.D. or Mara. Hadn't thought about Mara. And now all she wanted was to get back to the trailer. Maybe people like Jody and Irma, even Dirty Harry . . . and especially Cody, would wash the doubts and anger away. Maybe the ocean and *Sea Maiden* would rock the need for revenge from her body. *Love is a fishing boat.*

Jill heard the angry voices as she climbed the steps from the beach and when she reached the top there was no doubt they were coming from the trailer. She couldn't pick out Cody's among them. Her stomach tightened, remembering Billy Joe's anger at Marcia. Maybe Marcia was back. She hesitated at the door listening. No, they were all male.

The conversation stoped in mid-sentence and six heads turned to stare at her. Sorry now for intruding, she stepped away, "I'll come back later."

"No, no," Cody said, standing up and putting an arm around her shoulder, "This conversation is about over anyway." As he drew her into the crowded room, she could feel the tension in his

74

touch. When he made the introductions she realized she had walked into the middle of some crisis among the musicians.

"Meet Medic, our drummer." He looked no more than eighteen with smooth, beardless cheeks and gold-rimmed glasses.

"And John." The large bear-like man gave a first impression of nothing but a mass of curly, black hair. The eyes, nose, and mouth emerged when he smiled.

"Billy Joe, you met." Her new friend gave her a sheepish look, shrugged his shoulders.

Cody pointed to a slick man about thirty with a blond handlebar mustache. "That's Kevin, our manager."

"And last," he hesitated, then spit out the words, "And least . . . is Ron." The young man sitting crosslegged on the floor didn't look up.

She sat on an empty dinette chair in the corner, uncomfortable to be there and disappointed that she wouldn't have this time alone with Cody. She saw the twitch in his cheek and knew his mind was on other things.

"I'm telling you, Kevin, I won't have him in the group. It's nothing but trouble, man."

"Bullshit, Cody." Ron slowly stretched his legs out across the small room and pushed his straight, shoulder length blonde hair behind his ears before he continued, "You're making too big a deal out of it . . . just because of Marcia."

Cody looked quickly at her then dropped his eyes as the lazy voice continued.

"You know most of the musicians in the world

use something, man. I need it, man. To get up. I can't make those sounds without it, man." He looked in the manager's direction for help. Jill watched the late afternoon sunlight play through his beard, changing it from gold to caramel and back again. "Listen, I'll keep the stuff in the car from now on, man. No more bringin' it in, OK?"

Cody's fist smashed the table hard, set beer cans shaking. "No! . . . No way, man. I'm not gonna' have that shit around. Or you either." The tendons in his neck bulged. "I'll get someone else . . ."

Kevin interrupted, "Look, let's everyone calm down." He spoke with the same quiet authority she remembered in her trustee's voice: a friendly persuasion that triggered an instant dislike for him. When he reached to give Cody a pat on the arm, a diamond ring on his little finger and the manicured nails reinforced her opinion. The sincerity was merely a practiced habit.

"I know how you feel, Cody. And believe me, I see plenty of trouble when groups get mixed up heavy in the stuff. Some of my clients end up trafficking just to feed their musician's habits. Willie's had his troubles, so has Waylon. Now you know I sure don't want that from you guys." He paused, smoothed the front of his immaculate jacket. "But Ron told you, he only smokes some weed." He twisted the waxed moustache and smirked, "After all, half the doctors and lawyers in town do that . . . and he takes some uppers . . . they do that too. Now really, is that such a big deal?" *Don't listen to him Cody. Remember Marcia.* She clenched her fist and

76

looked down at the dime store ring on her finger. Good old Harry, not vain like this one she thought, as the velvet voice continued, "Cody, man, think about it. Ron is the best lead guitar and backup man in the business. You guys are on the verge of making millions. Just remember all those rotten nights in crummy honky tonk bars . . . fighting to even get paid." He lowered his voice, "Those guys at Country Records may not sign that contract if Ron isn't part of it. You don't want to blow it now, do you? Man, I'm begging you."

The room was quiet. Everyone sat with eyes downcast, waiting.

"I said no and I mean it. If you all want to operate that way, fine . . . then I'll get me a new band. But right now, just get out of here. I don't want to hear no more talk."

Ron stood, gave Kevin an insolent smile and walked out. Medic said a quiet, "See ya' tonight," and John exited with "Stay cool, man." Billy Joe gave her a shrugged shoulders, upturned palms, silent, "I don't know," from across the room. As the manager rose, she was pleased to see he was losing a battle with a receding hairline. Although the fine blonde hair was carefully styled and combed, and glimmer of scalp peeked through, making him less formidable. He tried once again with Cody.

"Come on, fella . . . Don't blow it all now." Then his eyes surveyed the room and he added, "Christ, Cody. You won't have to live in this dump any more. You can have a pad in the Hollywood Hills or Malibu."

Cody smiled . . . but it wasn't a smile. It was a threat.

"You bug the shit out of me, Kevin. You really do. Now get your fancy ass out of here. Excuse me, Jill." The $300 suit marched to the door; Billy Joe applauded, she joined him. *A leech, living off other people's talent. Cody means 10% to him, nothing more.*

The door slammed and Cody smiled for real at Billy Joe's, "Good work, buddy. You sure got that fuckin' mother fucker told. What an asshole!" He stood and stretched. "Come on, let's forget this shit for awhile. Jill here has been workin' her tail off all day, what say we take her out for a real nice dinner? We'd have time to go to The Cove."

Although she would have preferred the time alone, and Cody probably would have too, he mumbled an agreement. She exchanged her fishing clothes for a skirt and blouse, and in a few minutes was seated between the two men in Billy Joe's pickup. The commuter traffic was still heavy on the Coast Highway, but Billy Joe eased along in the right lane at thirty-five, oblivious to the darting Toyotas and surfer vans. Cody slumped beside her, his head back and eyes closed.

"I ever tell you my crazy dentist story?" Billy Joe said.

"No," he answered, "but watch what you tell in front of Jill."

"Oh hell, it ain't bad . . . . Well, you see I was workin' with this guy named Cheyenne Jones . . . at this dump of a club in Phoenix . . . strictly low class, low pay. Now Cheyenne, he was

78

the cheapest son of a bitch you ever met . . . . He had this thing, every night after closing he'd take a flashlight and go all over the floor . . . sort through the sawdust for dimes and nickels the customers might have dropped.'' He lit a cigarette and looked across her at Cody. ''You awake over there, Buddy?''

''Yea, yea. Go on.'' Cody sat up, took her hand.

''Well anyway . . . this guy, the crazy dentist, his ol' lady had left him, and he came in almost every night to watch the dancing . . . well, he found out about Cheyenne's scroungin' so he takes a hundred dollar bill and sticks it under the leg of a table and covers it up with sawdust real good. That night when Cheyenne found it, we thought the poor bastard was gonna' have himself a stroke . . . . So then this dentist, he tells him there'll be one of those bills hidden somewhere every week . . . . Well, he starts hidin' them and poor ol' Cheyenne, he would be in the club every night until four, huntin'. . . . The hiding places kept gettin' harder. Stuffed in empty beer bottles, between the paper towels, even in the urinal and toilets. This went on and it got so Cheyenne began dependin' on that extra hundred a week . . . . Then one night, this doctor dude come in and told him he was moving to Wyoming. Well, you should have seen poor ol' Cheyenne's face . . . Anyway, he says he wants to give him a final going away present and he pulls out a $500 bill . . . . Well, that sucker's eyes lit up . . . he was practically drooling . . . . So the doc, he says there's only one thing, he says he's run out of hiding places, there's only one left . . .''

79

Billy Joe started to laugh. "Maybe I better not tell the rest."

"You better," she said.

"Yea, come on, B.J.," Cody joined in.

"This doctor he says, 'Cheyenne, you gotta swallow this bill. Then hunt for it.' . . . Well, that cheap son of a bitch, he don't blink an eye. He rolled that fucker in a little ball and chugged it down with a beer. Then he shit in a bucket for two days until it finally came through. The doc he left town without ever knowing whether Cheyenne got it or not."

The small cab of the pickup rocked with laughter as Billy Joe changed lanes and braked, to turn into the parking lot of the rustic restaurant hanging on a low bluff overlooking the ocean.

When they came to a stop, Cody leaned across her and said, "B.J., you no good bastard, you have a way of talking me out of a mad every time." Instead of feeling left out, she sensed the privilege of being included in this deep and rare friendship between men. And comfortable. Without the pretenses of the country club society she grew up in.

They chose a table by the window where they could watch the surf smash and boil among the rocks below. The wood paneling and profusion of greenery in hanging pots, combined with the thick steaks and good wine to compress the triangular friendship into a circle. Billy Joe liked and trusted her now, and she him. Cody loved them both.

Between the two men on the way home, she lounged in the luxury of thought-to-be dead emotions. The only sour note was the memory of Mara's words. But the woman faded for the moment along with the hate and only the meaning seemed important. Love *is* everything. They parked in back of Cody's trailer. Billy Joe took their silent cue and left them at the door, saying, "I'll be back in an hour."


Cody's mood changed, his troubles returned, once they stepped inside. He walked through the hall and sat down in the darkened bedroom. She followed, leaned against the headboard beside him, took his hand, "Do you want to talk about it?"

He didn't move, neither removed his hand nor acknowledged hers. She felt both confidante and intruder as she listened.

"Sometimes I can't get a handle on it . . . this whole damned life. I come from nothing. Work those crummy, honky tonk bars Kevin talks about. Travel, struggle, sometimes don't get paid, like he said. But I liked it. Liked the people for the most part, just havin' fun, dancing, drinking beer. And when I was sick of it, I could pull out for a while, go to my buddies ranch in Wyoming. Work like an ordinary dude some . . . . But this scares me. All of a sudden—one hit record—and everyone else starts pullin' my strings. Kevin talks about big contracts, concerts. I don't know if I even *want* to get up in front of 30,000 people. Have ladies hangin' all over me. Shit!"

"You haven't signed the contract yet have you?"

"No."

*Then don't do it. We'll hitch up the trailer and drive off into the sunset together. The Lone Ranger and Tonto. Cody and Jill.* Head north. Leave our hurts and worried behind. She didn't say any of it.

"It's a decision you have to make yourself," she answered instead.

"I know." He squeezed her hand. "But I feel a responsibility to the other guys . . . . It's their big chance too . . . . But all of a sudden I'm losing control. Like with this Ron thing. I know they all think I'm crazy, but . . . Hell, I ain't no saint. Been in trouble some when I was younger. Even jail a few times. But these younger people, man . . . you excepted . . . they got me all screwed up with their drug thing." A far off siren stopped him for a moment, its wail adding to the gloom.

"Like Ron . . . . He started with me when he was just eighteen. He don't come from no trash family, dad's a big lawyer, his mamma is a teacher. Real nice people. When he didn't want to go to college, they gave him guitar lessons, new car, everything . . . wanted him to be happy, do his own thing . . . . And God, he's got talent . . . . But I've watched him. Go from an eager fun kid to a glassy-eyed, dull dopehead. He can still play now, but it won't be long before he'll fade but good. The dopers, they call it burn out when you smoke so much of that shit it dulls your minds."

She didn't answer, thinking about Sunday and the girl on the steps of the trailer. He seemed to read her mind.

"I was in love with a girl once. Marcia . . . .

Same fuckin' thing. She started smoking grass. Just once in a while. Got mad when I wouldn't do it with her. Thank God, I never got into that . . . . Anyway . . . pretty soon she was high all the time. Then started on pills, coke, dust, you name it. Didn't care no more about nothin' except that shit. Stole money from me, wrote prescriptions in her daddy's name—he's a doctor. I sat for three days one time waiting to see if she was going to live or die. And the first day out of the hospital she was hunting her pusher. Know where she is now?" He didn't wait for a response. "She's turning tricks on Sunset Boulevard . . . . Her mom and dad had her to clinics, shrinks, everything . . . . And she's out sleeping with dudes for money."

Jill moved closer and put her arms around his chest. He felt so strong yet was so vulnerable.

"I'm sorry, Cody." She held him, listening to his heart pound in her ear, reached to kiss his neck, longing to make the unpleasantness of his world go away. But he continued.

"And the guys responsible, sit out there every night and listen to us play."

"What do you mean?"

"I mean the God damned Fiends . . . . They're a motorcycle gang." She sat up, stiff and alert now. "They run the dope around here. They supplied Marcia and they're handling Ron. Scum of the earth."

His troubles took a backseat now to the question that rushed from her mouth. *Back to the hunt, ready or not.*

"Cody, did you ever know a girl named Mara?"

He stared at her surprised and confused, hesitated a minute, "No . . . why?"

Lie. Lie again. Jill wins the liar's award of the year.

"Oh, that mug I bought you. It was made by someone named Mara . . . and the man in the shop said he thought she was a girlfriend of one of the Fiends. Isn't that a coincidence?" She tried to bring the subject to a close. "Guess I shouldn't have told you. You won't like it anymore."

He pulled her back on the bed.

"Don't worry. I'll like it 'cause it came from you, not some biker chick."

There was a soft tap on the door. Billy Joe. Time for him to go. He kissed her quickly and said, "Take a nap, woman. Cause I'm gonna wake you when I get home," then he was gone out the door.

Jill wandered to the living room and switched on the lamp in the corner. Dude raised his head from his sleeping chair and wagged his tail but she still felt lonely. She considered calling Auntie Mil. No. Nine o'clock in California would be eleven or twelve in Ohio, she couldn't remember which. It didn't matter, both were too late to wake her. And she had nothing to say. The effort to sound cheerful would be too much. Her mind tried to digest the new information about the Fiends. Maybe one of them was the mysterious J.D. Maybe he sat in the Ranch every night and watched Cody. Maybe Mara did?

She picked up Cody's album and put on the side of the record she hadn't heard, hoping his voice would cheer her. It started with the hit song—and she realized immediately that it was written for Marcia.

"I'm not afraid of losing you,
I'm afraid of losing me."

She wished he would let her come to the Ranch with him, but each time she mentioned it, he refused. Despair welled up around her until she felt like a drowning victim . . . too late for CPR, or the paramedics. The breath of fresh air at the restaurant had disappeared. She was at the bottom of the well again. Inhaling water polluted with loneliness, lies, discarded friends—and the obsession that wouldn't let her rest; the obsesssion to find a chicano girl named Maria Rodriquez, alia Mara. The trail had been long and disappointing so far.

Jill eased out of bed before the alarm went off, eager for another day on the ocean. Her new job fitted as comfortably as an old pair of jeans, one she wouldn't want to give up even if a flaw or two should show up later. Even the chance encounters with other morning occupants of the beach didn't frighten her. They were mostly sad-eyed dropouts from the organized world who founded their breathing room on the deserted sand—and respected the similar needs of others. She sucked the chilly air into her lungs and paused to watch a pair of sandpipers pierce the tideline with their long bills. In search of a crab breakfast, they timed their puny-legged retreat perfect to avoid the next incoming wave. As the birds continued their assault and retreat, she acknowledged her buoyant feeling of affection for the ocean and *Sea Maiden*. Jody had expressed it well.

"I guess the ocean's so big, that when you're on a boat, even with all these other people around, you feel free. It makes you forget everything else."

The combination of days on the boat and nights with Cody was making it hard to concentrate on her search for Mara, even to question why she continued. She had to conjure up her father's skeletal face almost lost in the snowdrift of hospital linen—but his delirious tortured moaning grew quieter as time passed.

She hurried now to the boat and Jody. She wouldn't have to analyse or think about anything but her cooking and the sea.

"Howdy partner." The young girl's freckles danced a greeting. Their relationship reminded her of her teenage years with Mara, except for the role reversal. Now she was the confidante and advisor. As they prepared the galley Jody launched into a monologue about her favorite subject, Scott, one of the bait boys. He was tall, skinny, and wore braces—but Jill could see he would soon turn into quite a man and Jody could see it too. The young couple had an interest in anything that would float and often borrowed one of the dinghies after work to row out to the breakwater, drift around, and talk.

"Scott is going to be very successful, Jill. He's saving every penny he makes to buy small sailboats and start his own rental business." Her eyes twinkled. "And he says we will run it together."

The day assumed its soothing routine, and as they finished their clean-up, Jody asked her,

"Want to come to the penny arcade with me?" Jill was anxious to get home to Cody but a familiar plea in the girl's voice made her accept. The first mate came down the steps from the wheelhouse just then.

"Hey Rick, how about going to the arcade with Jill and me?"

She heard the instant's hesitation and saw the glimpse in her direction before his reply.

"Naw, sorry kid, I've got too much work to do. Maybe next week sometime."

*He avoids me.* The thought surfaced for the first time but didn't have time to be questioned as Jody dragged her off the boat and down the pier. The girl stopped a few feet farther on, hooked her arm in Jill's, suddenly serious.

"You know, Jill. I'm the luckiest girl in the world. Scott loves me and you're my best friend."

The pressure began behind her eyes as she heard the familiar words—and she had to look away before she could reply,

"I like you too, Jody. Very much."

The girl's mood changed again; she laughed and pulled at her arm. "Come on, let's skip."

Although people stopped to stare, made her feel a little silly, she had to admit it was fun. They panted to a stop in front of the penny arcade and Jody fumbled in her wallet explaining,

"This is my one vice. Scott says it's a silly waste of money but I've loved the noise and excitement of this place since I was a little girl." She advised

Jill to get four quarters and ten dimes from the change booth. "I always limit myself to $2.00. That's good for ten games of skeeball and four pinball games. Let's start with skeeball."

They each dropped a dime in side by side machines and ten balls rolled down a slot. Similar to bowling, she discovered the object of the game was to roll a ball up the alley and bounce it into the highest scoring area in the center. Jody scored 450 the first game and a middle-aged woman with red hair tore off a yard of coupons from a large roll she was holding and handed them to Jody. Jill's 80 score didn't win any prizes. But by the tenth game she had collected eleven tickets; Jody had 68. At the prize counter, Jody pondered for what seemed hours before she finally selected a plastic fold-up comb for her purse. Jill chose a tiny mouse that looked like blown glass, but turned out to be plastic. She slipped it in her pocket and decided to spend on quarter on a horoscope. But she was sorry immediately. The printing on the small card read: "Although many obstacles get in your way, stick to your primary goal." They used up their remaining money quickly, laughing hysterically at her uncoordinated attempts at pinball. It was dark by the time Jody walked her to the trailer and headed home.

Cody looked up from a stack of papers when she came in.

"Where the hell have you been?" She realized she'd been having such fun that she forgot he might be worried.

"Oh, I'm sorry. We stopped at the penny

arcade. You should have seen me trying to play those games.'' She reached in her pocket. "But I did win you a present.'' She put the small animal in his hand and bent to kiss him but he turned away.

"Who do you mean 'we'?''

*Don't spoil a nice day.*

"Jody . . . asked me to stop on the way home and play skeeball . . . . It was my first attempt and I was terrible.''

She watched him toss the plastic mouse on the table and felt the unwelcome tightness from his shouted, accusing question.

"Just who the hell is Jody?''

Although an inner voice said stay calm, she could hear her volume rise and each word was more shrill than the last.

"Jody, is the girl I've told you about who works with me. She's fifteen . . . . Certainly no threat to your masculine ego.''

His eyes were as steely as the set of his jaw.

"I don't believe you,'' he said quietly.

"Don't . . .'' She took a deep breath and ripped deeper. "What makes you think you have the right to get an account of my every move. What gives you the right to call me a liar?''

In one move he stood and grabbed her shoulders. Each word seemed to come from an inner ice machine. They froze his teeth and jaw and lips, making it difficult for him to speak.

"I just happen to be the dude you're living with, that's all . . . . I just happen to have been waiting and worrying about you for three hours . . . . That's all.'' He let go of her and stepped back.

"Thought we had more going together than you did, I guess. Should have known better." He glared into her eyes, the heat of his next words burned more than his fingers as they released her. "As my pappy said, 'Seen one broad, you seen 'em all'." His lips defrosted into a sneer. "Yep. My pappy said, 'Son, they're all alike . . . . All pink inside'. . . . One just like the next." He stepped back and waited for the impact.

She knew she could end it. Just by saying she was sorry. But the insults reinforced her own doubts and resentments. She remembered all the nights he went to work, wouldn't let her go along, of how she had forced herself not to ask questions—about the girls who hang around the Ranch, what he did until three in the morning, and with whom. She knew what she was about to do, and hated it, yet was powerless to stop.

"I'll find someplace else to live." The sharp sound of the door's slam on her way out announced a finality she regretted immediately.

Her car was sandwiched between the trailer and Cody's truck and angry tears welled in her eyes making it even more difficult to pull forward and back to get out. She didn't want to leave and hoped Cody would come after her but the trailer door remained closed. In a daze, she drove out of the alley, through Santa Monica and down the incline to Pacific Coast Highway. The lights twinkled along the shoreline, and Point Dume sparkled like a diamond necklace, but she didn't notice. When she turned into a campground above Malibu with no recolleciton of how she got there, the young attendant collected a $2.00 fee and directed her to a campsite at the back of the park. Only then did she realize she had no change of clothes or even a toothbrush. She unrolled her sleeping bag and crawled in, hoping for instant unconsciousness. But it was Friday night and the campground was crowded with congenial groups gathered around their fires laughing and talking.

She hated Cody for making her feel so alone; tossed in semi-sleep while thoughts cruised inside her head, one pushing another away before it had a chance to finish. Cody, Auntie Mil, Jody, and her father fought to have their say while she worried that without a watch she might not wake up in time to get to work. Finally, she gave up, climbed into the driver's seat and started the car. The neighboring voices were silent now. Curled up together snug and warm. As she turned into the deserted highway and headed back towards town she realized she thought of people in twos now—couples, lovers, Cody and herself. What happened to the vow of a few weeks ago not to get involved. The argument was silly. Why hadn't she just said she was sorry—instead of stomping out like a spoiled child? The stars were still out and the lights of the pier reflected in the surf as she pulled into the parking lot. She glanced up the cliff in the direction of the trailer although she knew it was hidden by the buildings on each side. He probably wasn't home anyway. Out with someone else. All alike, he said.

She pressed her face against the glass of the restaurant, and was just able to make out the time on the clock behind the counter. Three A.M. She pulled her jacket tighter against the chilly air and looked around. It was safe enough, with the few fishermen scattered about, to sit on a bench and try to catch a little sleep in the two hours before Irma would arrive. The quiet voices and the gentle waves washing the pilings below were more effective than 19 mg. of valium.

The chush, chush, chush was familiar and she knew before she opened her eyes it was the sound of a diesel engine at idle. The bait boat was tied up on the far side of the dock by the restaurant storeroom instead of in its usual place next to the bait shop. Rick stepped off with two young Mexicans—not the men she had seen him with before—and they disappeared from view behind the building. In a moment she knew they were in the back storeroom; the light had filtered through the crack under the door into the restaurant.

When the men returned to the boat and began unloading what looked like the five-pound boxes of squid she'd seen them use at times for bait on *Sea Maiden*, she questioned her intuition to remain quietly where she was. They carried as many as twenty packages at a time. A hundred pounds? By her calculations they unloaded over three thousand pounds of squid. The men seemed to tire towards the end, struggling with only half their beginning load each time. The light finally went out and as Rick paused on the dock and looked in her direction she froze in an unreasonable fear. He lit a cigarette, took a deep drag and then to her relief, untied the stern line and went aboard. One of his companions untied the bow and the boat chugged away from the dock and out past the breakwater. She was still holding her breath. Now they were going after live bait. Why didn't I want him to see me? Why the fear? She cloed her eyes, too exhausted to think anymore.

Irma arrived, surprised to see her asleep on the bench.

"Lordy, gal, you look like somethin' the old tom cat's been dragging around all night." The boisterous laugh jarred. "Or you been draggin' him?"

She tried to smile without success, impatient for the restaurant to be unlocked so she could try and make herself presentable. The restroom mirror confirmed rumpled clothes and circles beneath her eyes. Cold water and a hair brush didn't help much. The metallic taste in her mouth ruined Irma's fresh coffee. She gave up on it and carried her first load of food out to *Sea Maiden* as the bait boat came back into the harbor. Then she went to the storeroom for the meat. Both standup freezers were almost full of frozen squid and as she struggled to get a box of hamburger patties from behind the mountain of white packages, several fell out onto the floor.

"Having trouble?"

She jumped at Rick's voice behind her. The puzzling fear was in her throat again. He retrieved the boxes and shoved them back in place. Why did he make her uncomfortable? Perhaps it was his good looks. A deep seated attraction, maybe.

"The freezer is so full I can hardly get the meat out."

"That's our new supply of bait."

"Why don't you keep it at the baitshop?"

"Well . . . can you keep a secret? I cheated old Mr. Ferguson a little . . . . I got a deal on this for $2.00 a package. Now I'll charge him the regular price of $3.00 and make a buck for myself."

He put his arm around her sholders.

"You won't tell on me, will you?"

She relaxed. This explained his mysterious behavior and her apprehension.

"No, Rick. My mouth is sealed . . . . From what Irma says and what I've seen, you're getting a bad deal from him anyway."

For the first time since she'd known him, he showed some warmth towards her.

"Thanks. I can always use a little praise to start my day."

I could too, she thought, as she carried her carton to the boat. Jody looked up from her cooler loading chores.

"Well, you look bubbly this morning!"

The girl grabbed and whirled her around in the small galley, squealing, "Oh, Jill, I am, I am. Rick told Scott he didn't have to work the bait boat last night so he called and took me to a movie. Afterward we drove up the beach. Oh, Jill," she was suddenly serious, "I'm in love, you know. Really in love."

Jill thought of her own night then and responded unenthused, but Jody didn't seem to notice.

94

Rick came in and poured himself a cup of coffee.

"Better get everything stowed good today, girls. I think we're in for some rough weather."

Jill looked out the window at the sunshine and smooth harbor. "You must be kidding? It's like a pond out there."

"The radio says we might get some Santa Anas. You haven't been around here long enough to know what that means. But they're winds that come out of the East. Cold dry air comes this way . . . it's warmed by compression as it races down the mountain sides. It can be mild as a kitten here in the bay, but when the winds hit on out, they really whip things up." He motioned for her to come out on deck and pointed. "Look out there. That's Catalina Island. See how clear it is . . . . Well, there's a saying among the old salts around here. They say, 'When you can see the island, don't go.'. . . So just get ready to hang on."

She realized how much she had come to respect Rick's ability as a skipper. Irma was right. He was being cheated out of the job that should be his. So she was puzzled.

"You mean you take people out on the boat anyway? Even when you know about the bad weather?"

"Oh, sure. You don't think ol' Fergie would lose a day of profit, do you? But you can bet we'll have a boat full of sickies if the wind does what I think. So be prepared."

After a sleepless night and the disturbing events, this news wasn't welcome. Although she hadn't needed them lately, she decided to take two seasick tablets.

They didn't have a full load of passengers. Some of the regulars must have heard the weather report also. And as they headed out to the fishing area, she couldn't believe that Rick was right. The ocean was flat as a lake; no swells bounced them around and the tiny ripples flickered under a cloudless sky. But Jody pointed to what looked like a layer of smog hanging over the land towards Malibu.

"We're gonna have a zinger. That's a cloud of dust blown clear from the desert."

In two hours she believed them. The wind came—hot and dry as if it had just passed over a blast furnace. Great white-edged watery cliffs rose and swooped under them, sending her skillets skidding from one railing on the stove to the other and back again. The eggs slid up and over the sides, crusted and burned on the surface below. She blistered her fingers while trying to keep the bread on the griddle. At eleven, she breathed a sigh of relief and dropped the pans into the sink. Her stomach felt swollen—as if a balloon had been blown up inside her. Her own brand of *Mal de Mer*.

Most of the passengers weren't faring much better. The waves twisted their lines and threw the fishermen against the rails. Seawater and anchovies swished from the bait tanks on the stern, and washed down the decks and out the drainholes.

Moping and dull, Jill watched Jody bustle about, handing out 7-Ups to sick customers as if she was actually enjoying herself. Scott came in and publicly gave her a hug. It must be love, she thought as she ran for the restroom. The two pills hadn't worked.

When she came back, feeling much better, Jody announced that the boat was going in. It was blowing 35 knots at San Nicholas Island, according to the weather radio, and Rick said it would be doing the same there before long. He didn't care what Mr. Ferguson thought.

"Captain Green leaves all the decisions up to Rick," the girl said, "In fact whenever it gets rough, the good captain gets out his bottle of whiskey and drinks his way back to port."

For the next two hours, *Sea Maiden* fought her way through mountainous waves. With the passengers crowded into the salon to stay dry, it soon turned into a steambath. No one talked. Except Dirty Harry. The wiry old man told one war story after another . . . about the time they stayed out in 25 knot winds and lost 32 fishing poles overboard before the day was over.

"But I caught the biggest fish and won the pool." He grinned. "Only $16 though. Everyone else was too scared and sick to fish . . . Hey, Jill honey, how about putting on some water for my bran?"

She was unable to cope with the stove, so he mixed up his gruel with cold water and ate while she contemplated another run to the restroom. She grabbed the counter and forced her stomach to cooperate. Her head ached and she longed for a soft bed. Anywhere—except on this boat.

"You go on," Jody offered. "I'll clean up tonight."

She accepted, fought her way into line with the departing passengers, anxious to get her feet on solid ground.

Irma came to the door of the restaurant. "Lord bless you child. Can I get you something to eat?"

"I have to get out of here." Jill covered her mouth and, forcing the bile to retreat, raced for the sand. She passed Captain Green's broad rear as it moved more quickly than she'd ever seen. No doubt to the security of a bar stool in Chez Jay's across the street. Ignoring any misgivings about yesterday's fight with Cody, she unlocked her car and headed in that direction. Although she had been inside the boat all day, her lips tasted of salt, her hair was a sticky mass.

Cody was just stepping out of his truck when she drove up. With no thought of her appearance, she threw herself into his arms. She knew he had no love for the ocean or boats, and his alarm for her showed on his face. He held her as they went inside and once assured she was all right, he insisted she get into a hot shower. The warm water pricked at her skin until she felt almost human again. She wrapped her hair in a towel and hurried to get into bed beneath the warm comforter.

Cody laid down beside her on top of the covers, put his hands behind his head, and stared at the ceiling.

"Jill, I love you," he said softly.

Joy lapped at her like the kisses of a puppy dog. As much as she'd tried to deny it, this was what she had wanted since their first meeting on the beach. Mara seemed far away and unimportant.

He turned towards her then, his body warm even through the heavy cover.

"Babe, I swore I'd never let myself in for this kind of thing again. Couldn't take no more hurtin'. . . . And when you left yesterday, I made up my mind I didn't care . . . . But, shit, I couldn't sleep all night . . . . And when you drove up—all a mess and scared to death—I knew I was telling myself lies. I won't act jealous no more, I promise." He touched his index finger to the tip of her nose and grinned. "That is, if you'll just call and at least tell me if you're shacked up with some other dude, so I don't have to get myself worried sick . . . . O.K.?"

"You don't have any reason to be jealous, Cody . . . you're the only thing in this world that I care about." *It's true!* Yes, but it was true before, wasn't it? Didn't you leave someone in Albuquerque? Just drove off without a word. On your crazy Mara hunt. *Stop it* . . . . What, besides a Montgomery Ward car battery, comes with a permanent guarantee in this life, anyway?

She clicked off the annoying inner voice and snuggled into his arms.

The first light of morning pried at her eyelids, and she raised up, panicky that she had over-slept—then realized it was her day off. The cool pillowcase against her cheek emphasized the cozy warmth beneath the covers. Cody was asleep on his stomach with one arm thrown over his head. She enjoyed the chance to study him at her leisure. A cowlick on the right side of his head made a natural part; and silky strands, rumpled now, covered his forehead just touching the darker, heavy brows. The beginning of a beard announced a new day. She noticed for the first time a small indentation, probably a smallpox scar, above his cheekbone. Or maybe he had had acne as a teenager? No, she couldn't picture him with pimples. She ran her foot down the length of his bare leg, eager now to hear the country drawl that he hid behind. "Ah'm just a simple southern boy," he said. But she knew he was more—a talented writer, outstanding performer—and intelligent businessman.

"Hey," he opened his eyes and reached for her. "We got a day to ourselves, don't we? . . . And I got somethin' extra special to show you. What ya' think we stop at a store and fix us up a picnic lunch?"

They dressed, and she poured coffee into a thermos while Dude paced impatiently, somehow knowing he was included in their plans. They drove to the Greek delicatessen down the street and picked and chose an assortment of special treats. Marinated mushrooms, artichoke hearts, and fresh shrimp for her. Corned beef sandwiches and potato salad for him. A bottle of red wine for them both.

He remained secretive over her pleading and wouldn't tell her their destination. Maybe Bakersfield, she guessed, until they turned onto Coast Highway and continued past the campground where she spent that awful night, and on north past Malibu.

The ocean was back to normal with no signs of the turmoil it had put her through the day before. A few small fishing boats sat peacefully in the kelp off shore. They looked fragile compared to *Sea Maiden* and she wondered if they had been caught out yesterday and survived to come back again.

Halfway up a long grade, Cody turned off the highway to the right, onto a narrow two lane road that led away from the ocean. A few small homes nestled in private wilderness niches at first but as the road twisted and turned higher and higher, all signs of civilization disappeared. The hills were covered with bushy vegetation, broken only with an occasional outcropping of rock. After perhaps five miles, Cody turned again, this time down a narrow dirt drive. Dude stood up on the seat and began an excited whine while his tail banged her face. Cody slowed to a stop and leaned across to open the passenger door.

"We'll let him out to run. He knows where we're going."

The big dog disappeared and for the first time she noticed the change in vegetation. Although weeds grew everywhere, the large acacia trees lining the drive, and the palms and bottle brush didn't come from random seedlings. Someone had planted them.

As they wound through an arch of overhanging branches, Cody turned to her with the grin of a Little Leaguer after a game winning homerun,

"I found this place when I first came to California. I was so homesick for space. Hated the traffic and too many people. Could come up here and get lost for awhile."

They exited from the trees and she understood. He pulled up to a cement slab and shut the motor off; she gasped involuntarily and jumped out of the truck for a better look. They were on top of the mountain with the Pacific Ocean spread out before them, so far below that the breaking surf was silent. Only the sounds of birds, disturbed by their presence, broke the stillness. To her left, the coastline curved in and she could make out the buildings of Santa Monica and the pier. Farther South, Palos Verdes Peninsula jutted out as if trying to touch the two mounds rick had said yesterday were Catalina Island. Cody came up behind her and pointed out other islands to the right.

"The smaller one is Anacapa, the biggie is Santa Cruz. They're up off the coast of Ventura . . . . Today is really clear. If you look way out, this side of Catalina, you can even see Santa Barbara Island."

She searched until she found the tiny dot on the horizon.

"This must be God's view from heaven. We're not only on top of the world, Cody, we're above it."

Dude loped up to them with an excited greeting, then took off to leave his mark on the shrubbery as Cody laughed.

Dude loped up to them with an excited greeting, He grabbed her hand, "Come on, I'll give you a tour." They walked around the cement as he explained, "There was a big house here once. A man and his wife built it themselves. But it burned down about 10 years ago. The wife died in the fire and he never rebuilt. But he wouldn't sell the land either. In fact, he still came up here and took care of things."

"I see what you mean." Two freeform garden areas, one on each side of what would have been the front door were in perfect condition, as if the gardener had been at work yesterday. To her right was a rose garden, blooming white, red, salmon and yellow. The bushes were pruned and she could see the marks from a rake in the weedless soil beneath them. The other area was a cactus garden in the same well-tended condition.

"Cody, I don't think we should be here."

He put his arm around her shoulders and continued,

"It's all right . . . . You see, these were his wife's plants. So he came up here and took care of them for her. Let everything else go."

She became more insistent. "Cody, what if he comes? We shouldn't be here. It's . . . it's too private." A chill raised bumps on her arms but he continued as if she hadn't spoken.

"Ah learned what all these catcuses, excuse me, cacti, are . . . . This one here is a *Cholla*. That's the Spanish word for teddy bear . . . . Don't he look like one? All furry . . . . And that one over there is a mule ear. Can't remember his formal name." She could see the resemblance to the ears of a mule but she wasn't enjoying herself and begged again to leave.

"But Cody brought a blanket from the truck, spread it out in front of the slab, between the two flower beds and insisted that she sit. *What if the man drives in and they are here?* Cody sat down next to her, obviously unconcerned.

"This is mine."

*Oh no! More past she doesn't know about.* She tried to keep the emotion out of her voice when she asked,

"You mean you own this? . . . You were married to that woman? You come up here and take care of the flowers? Oh, Cody!"

She was further confused when he laughed.

"You're part right . . . An' part wrong. I do come up and take care of things . . . But no, I'm not the original cat. I told you, he wouldn't sell it . . . . Well, that was lucky, cause I couldn't have bought it then anyway. Didn't take two nickels to rub together . . . . But he died about six months ago. I knew because the weeds started growin' in the beds. So I kept coming up and cleaning. Got a book on how to prune roses . . . Then last week, after we signed our recording contract."

"You did? What about Ron? And those concerts you weren't so sure of?"

"Anyway, I found the realty guy and bought it. It's mine." His voice had a finality she didn't like.

"But Cody, I thought you loved Wyoming so much? Wanted to go back there? Couldn't stand the city?"

"Stop it, Jill, damn it. I didn't bring you up here to give me the third degree . . . . I'm stuck here for awhile. And this place is the next best thing to the wide open spaces."

He had made his decision and he wanted her to agree to its rightness not question.

"Oh Cody, it's beautiful. It reminds me of the song, 'On a clear day you can see forever.' "

"Jill, this contract . . . for recordings and concerts . . . It's for three million dollars . . . . Now no country boy could turn that down, now could they? . . . It'll work out okay."

*Money isn't everything. Believe me, I know.*

"I'm happy for you, cowboy."

"Jill?" He was tense, and his next words rushed out like those of a kid in a highschool play, well rehearsed—but anxious to be said.

"Jill, I'm going to move the trailer up here tomorrow, live in it while I get a house built. Will you come with me?"

His seriousness embarrassed and frightened her. Unable to match it she chose a lightness she didn't feel.

"That's an offer I can't refuse, cowboy."

He ignored her tone and kissed her hand. They laid back on the blanket tranquilized by the ocean breeze playing across their faces and bodies. Even the birds were quiet now.

"You can quit your job on that damn boat. Travel with me . . ." His voice trailed off.

She sat up, a feeling of doom grabbed her chest as she thought of her unfinished business.

"Cody, I can't."

He opened his eyes and squinted up at her. "Can't what?"

"I can't quit the job. I love it . . . even if I get sea sick once in awhile. I wouldn't be happy not working." *I'm getting closer to Mara.* "Can't I move up here with you, and still go to work? You're busy all day. We'd still have the evenings together."

She could hear the relief in his voice and hated

105

her deception.

"My God, Babe, I thought you'd like to quit. But I don't care if you think it's fun to scramble eggs for a bunch of old fishermen. . . . Just stay cool with that . . . what's his name? . . . Rick? . . . You know, that's who I thought you were with the other night. . . . And I was sitting home with the contract on this place waiting to tell you about it . . . . Hell, you can see why I was mad, can't you?"

"I'm sorry, Cody. And you don't have to worry about Rick. As a matter of fact, he makes it a point to stay away from me. . . . Hey, cowboy . . . I'm starving, thought you were going to feed me."

They spread their picnic out on the blanket and ate like a couple of truckdrivers. Dude trotted up for a taste of the leftovers but shook his head and sneezed at the vinegar on the mushrooms.

Cody laughed, "Just a country boy like me, aren't you Dude? Want plain food, no fancy stuff."

She wondered if Cody would stay plain with three million in his jeans. As if in answer to her question, he started talking about the house he wanted to build.

"What kind of houses do you like?" he asked her.

Jill had definite ideas. She loved modern designs of wood and glass. With two story ceilings and no corners. Balconies and towering fireplaces . . . and pillows scattered about—for sitting on the floor—and making love. But she answered,

"It's your house, Cody. You should built what you want."

His expectant expression clouded.

"I guess I forgot to mention one thing. I didn't mean for us to live in sin no longer. I want to make it legal. Do the right thing by you . . . So, it would be your house, too."

The old fashioned phrases must have been buried deep inside him, left over from childhood. She was touched but unable to stop her frivlous manner, her second choice of escape from serious emotions. First choice was always running away.

"I'll bet you say that to all the girls, cowboy."

He stared out to sea. "Why do you do that to me?"

*Why do I?*

"I never asked anyone to marry me before. It's not easy. . . . When I finally do . . ." Anger flared in his eyes, then the curtain dropped and dulled their blue and his voice. "Don't be a smart ass. Just say what you mean. . . . If . . . if all you want is a roll in the hay, just tell me. I can give you that . . . . Just tell me, Cody, all you're good for is free room and board and a fuck now and then . . . . Makes no difference to me."

But she knew it did. To her too. She wanted no repeat of another senseless fight. Why can't I let go and say what I feel—and feel what I say?

"Cody, I'm sorry. I want to marry you." The man beside her, the roses, the ocean and the unblemished universe overhead fought hard to wipe out every other thought—but they lost when she added, "but let's wait awhile."

"Whatever you say, Babe." He reached for her. Their lovemaking reminded her of yesterday's storm. The gentle beginning in the bright sunshine—building to a fierce, frightening pinnacle—then dropping back slowly to a body, mind, and spirit enveloping peace. As they laid motionless, their bodies massaged by the warm air, a warning—or maybe a universal truth—repeated again and again in her mind. She spoke the words quietly to herself.

"Love is fragile, especially now."

He asked without moving, "What'd you say?"

She repeated it, sure she had discovered an important secret of life.

"Love is fragile, especially now."

"Right on, Babe." Cody slapped her bare thigh and stood up. "Come on, get your clothes on before you shock ol' Dude there."

They sipped wine, and watched as the sun dropped in the water, then assumed the role of absentee artists, painting an abstract across the sky in front of them. They were silent, each lost in his own thoughts.

*I can't be a taker.* Mara was a taker. The money wasn't important. It was only a symbol. Mara was a taker of emotions. She offered love and trust and security. Then when she had it all, when she was sure you were hooked, she pulled it all away.

Jill shivered and Cody misunderstood.

"It's getting chilly. Let's head back."

As the headlights flashed from one side of the curving roadside to the other, casting eery shadows on the landscape, she moved closer to feel the warmth of his arm. Happy for herself, afraid for him.

She crossed the parking lot, unable to believe she would go home tonight to a mountaintop. As she walked the length of the pier, the locked doors of the various businesses made her realize she had no more idea who the mysterious J.D. was than the first day she came here. The casual questions of the people she'd met—other than the man in the pottery shop—had led nowhere. Mara was mixed up somehow with the Fiends . . . and Cody said they were involved with drugs. But that was about it.

Irma met her at the door to the restaurant, slapped her goodnaturedly on the back, ignorant of her own strength.

"Well, Girlie, you sure look a might better than when I saw you last. You was green as a frog's ass. . . . Day's vacation did you some good. Or was it the boyfriend? He give you any?" The huge bosoms shook with laughter, as Jill escaped to the store room.

The freezer was still full of Rick's bargain squid, and as she was silently congratulating him for his resourcefulness, she again knocked several packages to the floor. With a retrieved package in each hand, she realized something was amiss. One weighed only half as much as the other. Yet the boxes were identical, each marked $4.98. She checked the freezer. The packages toward the back were definitely lighter. Was Rick cheating Mr. Ferguson on the weight too? No. He could short them a few ounces maybe but not this much. The old man would be sure to catch such a large

109

discrepancy.

Her mind flashed to the argument between the two strange men and Rick that first morning, his telling Scott he didn't have to go on the bait boat the night the squid was unloaded, the strange way he'd looked when the packages fell from the freezer and his rush to pick them up before she did. The word in the letter to Mara—connection—it was all so obvious. She slipped one of the lighter packages under the hamburger patties and hurried to the galley, transferred it to her large purse and zipped it closed. Then she climbed the steps to the empty pilothouse. She had to see what Rick's full name was. Disappointment flooded through her as she looked at the framed Captain's license on the wall. Richard Lewis Cluny. No J.D. at all.

She was suddenly relieved, since she wanted to trust Irma's and Jody's judgement of him. Rick hadn't written the letter to Mara and he wasn't mixed up in drugs. It was probably the Mexicans, or maybe even Mr. Ferguson. She wanted to forget it all, even finding Mara. She was going to marry Cody, and be happy.

The rest of the day was routine; a full boat, calm weather and little time to think about anything but the time bomb she had foolishly stashed under the counter. When Jody started to move her purse to get an onion, Jill grabbed it from her and put it in the cupboard under the stove.

"What have you got in there, Jill, a million dollars?"

"No, but almost that much." Her throat constricted with the joke that wasn't.

110

"What's the matter? Don't you feel good today? Seasick again?"

"I'm all right. Just nervous that it might happen again, I guess," she answered.

She departed with the last passenger, glanced back to see that no one was following her, then hurried to her car. The parking lot was practically empty as she sat in the driver's seat and with shaking hands, unzipped her purse and took out the package. It was no longer cold. Felt soft to her hands—and had no fish odor. She peeled back the tape to each end and unfolded the wrapping. The contents did not really surprise her, only confirmed her suspicions. The light cardboard box held a plastic bag of fine white powder.

She sat catatonic with the package in her lap. It could be heroin or cocaine, she didn't know which, but whatever, she had stumbled into a first-class drug traffic operation. *Why did I take it and what am I going to do with it now?* And with the information? There was a good chance Rick didn't know he was a party to a drug-running operation, she kept telling herself. Mr. Ferguson was undoubtedly behind it? She remembered reading of innocent citizens being used unknowingly, or—remembering Rick's anger—maybe even against his will. When her hands recovered their ability to function, she carefully rewrapped the package, raised the sheet of plywood next to her, and placed it underneath. The compartment should be safe enough but she unrolled her sleeping bag over the top just to be sure.

The possibilities whirled around her as she drove

111

up the coast. No one could know she knew. But as she turned off the highway, a blue car followed her. It was old. Maybe a Plymouth. She couldn't see the driver. He stayed too far behind. But he was following her. She was sure of it. Her knees were weak, her thighs burned, and her hands felt glued to the steering wheel as she speeded faster and faster around the curves. The car disappeared then appeared again, closer now. She tried to concentrate on the road ahead and watch the rear view mirror at the same time. The memory of childhood games of tag flashed before her. The panic of being chased that always made her stop and be caught. Just when she knew she was about to do the same thing now, the car vanished. She slowed to twenty and watched, but it was gone. She pulled over and waited. Nothing. *Just someone going home from work.* She felt foolish now and anxious to reach Cody and their new home.

The trailer looked small and lonely, sitting on the giant cement slab, and she wished for a moment it was back in Santa Monica. But as she took a deep breath and opened the door, Dude almost knocked her down, and Cody whirled her round and round in the small room in an unusual display of exuberance.

"Just look out there!"

The drapes were open and he had placed the trailer so the front windows offered a awe-inspiring view of coast, heaven and sea.

"I bought steaks for dinner and you're going to The Ranch with me tonight. It's about time you see how I earn my living."

112

She wondered at his change of heart. Perhaps it was the promise of marriage. He must have need that. She stopped herself before she began to analyze. Remembering the car, she was just thankful she didn't have to stay alone tonight.

They ate and drank and made love. She had never seen Cody happier. She decided to throw the cursed package over a cliff on the way to work in the morning. When she came out of the bathroom after showering, he handed her a gift-wrapped box.

"It's not my birthday."

"Naw, this is an un-birthday present. Open it."

A film of organdy nestled in the crinkly tissue and floated as she lifted it, only then recognizable as a blouse made out of delicately flowered hand-kerchiefs. The material ended in points at the front and back, and the sleeves were wide and flowing. Although it was a contrast to the tailored clothes she was accustomed to, she experienced great pleasure when she put it on to see the look of satisfaction on his face.

"You know, Babe, you are one beautiful lady."

The sleeves tickled but she enjoyed their flutter when she moved her arms. She felt like a butterfly erupting from a cocoon.


The side lot was already jammed with cars and tucks when Cody parked, and they went in the back door of the club. Billy Joe and the other members of the band were gathered at the far end of what appeared to be a large storeroom stacked with cases of beer. Jill was surprised to see Ron,

113

and commented on it.

Cody's face tenses as he replied, "It was part of the deal. Had to keep him." They joined the group.

"Hey, Medic," Cody slapped the thin drummer on the back. "How's it goin' tonight?"

The young man pushed at the bridge of his glasses.

"Well, Cody, not so good. Can't seem to wake up. You know, I haven't been getting enough sleep lately. . . . So I decided to take a little nap about six. But I slept maybe about an hour too long. . . . Now I feel kind of tired."

The others roared with laughter as Jill watched, confused. B.J. slapped his thigh.

"Oh, come on, Medic. We know what's wrong with you. . . . It's that god damned bran you're always shovin' down your throat. You're shittin' so much, it's making you weak."

The owl eyes stared at Billy Joe, serious.

"No, you're wrong. I've read a great number of scientific papers on the subject of bran. It's not that. I think I just slept maybe an hour too long, that's all."

Cody grinned at Jill. "You see why we call him Medic, don't you?" He gave the drummer an affectionate nudge. "This guy monitors his body, every minute and hour of the day."

"Well, Cody, I'm going to be healthy when I'm eighty and the rest of the guys . . . the way you abuse your bodies . . . you're probably never make it."

"Whatever you say, Doc. Anywawy, you're a

fuckin' good drummer."

"That's because I take care of myself."

"Hey, Janice," Cody called to the cocktail waitress coming through the door from the bar, "Come on over here. I want you to meet Jill."

The girl looked her over from head to toe, but if she wasn't pleased, she hid it with a smile.

"Hi, Honey. I've been hearing lots of good things about you. Now I know why."

Billy Joe interrupted. "Janice, you be nice to this gal, hear? Or I'll beat you up." He raised a fist playfully in her face.

The tiny girl, looking no more than eighteen, turned angelic blue eyes and an innocent smile towards her and said, "Show me a guy with a beard and I'll show you an asshole every time." Then she laughed and there was no mistaking the adulation in her voice as she asked Cody, "Want me to get Jill a good seat?"

"Sure do. Go on with her now, Babe, and I'll see you at the break."

"Yea, Janice." Billy Joe swatted the girl's rear. "And I'll take you out back and give you a break you'll never forget."

Janice pushed open the swinging doors, and without looking back, gave a flip of her hips and answered, "Fuck off, jerk."

Laughter followed them as she trailed behind Janice like a puppy, through the crowd of loud voices and clinking glasses to a table against the back wall. She squeezed into a chair as directed; Janice perched on the table beside her.

"Don't pay any attention to me. I just like to kid

with those guys. Especially B.J. . . . Me and him got a good thing goin' . . . And that Cody, he's the greatest . . . . I hope you know that.''

"I know that," she answered, wondering at the same time if she had been put in Marcia's regular seat. If Cody ever returned Janice's admiration? Now who's being jealous? This place was raising all sorts of questions and she wasn't sure she wanted to know the answers. Maybe that's why Cody didn't want her to come here before.

Janice stood up. "Gotta' get to work. I'll stop by later." In a few minutes she returned, set a glass of white wine on the table, and left again without a word.

She looked around, feeling out of place by herself. Most of the customers were couples in their twenties and thirties. A few tables were occupied by two or three girls, and several by stags, but none by women alone. The room rustled with excitement as Cody and the others came onto the bandstand. Conversations continued as they turned their instruments and adjusted the sound system, but when they hit the first note, the audience was immediately quiet. Cody sang the first phrases and the crowd erupted with wild applause and whistles. The song was obviously a favorite, Jill listened to the familiar drawl manipulate the words, tell the story of a man tormented by a unfaithful woman. Like a good novelist, he forced his audience to love, and hate, and care. Ron joined in on the chorus and she could see why he was such an important part of the group. His instrumentals accented and enchanced Cody's while the dream-like quality of his voice—although probably induced by drugs—added an undeniable emotional impact. They finished to a deafening roar from their admirers.

When the noise died down, Cody spoke softly into the mike, "Ah just wrote this one . . . And it's the first time we've done it for an audience. So bear with us. It's called 'I Can Wait'." He never looked in her direction, just began.

When I asked the question
I just
Hung my head in gloom
'Cause she's a free style city gal
You gotta give her room.

When I asked the question
She thought it was all play
But she's a crazy lovin' city gal
Who don't understand
My way.

Ron joined in and they boomed out the chorus,

But I can wait
I can wait.

The rest of the set was a blur. 'I can wait' was the only message she'd received. Janice appeared to tell her Cody wanted her to come to the back room. She moves self-consciously past the stares from the bar and through the rear door.

He smiled and said they could go sit in the truck

117

out back. She studied his face. He appeared to be the same man she'd been living with, a little shy, quiet, serious much of the time, different from the dynamic performer she'd just watched.

"Cody Williams, you are the greatest. No wonder they're fighting to give you three billion dollars. Do you realize how much pleasure you give people? What your singing does to hearts and pulses?"

He leaned back against the seat and grinned.

"Hey, hang on. You'll give me such a big head you won't be able to live with me." Then he asked quietly, "Did you like the new song?"

She moved closer to him, took his hand. Feeling hard calluses on his fingers from a lifetime with a guitar, she wondered how he managed to stay so soft and gentle inside.

"I like the song . . . But . . . Cody . . . I never thought of myself as a slick city girl and you as some country bumpkin. . . . Never. That's not why I wanted to wait to get married. . . . There were other reasons. . . . But they don't matter anymore. I love you. . . . Let's get married right away."

Before their lips touched, he murmured, "Sure, Babe, that's cool."

*I said it*! I said I love you. And it wasn't a lie.

They jumped like teenagers necking on the sofa when Billy Joe pounded on the door and shouted, "Who the hell is working here tonight, anyway?" As she smoothed her half on the way in, B.J. commented stone-faced, "I thought I told you. Janice and I had first dips on the truck."

Jill blushed, then embarrassed as blushing, reddened even more. Everyone laughed and she felt more at home, less conspicuous when she returned to her table alone.

Engrossed in the music, she hardly noticed someone slipping into the seat next to her.

"You a friend of Cody's?"

She turned toward the voice and met a pair of piercing brown eyes. The man looked about thirty. A fine scar cut across his right eyebrow and disappeared in wavy chestnut hair, adding distinctiveness to an otherwise average face. A black, size extra large, teeshirt revealed bulging biceps as it advertised in bold letters *Two Fingers Tequila*.

She answered a curt "Yes," to his question and returned her attention to the bandstand.

"Cody and I are old friends, go back a lot of years. . . . Name's Neal," he shouted over the music. When she looked again he put out his hand. She hesitated, then took it.

"Hi, I'm Jill."

He leaned back in his chair, took a swallow of beer and moved his head to the beat of the music, singing the words under his breath. She paid no more attention to him, more excited with her decision to give up the Mara thing and make a life for herself with Cody. Auntie Mil would be happy. She would call her tomorrow.

Janice interrupted her thoughts as she set her tray down on the table and said,

"Vanish, asshole. You're sitting in my seat."

Jill looked at the empty chair in front of her.

Cody's friend picked up his beer, shrugged his shoulders and stood up. He looked at Jill with a half smile and said,

"Don't argue with the help around this place. I learned the hard way. You end up 86'd or out in the street on your ass." He threaded his way to the bar.

Janice turned to her, "Don't mess around with that creep. I'm telling you, he's nothing but trouble."

Jill answered what seemed an unreasonable anger with the only thing she could think of, "But he said he was a friend of Cody's." She was slightly angry herself. "And I wasn't 'messing around' with him. He just came and sat down."

Janice exploded, "Holy shit. That cocksucker! He ain't no friend of nobody's." Several heads turned in their direction. "He's one of the Fiends." Jill needed no explanation but Janice didn't know that as she continued, "That's a motorcycle gang. They're bad cats to fool around with, believe me. And Cody hates them."

She resented all Janice seemed to know about Cody, what he liked and didn't like, but she realized the girl was only being nice.

"Thanks Janice. I appreciate your telling me."

This encouraged confidence and when the music stopped, the girl leaned over and whispered in her ear.

"You know, Cody had a girl before you. Her name was Marcia."

*Not again.* Jill was sick of hearing about Marcia. Resented the snapshot that was still pinned to the

120

wall in the trailer. Marcia even went with them to the top of their mountains. Those drugged, dreamy eyes were right now staring out at the starfilled skies.

Janice continued, "Well, she got mixed up with the Fiends. Really went on a trip. In fact, I heard she was fuckin' that asshole Neal for her dope. So Cody's real sensitive like, you know, about them dudes."

Janice hopped up to take care of her tables while Jill wished the conversation hadn't taken place. Her joy was gone.

When Cody started his end of the night fadeout—introducing the members of the band and reminding customers to come back tomorrow night—Jill wormed her way through the tight tables to the back room, anxious to leave the evening's confusions behind. The five musicians followed in a moment, joking and laughing together. And although Cody put his arm around her, he was absorbed in music talk.

"Did you hear that lick, man? I picked that up from Buckles Sullivan. Deedle-de-deedle-deedle-de-dah." He strummed an imaginary guitar. "Man, it is so good, shit."

B.J. slapped his hand. "Yea, I heard it. Ol' Buckles is all right. He can't fuckin' talk, but he sure can play."

She stood excluded and tired, unable to listen to the words, most of them foreign to her. Ron did not join in. He picked up his jacket and exited through the back door without a word.

"Can we go now, Cody?"

He frowned at her. "B.J. wants us to wait for Janice." The girl walked up as she protested silently to herself.

B.J. said, "Janice and I are going to Gene's for scrambies. He asked you guys to come too." Jill said nothing, sure Cody would refuse—but instead, he answered,

"Sure, OK, Babe? That wife of his makes the best eggs in town."

B.J. ordered them to come on and follow him as Janice went out the back first, moaning about "the shit eating crowd that must have their tip money stuck up their asses."

Jill wallowed in self pity and disappointment as they drove behind B.J.'s pickup through a maze of dark, residential streets. She wanted to be alone with Cody. But he was wound up, eager after a long night for his turn at some fun. And she did realize that while everyone at The Ranch was playing, Cody was working. But she was also jolted at the thought of how early she had to be at work herself in the morning. Oh well, one night wouldn't hurt.

They turned off onto a tree-lined street of very expensive homes, similar in size to the one she grew up in.

"Where are we going anyway?"

They pulled into a circular drive in front of a large two-story English style home.

"This is Gene and Marion's. He's a big shot lawyer. Likes our music and is handling some legal things for us. A real nice guy. And his wife is great too. You'll like them."

Billy Joe and Janice had already gone inside as they followed the used brick sidewalk toward the front door. She reached for his arm to stop him.

"Cody? . . . I . . . I just want to tell you . . . How much I love your music . . . and you."

"Yea, Babe. I love you too. And I'm glad you like the sounds. Come on." He was distracted and in a hurry to get inside. His indifference hurt but the door opened then, making any more private conversation impossible.

Although he was a picture of physical fitness, Jill was certain upon close observation that the man inviting them into the large foyer was fifty or more—and didn't want to be. His thick grey Prince-Valiant haircut and the western shirt and jeans, probably custom tailored, denied the staid lawyer image but failed to disguise either age or wealth.

Cody made the introductions and Gene held her hand just a fraction too long, then gave it a squeeze as his mahogony eyes searched hers to give extra meaning to his, "*Very* happy to meet you." Cody didn't seem to notice. He started toward the back of the house.

*Relax*. You're just tired.

But when Gene said, "Come meet the ol' lady," took her arm and smiled—his canines, just a shade too long in an otherwise perfect dentition, reminded her of the vampires in the old horror movies. I vant to suck your blood! She shuddered and pulled her arm away without looking at him. His wife, Marion, was at the stove cutting bacon into a skillet with a pair of kitchen shears. The woman's

123

friendliness reassured her as Gene introduced them quickly and left.

"Can I help you?" Jill asked the woman.

"Oh, heavens no. I love to cook and these late night get togethers are my only chance. Otherwise, Edna, our housekeeper, won't let me near the kitchen." The small woman insisted that Jill go join the others, but not before she noticed that Marion looked older than her well put together husband. Although Jill was sure she wasn't. The slim figure and tanned, lined face; the grey hair parted on one side and falling straight to just below the ears, reminded her of the women who belonged to her father's country club in Columbus. Not the loud-laughing neuvo riche in their mink stoles. But the old members. They were so secure with their stature that they played their golf and tennis and wore drab tweeds and baggy Bermuda shorts without any thought or worry toward their aging. She had liked them. The Auntie Mils of the world.

As she passed the massive stone fireplace in the living room and went on into the dining room, the porcelains and paintings—the crystal and silver reinforced her intuition that this home and its contents didn't come from a lawyer's earnings, no matter how successful. They had been purchased generations ago and lovingly passed down to—no doubt about it—Marion. She recognized the banquet table and high-backed chairs as 17th century English oak. Admiring the wood's beauty, made more so by age, she realized why she felt a closeness to the woman in the kitchen and a wariness of her husband. His office was probably chrome and plastic and Naugahyde—with flashing disco lights.

As she entered the party room, she was aware of the same good taste in furnishings. More Marion. Soft lights were absorbed by the routed walnut paneling and except for the brightness over the pool table, the room had a warm, cozy feeling. Cody and Billy Joe were engrossed in a game of pool; Janice sat on a high stool kibbitzing. Gene motioned her to a seat at the bar and although she didn't want to join him, she didn't know how to refuse without being rude.

"What can I get you?"

"Just a plain tonic water, Please." She was tired. Cody missed an easy shot and she was ashamed at her silent delight. Billy Joe followed with a spectacular combination shot but left the cue ball blocked against the far rail. Janice downed a shot of tequila and laughed,

"Boy, you sure fucked yourself this time, sweetie."

B.J. bent over to take an exaggerated look at his crotch, at the same time drawling, "Did I really? I didn't even notice. Must be taking lessons from you."

Janice climbed off the stool and hit him on the shoulder. "You shithead! You know I'm the best piece of ass you ever had." She bent his arm behind him. "Now admit it." He faked he was hurt and agreed.

*Out of the mouths of angels*! Cody never looked her way just continued with the game.

When Gene handed her a drink, he reached for

her other hand, stroked the back of it with his index finger and with the confidence of a professional Romeo, spoke in a half-whisper, "You know, you're something else." He reached up and let his fingers glide through her hair. She glanced in the direction of the pool table but Cody was still unaware of her.

The vampire teeth appeared again as he continued with frank assurance of a man who was never turned down.

"I'm attracted to you. If you ever get tired of the cowboy scene, my office number is in the book. We could arrange a weekend somewhere." He reached for her hand again but she pulled away. "You know. Get it on some and then just kick back, with a little weed, maybe. I know a great spot in Laguna."

The anger boiled in her. She wished she could be like Janice and tell him to "Fuck off," but he was Cody's friend. So instead, she mustered enough dignity to turn her back on him and walk over to Cody without a word of response. Cody seemed surprised, as if he'd forgotten she was there when she came up from behind and put her arm around his waist.

"Oh, hi Babe, where you been?" She wanted to tell him but he moved away for his next shot.

Marion came in then with a large tray of scrambled eggs and toast, called them all to sit at the game table in the corner.

Jill made sure she was on the far side of the table from Gene but each time she looked up he smiled, smirked, or stared at her. To make her discomfort even worse, she could see Marion watching her husband closely. *And Cody didn't even notice!* She picked at her food, eyes riveted to her plate. The eggs seemed to stick in her throat. Billy Joe excused himself to go to the restroom and when he came back said:

"Marion, that sure is a pretty bathroom."

Janice looked up, her fork stopped, halfway to her mouth.

"Well, Billy my boy, if you think it's so fuckin' pretty, why don't you go back in there and take a shit."

"Good Christ, Janice," he answered, "you really are a garbage mouth." He glanced nervously at Marion. Jill did too but Marion laughed and threw an arm around the young waitress.

"Don't pick on her, B.J. Janice is one of the funniest people I've ever known—and one of the nicest. . . . And you know whatever she says is honest." She looked directly at her husband. "More than we can say about most people wouldn't you say?"

"Thanks, Marion." Janice pointed her fork at B.J. "See asshole," then she looked serious, about ready to cry, "Marion knows I'm honest. That my kidding around doesn't mean anything. That I would never fool around on you if we got married."

B.J.'s face tightened but whatever he was about to say was interrupted by Gene.

"Married? Jesus Christ! Don't you know marriage is an outmoded institution."

Jill glanced at Marion but the woman's face was

127

a blank.

He continued, "Marriage, divorce, marriage, divorce. That's all I see in my office every day. Fights and arguments over kids and money. But the money is the most important. Believe me." As he paused Jill could feel the tension around the table but Gene continued, "Let's face it. A lifetime is too long to be tied down to one person. Serial marriage is the answer. When one party or both are tired of the relationship they can feel free to walk away without guilt."

Cody reached for her hand under the table, his first show of affection since they had arrived. She could see the now familiar twitch begin in his cheek as he stared at Gene.

"Jill and I are getting married. And it's by God gonna be for a lifetime. None of your serial shit."

She was proud of him, yet the words frightened her. Marion stood up and began stacking plates. She hurried to help her carry the dishes to the kitchen. The older woman kept her back to her as she said,

"Don't let Gene bother you, Jill."

Jill tried to deny knowing what the older woman meant, embarrassed for Marion, but she stopped her and continued,

"He's a good man, Jill. We've been married thirty years, raised two sons, had a good life. But poor Gene can't face getting old." Marion turned from the sink.

"Just try to be nice to him, and understand."

*Nice? Understand?* She searched for a way to end this conversation but failed. Marion scraped leftovers into the sink and continued.

"If you would enjoy it, go meet him someplace. He's asked you, hasn't he?"

"Marion, no!"

"Go off with him. . . . Because if it isn't you, it will be someone else?"

The roar of the garbage disposal vibrated her nerve endings as the woman attempted to dispose of the more than just what was left on the plates.

"He tried Janice. But she turned him down as only Janice can turn someone down. Now, you're the target. And if an 18-year old walked in, you would be forgotten. . . . You see, it's just your youth he's after. The younger the woman, the farther he feels from that inevitable end of the line.

"He looks at me and feels his age; he looks at you and feels twenty." Marion laughed, "I guess he never looks in the mirror."

"Oh, Marion." She hugged the woman to her. "It will pass. I know it will. . . . And don't worry about me. . . . I'm in love with Cody." They parted and stared at each other for a moment.

"I know it will too. He could never give up the security of this house. . . . You're a nice girl, Jill. I always wished I had had a daughter."

Every profanity she'd ever heard, surfaced, as she hurried to the pool room—and insisted they must leave immediately. Amusement twinkled in Gene's eyes and she realized this was a game he must play regularly, getting a cheap thrill out of maneuvering under his wife's nose—and at her expense.

As they left, he stood in the doorway with his

arm around Marion, and the last words she heard as she walked down the driveway with Cody was,

"Remember. *Anytime.*"

She wished him a slow and painful death.

Cody was quiet on the way home, allowing her mind to wander back to another time, another older man.

She had been eleven, the year before her father married Mara. Her best friend, Julie Evans, invited her home after school for dinner and to spend the night. Julie's parents went to a country club dance, and the girls spent the evening watching TV, and later making the typical crank telephone calls of girls their age. To the drugstore: Do you have Prince Albert in the can? Yes. Well, why don't you let him out?

They went to bed and giggled until they heard the car drive in, then feigned sleep as the parents climbed the stairs to their bedroom. A few minutes later she had whispered Julie's name but her friend was already asleep in the twin bed across the room. Over-excited by the fun of the evening and unable to drop off, she lay listening to the pre-retirement sounds from the master suite; water ran, the toilet flushed, then the muffled voices ceased. She closed her eyes, finally drowsy. The crickets played their leggy tune outside the window.

She was almost asleep when she sensed or heard something. Terrified, she opened her eyes a crack and tried to keep her breathing steady like she'd seen actresses in the movies do when they fell victim to a cat burglar. It took a second for her eyes to adjust to the darkness but when they did, she found herself face to genitalia with a naked Mr. Evans. He stood motionless, his penis (the first she'd ever seen) erect and inches away. She clamped her eyes closed while his uneven breathing thundered in her ears. After what seemed an eternity, she peeked again and he was gone. She lay stiff, frozen to one position the rest of the night.

The next morning she told Julia she was sick and had to go home, but when they went downstairs Mrs. Evans insisted she would feel better after breakfast. She toyed with her cereal, not daring to look up, as Mr. Evans sat down opposite the girls.

He was jovial. "Morning, girls. Have fun last night?" She found it hard to believe that this father in the business suit—was the same panting man in the bedroom. When he heard she wasn't feeling well, he offered to drive her home on the way to his office.

She screamed, "No," and ran from the room. She never went to Julie's house again. Many years later she read a magazine article about men with a Lolita complex. Men who only like young girls. *Maybe that was Gene's problem.*

The moonlight gave the trailer a patina of old sterling; and after the long night, it was a welcome sight as she'd ever known. Cody switched off the ignition and pulled her closer to him.

"You're awful quiet. Something wrong?"

"No, just tired, I guess."

"Well, I'm sorry . . . . Know you have to get up early. We'll keep better hours from now on."

Everything was fine again. She decided not to tell him about Gene, or her annoyance and hurt at being ignored all evening. As they stopped at the door she leaned against him and sighed.

"I don't know why anyone needs drugs. You know, Cody, I get high on you."

To her surprise, he shoved her away.

"What put that in your head? Was Janice filling you full of a bunch of bull about Marcia?"

He threw open the door and marched into the trailer while she hurried to catch up. Ignoring Dude's excited welcome, he flipped on the light, stomped to the far wall and ripped the photograph from under the thumb tacks. He shoved it under her nose.

"There. That's Marcia. See . . . see her . . . . Well, we're going to get rid of Marcia." He tore the picture into tiny pieces, walked to the kitchen and tossed them into the wastebasket. "Now Marcia is gone, out of our lives. And I don't want to hear any more references to her—or to drugs. No more."

Jill wanted to explain. She hadn't been thinking about Marcia when she made the remark. Or had she? Anyway, she breathed in relief, Marcia and her picture were gone out of their lives, just as he said. The mountain top was theirs alone.


Begin with ghosts from the past. Add advice from a questionable new friend. Stir in neglect, a flirtatious husband and jealousy. Add two hours' sleep, a touch of white wine and simmer. Not an ideal recipe for a boat cook. Jill emptied the remains of a bottle of orange juice into a glass and swallowed two aspirin. The four thumbtacks, still holding corners of the picture that had been ripped from their grip, mocked her further as she hurried out to her car.

The package was still there, under the plywood. In the half light, the white paper glowed an icy blue. What should I do? Throw it away or tell the police? Tell Cody? Confront Rick? The ache in her head dulled her mind and she could not make a decision. She eased the board back into place and repositioned her sleeping bag over the top. The hiding place looked less vulnerable.

A new doubt flooded the small sedan at each curve in the road. Agreeing to get married, was a mistake. Too much unfinished business. By the time she turned onto the Coast Highway, she had made a decision. She would ask questions of everyone. Do you know a J.D.? Or a Mara? She would go back to the ranch with Cody. Talk to Neal and the other Fiends. She would give herself a week. If she was no closer to Mara by then, she would definitely forget it this time and get married.

But . . . what if she was closer? Cody's face swam in the tail lights of the other cars making their early morning sojourn toward the city. He kept saying, I can't stand to be hurt anymore. She slammed on her brakes, narrowly missing the rear end of a truck stopped for the red light in front of her. The Pinto's tires screeched and the driver rolled down his window to let go with a volley of curses. But she couldn't hear them in her closed car. Just Cody's voice, over and over. I can't stand . . . I can't stand . . . .

She was later than usual. Rick and six or seven other customers were drinking Irma's coffee when she arrived. She ordered bacon and eggs, hoping they would counteract her headache, shaky stomach, and case of nerves.

Rick moved down two stools to sit beside her, and she had the sudden feeling she was looking at him, really seeing him for the first time. By Hollywood standards, he was as handsome as any director could hope for. Her high school friends back in Ohio would have made him their instant box office favorite had he been the star of a surfing movie. But imagined or not, his wide grin and easy manner seemed to clash with the hardness of his eyes. They refused to smile with the rest of his face even as he joked.

"You're going to lose that girlish figure if you keep eating Irma's greasy potatoes and eggs."

She tried to match his lightness, even with the anxiety and confusion ballooning in her stomach.

"I was out later than I should have been last night. Needed some nourishment this morning."

"I know." The cold eyes continued to penetrate.

"You know?"

"A friend of mine said he saw you at The Ranch. Recognized you from the boat." He hesitated. "Said you were with Cody Williams. Are you and he . . . a thing?"

Since she and Cody hadn't been in the club together at all, only in the back room, she wondered how "the friend" knew they were together. She was surprised at her own answer.

"Oh, not really. I just enjoy his music."

Rick reached across the counter to lay some change on his check. His hand brushed hers and stopped for just an instant as he said, "I'm happy to hear that." He stood up. "Can I help you carry your stuff out to the boat? I finished my chores early this morning . . . . And I got more sleep than you probably did?"

The sudden attention frightened her, but she cautioned herself not to over-react. He might just be attracted to her.

When she opened the freezer, its nearly empty innards blurred before her eyes. The white packages were gone. She was sure now that Rick offered his help so he could watch her reaction. She willed her hands to remain steady as she reached for the food, but it seemed unnecessary since Rick had his back to her, loading paper cups into a carton. He turned as she did, glanced casually in the open door.

"Made you some room in there. Sold the squid to Fergie and we moved it to the baitshop. Made a nice pile of change on it, too."

"I'll bet you did." She couldn't believe her own stupidity as the words popped out, but Rick only laughed. If he suspected her of knowing more, he was a better actor than the professionals and should be a star. He appeared completely relaxed as they carried their loads to the boat. She was relieved when Jody walked into the galley to take her mind off the hundreds of questions without answers.

One look at the girl, however, and she forgot them all.

"Jody! My God. What happened?"

Four dark-red welts traveled through the freckles on the girl's right cheek. An ugly purple bruise at the top of her cheekbone was swollen and beginning to turn dark. She winced as she moved—tears welled in the corners of her eyes.

"Jody, what happened?"

The girl's eyes darted like those of a cornered animal. She whimpered, "Come in the bathroom with me." The young girl walked with effort, but when Jill tried to help her, she could tell any touch only increased the pain. Jody waited for her to step through the door, then closed and locked it, leaned against the wall. Tears poured down her cheeks.

"Oh, Jill. It's my mom."

"Were you in an accident? What happened to your mom? Is she all right?"

Jody sobbed, unable to talk. She waited, afraid to hear. Jody's mother was dead, she was sure of it. Finally, the girl winced, wiped at her face, then wailed.

"She's not hurt. She did this to me."

"What do you mean, Jody. I don't understand."

"She's an alcoholic, Jill . . . . Not . . . not all the time. She can go months sometimes without drinking." Her sobs began again, dry this time, the tears all gone.

"But then something sets her off. Last night, I went out with Scott. We just went for pizza. I was home early. Because we both had to work . . . but

136

after he dropped me off, she was waiting for me
. . . . Started screaming . . . that I was a . . . was
a whore. Said I was just like my sister." Jody
looked up defiant. "I'm not. Maureen got pregnant when she was fifteen . . . . Ran away . . . .
Anyway, my mom said I was no good . . . Awful
things." Jody melted into her arms. "She said she
wasn't fooled. She knew I was out screwing every
night . . . . Then she started to hit me." Jill held
her gently, but the girl pulled away and slowly
unzipped her jeans and pulled them down around
her hips. Her face contorted as she screamed,
"Look!"

The bile rose in Jill's throat and she swallowed
hard, not wanting Jody to see her gag. The girl's
flat stomach and slim hips, once smooth and tan,
were a mass of cuts, welts, and oozing burns. She
felt faint, asked in a whisper, "But how? How did
you managed to get here in that condition? How
could she do that to you?"

Jody continued, as if to herself.

"She just hit me and hit me. I was half unconscious. It was like a nightmare. She weighs 250
pounds . . . . Then she pulled my pants down and
said she's make sure no boys ever got near me
again." Jody slid to the floor, her long hair falling
across and hiding her face. Her voice was barely
audible. "She used a spatula."

Jill could see its pattern in the ugly broken skin.
Where it had been turned on edge and cut deep.

"But the cigarettes were the worst. I begged her
to stop. Then I guess I passed out. When I woke
up, she was asleep in a chair . . . . I just got up and

ran out.''

Jill had never felt such rage. Not at Mara. Not at God, if there was one, who made her father suffer so before he died. Not at anything or anyone. Her chest heaved and fell like it would explode.

"Jody, sit right there," she ordered. "Don't move. I'll be right back."

Jody reached for her arm. "Don't tell Scott." It was a wail. "Don't tell him."

"Stay right there. I won't tell Scott, I promise."

She unlocked the door and raced past the galley and up the steps to the pilothouse. It was still early. No passengers were aboard yet. Rick looked up from a chart as she entered. Her alarm must have showed. He jumped up and came toward her.

"What the hell is wrong?"

She forgot any fear or doubts she had about him. He was help. He would know what to do. She told him quickly what had happened and watched his anger tighten the muscles of his jaw. She knew Jody was very special to him.

She said, "I have to get her to a doctor. We can't work today. Is Scott here yet? Jody is almost hysterical that he will see her. I promised her we would keep him away."

Rick stood immobile, mumbling over and over, "God damn it, God damn it."

"Rick" she shouted, "Stop it. We have to get her help."

He wiped at his face. "I'm sorry. I'll keep Scott busy on the bait boat. You take Jody to Doc Adamson. He's at the corner of 16th and Arizona." He started down the steps, then turned

138

back. "If she needs the hospital, I'll pay for it. If not, when you get through at the doctor's, bring her back and put her in my bed."

"Where's that?"

"On the bait boat . . . . After I give Scott some chores, I'll call and tell the doctor that you're on the way."

Jody was sitting in the same spot, her head on her knees. They managed to zip her jeans, then made their way slowly off the boat and down the pier. Jody glanced behind her several times. The girl's eyes reminded Jill of the time her horse stepped in a coil of bailing wire and became entangled. She knew Jody was terrified that Scott would see her.

She unlocked her car, and Jody stretched out on the sleeping bag. She tried to stay calm, and drive carefully through the going-to-work traffic, but Jody suddenly sat straight up and asked, "Where are we going?"

She reached to smooth her hair, "Just relax, Jody. I'm taking you to a doctor."

The girl screamed and began to sob, hysterically for the first time. "No! No, I can't go to a doctor. Stop the car. Turn around. Go back." Jody grabbed the steering wheel then, surprising her. She held tightly and swerved to avoid a head-on collision. She managed to dodge out of traffic and pulled to the curb.

"Jody, what is the matter with you?" Her heart was pounding at the close call.

"No! I can't go to a doctor . . . . He'll know . . . . He'll know how it happened." Jill grabbed the girl's hand on the door handle.

"Stop it, Jody. You have to see a doctor."

Jody, amazingly strong, swung at her and managed to get the door part-way open. But Jill's strength finally prevailed. She closed the door gently as Jody collapsed on the sleeping bag sobbing.

"You don't understand, Jill. She's my *mom*."

*No, I don't.* But maybe because I've never known my mother. She tried to imagine her father ever doing any physical harm to her but she couldn't remember even a spanking. She sighed.

"All right. I understand. Look, we will tell the doctor you were coming to work across the beach this morning and two men attacked you. How's that?"

Jody was quiet, thinking.

"I don't know. Maybe he won't believe us. And if he calls the police, they'll call my mother. And she's been arrested once before."

"You mean this has happened before?" Fury pounded at her temples, begging to be unleashed, but Jody was defiant.

"You just don't understand."

She forced herself to be rational, to try and solve this problem.

"All right. If the doctor insists on calling the police, we'll walk out. I promise. We'll give him a phony name and address. And say you're eighteen. That way he won't need a parent's consent."

Jody smiled for the first time. "You sure seem to know a lot about these things."

Jill started the car and pulled out into traffic.

"Yes, I do." From years of my own lies. Yes, too much.


The middle-aged receptionist hurried to open the inner door when they walked into the small waiting room. Rick must have already called.

"Come right on in, dear." The woman walked ahead of them down a narrow hall and into a small operatory. "Just remove your clothes, child, and put on this gown. It opens down the back. Then stretch out on the table. Dr. Adamson is still at the hospital but I called and he'll be right over," then to Jill she said, "Will you come out to the desk with me please?"

Jody grabbed at her, wildeyed again. "Oh, don't leave me, Jill. Please."

She gave reassurance she didn't feel. "It's all right, Jody, I'm sure I just have to fill out a form or two. Then I'll be right back."

The girl took the gown and began unbuttoning her blouse. Jill followed the white uniform to the front desk. The woman spoke in a low voice, obviously so Jody would not hear.

"Are you are relative?"

"No, a friend."

"How old is she?"

Jill looked her straight in the eye and answered, "Eighteen."

"Oh, really. She looks much younger." The woman paused. "You know, we can get in considerable trouble if we treat a minor without parental consent."

*Maybe this was a mistake.* Maybe no one will help. She blurted out, "Oh, you have to take care of her. This is a doctor's office isn't it? We're not going to get you in any trouble. She's eighteen. Believe me, please."

The woman was unmoved. "Well, with all the malpractice suits nowadays, we have to be awfully careful."

The anger was obvious now in Jill's voice as she said, "I'll talk to the doctor about it."

The woman's lips tightened, "As you wish . . . . In the meantime, please fill out this information sheet and health history." She handed her a clipboard with several questionnaires attached.

"Do you mind if I take this back to the examining room. Some of the questions, Jody will have to answer." They needed to get their stories coordinated.

"As you wish, then bring it back to me."

Jill realized she had made a mistake. The annoyance in the receptionist's voice reminded her of the inflated sense of authority she ran into over and over in civil servants at the various government offices she'd scouted through in her search for some lead on Mara. Stern-faced women of marginal intelligence made $65 a week and thought they owned the Bureau of Vital Statistics. But she had learned to be nice since they loved nothing better than to refuse whatever it was you requested, and the more angry you became, the more stubborn their negative was. *Change tactics.*

"What's your name?" She forced a polite calm.
The woman made it obvious with a loud and

annoyed sigh that this was not the way she chose to start her day.

"I am Mrs. Collingswood."

"Well, Mrs. Collingswood, I'm sorry. I didn't mean to sound rude. I know your problem. It was just the shock of Jody's condition . . . . You can understand . . . . But really, the doctor hasn't anything to worry about from us. And there is no problem with money to pay him . . . . We just need a doctor." Then surprising herself—she hadn't planned it—she began to cry. But it was the clincher.

Mrs. Collingswood stood up and came from behind the desk to put her arm around her.

"Now, now young woman. Don't worry. I'll explain to Dr. Adamson . . . . We'll take care of the child . . . the young lady . . . . And don't worry about the bill. Treatment is what's important now."

Jill thanked her, wiped her eyes and walked to the back room. Jody was stretched out on the examining table, the wounds on her face exaggerated by the stark white of gown and pillow. She squeezed the clipboard and clenched her teeth to control the anger that threatened to boil forth again.

"Jody? If you can, we have to get this redtape over with. Now what would you like for a last name?" She tried to laugh and Jody smiled with her as they made up an address and phone number. Mrs. Collingswood wouldn't question now, she was on their side.

There was a soft tap on the door, and Dr. Adamson strode into the room. The young man with below-the-collar brown hair and a mustache looked more like a beach pal of Rick's than a physician. After a gentle smile and greeting for the girl, he turned to her,

"I understand Jody here ran into some problems."

His eyes were piercing and she couldn't match them, had to look away, at the wall just to the right of his head.

"Yes, Doctor. She was coming to work on the beach . . . and two men . . . you said they were young didn't you, Jody? . . . well, anyway, they grabbed her. You can see the results."

"And Mrs. Collingswood said she is eighteen?" The brown eyes forced her to look at him.

"Yes, sir. She is just eighteen."

"I'll have to make a police report." He continued to watch for a crack in the tale he knew was untrue but she stared back now undaunted. They had decided a police report would mean nothing with a false name and address on it. When she didn't respond, he cleared his throat and continued,

"If you'll wait outside now, I will complete the examination and then talk to you."

Jody spoke for the first time since his entrance.

"Oh doctor, please, can't Jill stay?"

While his hand was gentle on the girl's head, his voice was firm, "No, Jody. She can't stay while we're looking you over. But your friend will be right outside. Don't worry, I'll be nice to you."

Jill squeezed Jody's hand. "The doctor knows

best."

After what seemed like hours of leafing through old *Newsweeks* and *Redbooks*, Mrs. Collingswood told her the doctor would see her in his private office. It had only been twenty minutes!

He motioned her to a seat across his desk and although he kept the volume of his words low, there was no mistaking the harsh anger as he asked, "Who did this to her?"

She watched the tremor of her hands in her lap.

"I told you, two men on the beach."

"Bullshit!" The obscenity coming from a doctor surprised her.

"Someone in the family did it, didn't they?" He didn't wait for a response. "Her father did it, didn't he? I've seen these cases before."

They both jumped as the phone on the desk to his right pierced the room with a staccato buzz, then sat transfixed until the caller either gave up or Mrs. Collingswood handed it.

"Why are you protecting the bastard? Is he your lover or something? . . . He should be strung up by his nuts." The doctor's face was flushed and to punctuate the accusations he picked up a letter opener and slammed it into the desk blotter. Jill stared at the jagged slice, feeling her fingernails dig into the arm of the chair.

"Did you see her body? Did you see it?"

She nodded. The tears were rolling along again, down the familiar channel between cheeks and nose.

"Well, you didn't see it all . . . I don't know how much you know about anatomy, but that young girl in there even has cigarette burns on the labia and the mouth of the vagina . . . . Now, how can you protect a son-of-a-bitch that would do that to her?''

*Oh, Jody*! Sweat broke out on her forehead. As he waited, his face a mask, it was suddenly important that he know the truth. That he didn't think she had anything to do with such atrocities. She broke her promise, whispering.

"It was her mother."

She watched his face crumble. He covered it with his hands, slumped over his desk and cried. Jill sat stunned. We should have gone to someone older, she thought. Someone more hardened to the realities of life.

He recovered then, wiped at his eyes apparently unashamed, and asked, ''My God, what kind of a world do we live in? When a mother would do this to her child?''

Jill straightened. She had to make him understand, for her friend, even though she didn't.

"I promised Jody I wouldn't tell you. She just keeps saying, 'She's my mother,' . . . so doctor . . . Please . . . no matter what you think . . . PLEASE . . . for her sake, don't report it." She hurried now, determined to convince him. "I'll see that she never goes back there. I'll take care of her. And Rick will . . . . You know him, don't you? . . . We'll make sure nothing happens again . . . . But doctor, how is she going to be?''

The human being, capable of tears, lept back into the security of his professionalism, grasping for the non-involvement of a vocabulary of diagnosis and treatment that allowed him to survive the pain and dying he must see every day.

"Her face will be fine. I've cleaned and treated the other wounds and I'll give you medication and pain pills for her. She may run a temperature for a while and she's going to have considerable pain." Jill could see his anger surfacing again in the form of a bulging vein on his right temple. "There will be some scarring. Some of the burns are second, maybe third degree. But after the primary healing period we'll see if plastic surgery can almost erase them . . . . Internally, we're lucky. She should have no problem with either intercourse or child-bearing."

"God, it's just not fair. Jody, is the sweetest, kindest girl I've ever known." Then she remembered to ask, "What about the police?"

The only sound in the room was their breathing and the tick of a small clock on the desk.

"I won't report it."

She stood up and put out her hand. She wanted to say so much. Tell him what a wonderful, under-standing, sensitive human being he was. Instead, she simply said,

"Thank you, doctor."

He took her outstretched hand and tried to smile but his face wouldn't cooperate.

"I'm sorry I said the things I did to you, accused you. And I apologize for being so professional. But I'll never understand these things . . . . And worse yet, here I am . . . here we are . . . a party to letting someone like that go free, without punish-ment." She tensed, afraid he was changing his mind, but he finished, "I just have to tell myself that in this case it's for the best."

Jody joined her at the reception desk, they gathered up the medicines, thanked Mrs. Collingswood and drove silently to the pier.

Thankful that *Sea Maiden* was already out for the day, they climbed aboard the bait boat and went below. She was surprised. The rusty, rundown exterior did an excellent job of camouflaging Rick's small but comfortable living quarters. The cabin housed an attractive blue and white plaid settee on the port, a tidy galley on the starboard. Two vee-berths in the forward compartment had been converted to an ample double bed. Rick's wardrobe—cotton teeshirts, shorts, and jeans—snuggled together in tight, navy-style rolls on the shelves above it to each side.

She reached for a red and white striped shirt.

"Come on, Jody. Let's get your clothes off. We'll borrow a nightgown from Rick." She helped the girl out of her clothes, tried to joke about the huge shirt that hung to Jody's knees; but as she climbed into bed, Jody sank once again into a tearful depression.

"Jody," she smoothed the girl's hair, mimicing the comfort Auntie Mil used to give her, "Jody, it will all work out. The doctor said you may not have any scars at all."

"But . . . But what about Scott?"

"Scott? . . . Jody, from what I've seen of you and Scott . . . the way he looks at you . . . why, if you had tattoos from head to toe, he'd still love you."

The girl finally smiled and closed her eyes. Jill held her hand until she fell asleep, then stretched out on the settee and sank into her own unconsciousness.

When Jill's eyes opened again, Rick was standing in the center of the cabin looking ill at ease. She sat up quickly and looked forward. If *Sea Maiden* was back she must have slept all day. But Jody was still flat on her back and fast asleep. Rick closed the door between the two areas then whispered, "How is she? God, I've been going crazy all day wondering."

She told him what the doctor said, leaving out only the most intimate details. He was relieved yet angry again about the possibility of scars and plastic surgery.

"Scott has been like a wild man all day but I made him stay away until I talked to you. I'll go tell him to come over now and wait until she wakes up." As he disappeared up the companionway steps Jill splashed water on her face to try and clear her lethargic head.

The boy's bare feet appeared on the steps immediately. His gangly arms hung uneasily at his side, and somber eyes darted from her to the closed door. As if on cue, Jody called her name. Jill could hear the slight panic and hurried in, shutting the door behind her.

"How do you feel? You know we both slept all day."

"I'm hurting now. Bad. Can I have another pain

149

pill?"

"Of course you can . . . Jody, Scott is out there to see you."

The girl winced as she sat up. "Oh Jill, I must look awful. Tell him to come back tomorrow."

"Jody," she whispered, "He's been worried sick all day. He doesn't care how you look. Now come on, we'll brush your hair . . . . Let me prop the pillows behind you . . . . Now, I'll get your pain pill and have Scott bring it in to you."

The girl's desire to see him overcame her concern about appearance.

Both men stared anxiously when Jill came out and closed the door again. She filled a glass with water, took one of the codeine tablets from her purse and handed them to Scott.

"Here, take these to your friend in there. Rick and I are going to take a walk." She could see Rick's disappointment, but he followed her out and down the pier. "Scott is the best medicine she can have right now. I hope you don't mind?"

"No, I understand. I'll see her later."

As they passed one of the open air cafes he took her arm and asked, "Can I buy you a beer?"

"No . . . But you can but me the biggest cup of coffee they serve. I need to wake up."

She sat down at the nearest table and looked about her at the beautiful day she'd almost missed. The sun, low now, had turned the ocean facing windows of the tall Santa Monica buildings a bright gold. Rick came back with his beer and set a milkshake size cup of coffee in front of her. "You said big."

"Delicious, thank you."

He told her Scott managed the galley all right. Not really, but they had made it through the day. He said he had another boy coming tomorrow to help out.

"But I'll be back tomorrow?"

"No, I want you to stay with Jody." She heard the uneasiness most men have about their abilities with illness when he asked, "I was hoping you would stay tonight too?"

"But where?"

"Well, the forward bunk is plenty big enough for you and Jody. And you would be right there if she needs something in the night . . . . I can sleep on the settee. Done it before, lots of times."

She thought of Cody for the first time since morning, then remembered he said they were recording today and he would have to go straight from the studio to The Ranch. She could call there. "I guess it is a good idea. Jody is still terribly upset emotionally."

Rick covered her hand then and squeezed it. The relief in his voice was obvious as he thanked her. Neither of them moved. She was surprised and guilty as her body responded to his touch; he seemed to wait for some outward acknowledgment. The instant passed and they both let it go. Rick took a last swallow of beer and stood up. The sun back lighted his hair, turning it gold like the panes of the windows and Jill listened to herself talk too fast and stammer,

"I have to make a phone call, Why don't you go back and see Jody. I'll be right along."

151

He agreed and left quickly. Feeling disloyal to Cody, and remembering his warning about Rick, she hurried to the phone booth and looked up the number of the Ranch. He wouldn't be there yet but she would leave the message with Janice.

It took several minutes for whoever answered to find her.

"Janice, this is Jill."

"Who?"

"Jill, Jill Kerry." The line was silent still. How should she describe herself? Cody's Jill? She tried again. "Remember me? Cody's friend." She could hear whispering and Janice giggled.

"Oh, yea. Jill. . . . How are you honey? . . . Cody isn't here yet." The girl laughed again. "Get out of here shit ass, I'm trying to talk. . . . Oh, Jill don't pay no attention. Some cat is here bugging me. . . . Cody's not here."

Jill hesitated, wondering now if Cody would get a message, decided to try.

"Janice, this is important. Will you write down a message and be sure Cody gets it when he comes in?"

"Oh, yea, sure. . . . Wait, gotta get a pencil." The waitress laughed, "and a piece of paper." Jill listened to the bar sounds; the clink of glasses, voices and laughter, juke box music.

"O.K., I got them. What do you want me to write?"

Until now she hadn't thought of what she wanted to say. She didn't want to tell him she was staying at Rick's. Innocent or not, he wouldn't understand.

"Tell him that Jody, the young girl I work with, had a bad accident . . ."

Janice interrupted, "What kind of accident."

She sighed, "I'd rather not say. Just tell him I'm going to stay with her tonight and tomorrow. That I'll be home tomorrow night. O.K.?"

"You're crazy."

"What do you mean, Janice?"

"I mean he'll blow his god damned top, that's what I mean. You sure don't know that man of yours very well do you?"

She had had enough. All of the traumas of the day boiled out of her and into the mouthpiece of the pay phone.

"Look," she shouted, "I don't need any more advice from you about Cody! I don't want it! Just give him the message, tell him I love him and will see him tomorrow night."

She could hear Janice's breathing.

"Sure, sweetheart, I'll give him the message. But he isn't gonna believe that cock and bull story. . . . Who you shackin' up with anyway?"

She slammed the receiver into its cradle, her hands shaking at the accusation, especially coming so close behind the incident with Rick. Dr. Adamson's question popped into her head.

What kind of a world *do* we live in?


As she hurried back to the boat, her thoughts waged guerilla warfare, one side firebombing the logic of the other. Janice is crazy, Cody will understand. Then why not tell him where you're spending the night? And with whom? He knows he can trust me. Promised he wouldn't be jealous anymore. What about the hand touching? Would he understand that? Yes! No! She called a cease fire. Jody needed care and dinner.

As she stepped down into the cabin she could see the food had been taken care of. Irma, Hugo, and Rick were squeezed together on the settee; Scott's lanky frame slouched opposite Jody in the forward cabin.

The girl sipped a milkshake and smiled, relaxed now. "See what Irma brought us."

They were all eating from a large package of fried fish and chips. Irma, quieter than usual, yet trying to be jovial answered, "Yep, young lady. A hearty meal of junk food is just what the doctor ordered. . . . Help yourself, Jill. You gotta keep up your strength so you can take good care of my girl here."

She didn't want to eat, but at the older woman's insistance took a bite of the hot, crisp fish and realized how hungry she really was. Between them, they finished every crumb. Jody enjoyed the small talk but after coffee, Irma rose and pulled at her small husband's shoulder, "Time we get out of here and let the child get some rest. Come on. You too, Scott."

The boy kissed the unbattered side of Jody's face and said, "See you tonight, maybe."

Jill started to tell him that wasn't such a good idea when the realization hit her. The boat they were on would be going out for bait tonight.

Rick walked out with the others as she cleaned

up and prepared to follow Dr. Adamson's orders. She took hot water, clean towels, salve and medications into the forward cabin and closed the door.

"Well, how did it go with Scott?" She knew or she wouldn't have asked. She began sponging the girl's face.

"Oh, Jill. It was just like you said. He's so wonderful." Jody was her old self again, bubbling with enthusiasm, even as she winced at her treatment. Jill finished, gave her the four before bedtime pills as directed, plumped the pillow, and although she was sure one of the pills would take care of it, ordered the girl to go to sleep. She turned down the other side of the wide bed and said, "I'll be staying right here beside you tonight, O.K.?" Jody closed her eyes, then popped up again at the soft tap on the door.

Rick peeked in. "Just wanted to tell you goodnight and not to worry about anything."

Jody opened her arms to him. "Rick I love you." He hugged and kissed her.

"I love you too, kid. And I need you back in that galley. So go to sleep now." He reached over her head and turned off the light. Jill and Rick went out and closed the door.

"How about a drink?" He poured red wine into a plastic glass and handed it to her, before she could refuse; then filled a mug for himself and sat down on the other end of the settee from her.

"I talked to Irma. She wants Jody to live with her and Harry. I think it would work, don't you?"

"Oh, that's wonderful." It had been in the back of her mind all day. She'd told the doctor she would take care of Jody, but there certainly wasn't room in the trailer—or her Pinto. "I know she'll be happy, she loves Irma so much."

A siren whined in the distance, probably another accident on the coast highway. She thought of Cody and hoped he was safe at the Ranch by now and had her message. Then except for the lap of ripples on the hull and the occasional groan from the pier's ancient wood pilings, it was quiet. Rick lit a cigarette and she took a sip of wine. He leaned back, his legs sprawled almost across the narrow room.

"What the hell are you really doing here?" His voice boomed in the still cabin.

"What do you mean?"

"I mean, I've watched you, listened to you. You don't fit the hippie-girl category . . . roaming around the country, sleeping in one guy's bed then another. . . . When I hired you, to be frank, I didn't think you'd last a day. Had you pegged for some poor little rich girl getting her kicks from a variety of experiences. . . . But you did stay, and you work like a mule." He seemed to look through her. "What I mean is, you sure as hell aren't the type to make cooking on a fishing boat your life long occupation. So what's behind it?"

She tried to keep it light as she answered.

"I just fell in love with you at first sight, that's all."

A fragment of light, the beginning of a flicker began in his eyes as he half smiled; then it died as he murmured,

"Just the truth. No jokes."

*The truth?* Why not? She thought of the white package hidden in her car. Her decision to ask questions. Why not start here?

"I'm looking for someone."

He straightened, asked, "Who?"

"I'm looking for a woman. Someone . . . someone who hurt me and I'm determined to find . . ." She stopped.

They both felt it. The almost inperceptable list of the heavy boat towards the dock. Someone was coming on board. Rick sprang from his seat and was up the steps before she could set her glass down to follow.

Jill knew immediately who the woman was, even before the slurred words reached her ears. The elephantine flowered muu-muu did not hide the mounds of flesh lurking underneath, oozing out the sleeve and neck openings—or the alcohol saturation. At least 250 pounds, tried to step through the opening of the boat's railing.

"She's here, isn't she? . . . My baby. I want to see her. Want my baby back."

Before they could respond, Jody's mother reached for a handhold and attempted to lift her tremendous weight on board. With one foot still on the dock, the strap of her large purse caught the rail and spun her back and halfway around. For an instant she swung like a carcass on a meathook—then the leather handle gave up and the heavy body fell sprawling onto the dock, the dress waist-high exposing spongy thighs and dingy, loose panties.

Jill and Rick stood frozen as the grotesque scene continued.

The woman struggled onto one elbow and attempted to lift the pounds of flesh, to cover them again with the Hawaiian print. Her watery eyes pleaded as she wailed, "Help me. Somebody help me."

Rick, finally released from his shocked immobility, stepped off the boat and reached for her.

"I'll help you. I'll help you, you sadistic drunken pig. . . . I'll help you get your ass out of here and I don't want to ever see you set foot on this pier again."

As he leaned over, the woman swung the purse. The broken strap hit Rick on the ear. Surprised, he stepped back, just in time to avoid the ham-size forearm aimed at his head.

The woman hugged her purse to her giant bosom and rocked it, moaning, "I want my baby. She's mine. . . . You can't take my baby away form me. . . . She's my baby." She wiped her runny nose on the sleeve of her dress. The slobbery sobs increased in volume.

Rick glanced back at Jill and she looked quickly down below but there was no sound from the forward cabin. The sleeping pill must have worked. He kept his voice low, almost a whisper.

"You bitch! You sick bitch. You're lucky you're not in jail this minute. We only protected you for Jody's sake." This time he grabbed her from the back, under the arms and stood her on her feet. "Now you are going to stagger your way right back the way you came. From now on, you are not Jody's mother." He turned her around, pinched her soft chin between his thumb and fingers, jerked her face up to look into his.

"If you ever come near Jody again I will personally kill you."

He jerked her neck again.

"Do you understand me, lady?" His voice was a hiss, and left no doubt in anyone's mind that he meant what he said.

"I will kill you."

He let go of the puffy face, and in one motion turned the woman around. With his fist in her back he shoved her in the direction of the parking lot. She staggered forward, bumped a fisherman who was pretending not to listen, then continued on. They watched until she was out of sight.

Jill hurried below and opened the cabin door just a crack. Jody was sleeping soundly, oblivious to "Mom's" arrival or exit. She gave Rick the "it's O.K.," sign as he came down the steps. His hand trembled when he poured himself another cup of wine.

"You were wonderful." She sank onto the settee.

He bowed his head without comment, then tipped his cup and downed the contents in one gulp. "We won't say anything about this, all right? It will be our secret." He stood, "Time for bed. Scott and I will be going after the bait at three. It's usually calm, no wind, so I don't think the motion will bother Jody or you. Just stay in your bunks."

"Goodnight, Rick." She opened the door to the forward cabin and climbed into the bed, being careful not to disturb her sleeping patient.

The vibration of the diesel woke her. She heard the thump as Scott threw a dockline ashore and muffled voices from above as they motored out of the harbor. But as soon as she checked Jody, the motion lulled her back to sleep. When she woke again, they were back at the pier. She climbed out of her bunk, pulled the covers up under Jody's chin and quietly left the cabin.

Since the first morning after she'd driven away from her home in Ohio, she had loved this pre-dawn hour of the day best. She thought of other mornings as she climbed the steps to the deck and stretched, remembering the farmer's campground in Kansas. Somewhere around Wichita, Bucklin was it? The rural entrepreneur had set a few picnic tables and trash barrels around a small pond in his meadow, hung a hand lettered sign, Camping $1.00, on his fence, and put his wife in charge of collecting the fees. Jill had stopped there after leaving Kansas City. The heavy set woman in a print housedress came out of the small frame house when she drove in but hesitated on the porch when she saw the small car.

"You ain't a camper are you?", she'd shouted as she peered through the dusk.

She could hear the fear in the woman's voice and got out of the car and walked up to the house.

"Oh my, just a young girl. Had me scared for a minute. Harry likes this business, but I don't. Never know who's going to drive onto our property now since he put up that blasted sign. . . . But you look all right." She shoved a wisp of grey hair back under her hairnet. "I guess so . . . just a child you are. . . . What you doing out alone, way out here?''

"I'm on a vacation. To see the country. Do you have a spot for me?''

The woman laughed sarcastically, "Have a spot? You can take your choice. I told Harry this cocka-mammie idea of his wouldn't work. We're too close to Wichita and too far from Albuquerque. All we get are misfits who don't know where the heck they are, or where they're going.'' She caught her offense then, "Oh, sorry, child. Didn't mean nothing personal. Follow me and I'll show you where to park.''

She had pulled the Pinto in next to the water faucet, paid her dollar and said goodnight. A dim bulb in the tree branch overhead cast its pale security inside the Pinto, and the crickets, plus a baseball game broadcast from the farmhouse radio sang her to sleep. A clatter woke her. She sat up, fright closing her throat, stopping her breath. Four pairs of eyes gazed steadily into hers. Two belonged to housecats, two to a pair of racoons. She had disturbed their raid on the garbage can beside the car. They waited for a moment, then with no apparent fear, continued their food gathering. Size seemed to dominate in this odd community. The calico and black cat sat patiently on the ground while first one and then the other masked bandits hung upside down, with only back feet and tail showing, and rummaged through the remains of someone's picnic. They came out with orange peels and scraps of bread held daintily in their long black claws. She missed whatever sign

161

they gave which allowed the felines their turn. They leaped easily to the rim of the can and then inside but returned shortly with nothing but sober faces. They watched the raccoons for some time then darted away into the dark. Shortly, thereafter, the broad rears lumbered off in the same direction. She let out a breath and wondered if she had been holding it the whole time. Refreshed by the sleep and the privileged glimpse of animal life, she climbed out of the car, wrapped her jacket around her shoulders and sat on the picnic bench paralyzed by the stillness of the dark pond and the sense of knowing, without a watch, that the sun was about to rise gently and blot out the sea of stars and planets overhead. There had been many early mornings since then, but few had been as magical.

She stretched now and sucked in a lung full of cool marine air with its faint fish aroma. Rick and Scott were in the bait shop; the light seeped out from under the door.

"Hey, lady."

Jill recognized the eavesdropping fisherman from the night before. The seedy old man came close, smelling of tobacco and anchovies.

"Lady," a gap from a missing front tooth leered at her, "there was two guys down here looking for you. Cowboys. Both kinda short. They asked me if I'd seen you."

"And?" Her chest tightened as she asked the question.

"I told 'em, yes. I'd seen you. When the one said, a gal with long, kinda red hair, I remembered.

162

. . . Told them you were on the boat. . . . That it had just gone out before they got here.'' She could sense the excitement to continue, "The one, the taller of the two . . . he just said to tell you, 'Don't come back.' That's all he said, 'Just tell her, don't come back.' ''

Jill stood catatonic staring at the motheaten sweater and five days growth of beard while deep lines pulled the old man's parched lips into a wide grin. They gave way easily, happy it seemed to be the messenger's of ill tidings. "That's all he said lady.''

*Get away.* The panic followed her down the dock and into the cabin. It tightened wire strings across the frets of her mind. Shoved at the back of her eyes until they wanted to pop like the seeds from a lemon. They changed to anger. I won't go back. Who needs a jealous man. I don't need anyone. I'm alone. Always have been. *Always will be.*

The strings changed key. I'll explain. He'll understand.

Then played a different song. I don't deserve him. I'll only hurt him again. The moment of response to Rick's handholding added a guilt accompaniment to her internal sonata. Anxious for something to do, she turned on the cabin light and washed the cups and glasses from last night. Rick clumped down the steps with two styrofoam cups of coffee from Irma's.

"Good morning," he was jovial, as if energized by last night's confrontation. "Irma says as soon as Jody wakes up she will fix you both a big breakfast . . .here.'' He reached to hand her a cup, stopped when he saw her face. "What's wrong?"

A twitch began in her right eyelid and she turned back to the sink, trying to sound normal, "Nothing is wrong. Jody slept fine all night. Is still sleeping."

From behind, Rick wrapped his arms around her waist and drew her close, his voice was gentle in her ear, "Look, I know it's been a bad time . . . but it's all over now. . . . We'll . . ."

It was more than she could take. Her elbow in his stomach shoved him away as she shouted, "Don't"

He backed up and mumbled, "I'm sorry."

"Oh, Rick. Forgive me. Too much has happened that's all. I didn't mean that."

A shield dropped behind his eyes when he answered, "That's O.K., I get the message." He picked up his coffee cup and left.

Scott ran over to see Jody but she was still sleeping. *Sea Maiden* perked out of the harbor and by the time Jody finally woke up Jill was able to greet her with some facsimile of normality. She cleaned the girl's wounds as directed by the doctor and applied the prescribed cream. The burns were crusted over and oozed a clear fluid; the rest of the area was a grotesque combination of red, orange-yellow, and various shades of purple. But the pain pills seemed to be doing their job; Jody talked continually and wanted to get up. Jill helped her to the settee and brought a breakfast from Irma's. Jody ate like a ranch hand, even wiped at the plate with her last bite of toast. With the meal out of the way she asked expectantly, "Jill, can I live with you?"

Jill looked at the ugly swelling, the welted cheek

164

and wondered how she could avoid dealing the girl anymore blows. "But Jody, Irma wants you to stay with her."

The girl looked away, fidgeted with her hands before saying,

"I know . . . and I love Irma . . . But I love you more."

"Oh, Jody," She slid down the seat to take the girl in her arms. "I love you too. But I have no place of my own. Except my car. . . . And we certainly can't live in it."

"You could stay here. . . . You, and me . . . and Rick."

"I've told you about Cody. . . . I can't move in here." Cody. She had to talk to him. Make him understand.

"But Rick likes you. I know he does . . . A lot . . . I can tell. And anyway, I bet he's more your type."

Jill sighed, remembering her own attachment to Mara, the emptiness when she went away. She was determined not to hurt Jody the same way.

"I'm going to tell you something, Jody. . . . Something I've never told anyone else. It's a secret and I know you'll keep it."

The girl sat up, alert and anxious to hear, "Oh, I'll never tell a soul, Jill. I promise."

"Well, there was a girl in my life once. She was ten years older than I was, but we were best friends. I told her everything. And she gave me advice, not like a grownup but like an older and wiser friend. Everything we did together was fun." She could hear Mara's easy laugh as if she were in

165

the room. "I became very attached to her, loved her. . . . Then, one day when I needed her most. . . . When I was very unhappy. . . . She vanished. Just left, disappeared." Her insides churned and she almost forgot Jody's presence as she continued. "She let me down. . . . And I've been looking for her ever since." For what? So what if you find her? She couldn't hear the answer in the quiet room. Jody seemed to shrink in her arms, smaller, more vulnerable.

"What you're saying is, you don't want to do the same thing to me. That you're going to go away . . . and I'll never see you again. That's what you're trying to tell me, isn't it?"

"Jody, what I'm trying to say is . . . I don't know. That you can't count on me."

The girl pulled away, her body tense inside Rick's huge shirt. "Well, that's life, isn't it? You can't count on anyone. . . . I can't anyway. Not on a mother, or Rick, or Irma . . . or you." The battered young face puckered. "Not on Scott either. He'll probably drop me too."

The words carved and sliced, tore at the same emotions she'd kept so carefully wrapped inside herself. Emotions she had protected for so long, fed and nurtured until they grew strong enough to, in turn, feed every relationship with fear, suspicion and doubt. The same thing couldn't happen to this positive, lively girl.

"That's not true and you know it. I was only trying to explain why you are better off with Irma. She has a home for you. I'll never vanish from your life, I promise. . . . But I may go away for a

166

while. Rick and Irma and Scott won't."

Jody's curiosity overcame her personal doubts for the moment as she asked, "Who is the girl? Are you looking for her here?"

*Plunge in, like you promised yourself.*

"You promise you'll never discuss any of this. Ever?"

Jody nodded.

"Her name is Mara and here is a snapshot of her. The last name doesn't matter. She's changed it several times." Jill looked hopefully at her young companion as she asked, "Did you ever hear that name around here or see that face?"

Jody shook her head. "Nope. And you'd remember a name like that. . . . She's really pretty!"

The dark eyes flashed at her from the picture. "Oh, yes, beautiful. . . . Jody, did you ever know anyone called J.D.?"

The girl shook her head again as she answered. "You mean like two initials? . . . J.D. . . . No, why?"

"Mara received a letter from someone by that name." She reached for her purse and unzipped the inner pocket. Jody was the first person she had ever shown the letter to. As she handed it over, she continued, "It seems to have come from the pier. And from some of my sleuthing, I think this person may be involved in something illegal." She hesitated, "Maybe drugs." An idea surfaced. She asked, excited, "Jody, how about Ferguson that owns this place? Anyone in his family? Or one of the Mexican fellows I've seen around here? Could

167

any of them be J.D.?''

Jody sat very still, staring at the envelope. The anger in her voice was apparent when she answered, ''I don't know anything about any of this. And I don't know a J.D. . . . Probably some transient worker who hung around here for a while. You'll probably never find him and I think you should stop trying. The whole thing is dumb.'' She tossed the envelope into Jill's lap.

''I'm sorry, Jody.'' She returned the letter to its zippered safe. ''I didn't mean to upset you. But, please, keep my secret.''

The girl looked steadily into her eyes when she answered, ''Don't worry. I will.'' Her voice softened then. ''But I wish you would stop looking. You're only hurting yourself.''

The advice was sound and she said quietly, ''You're right. I may forget it all very soon. . . . It's time for you to take a nap. . . . I'm going over to Irma's for a few minutes.''

This isn't summer, she thought, as she stepped onto the dock. A light fog coated the sky with off-white, blotting out any blue or sunshine. It captured her with its gloom as effectively as the walls of a prison. She shivered in the clammy air, then headed for the phone booth. Maybe a call to Auntie Mil would help.

The prolonged ringing compounded Jody's words, and as much as she wanted to deny them, they kept repeating. *You can't count on anyone.*


When *Sea Maiden* docked, Jill hurried over.

Rick and Scott were fileting fish for some passengers.

"Looks like a good catch today." Rick continued without looking up. "Rick, I have something important to take care of. Can you stay with Jody until I get back?"

"Sure, sure. Go ahead." His coldness was obvious, a natural reaction to her unfortunate forceful rejection this morning. *Explain later.* She had only one thing on her mind as she hurried to her car and drove to The Ranch, hoping Cody might be there early. His truck wasn't in the back and with two hours yet until the music started, she was surprised to see a line of customers at the front door. She looked up at the billboard. "Last week for recording star Cody Williams." Where was he going? What had happened? Desperate now to talk to him, she reacted to every tire and motor sound until his truck pulled in a little after eight. She jumped out of the car, slammed the door—then stopped. A tiny blonde in a long print peasant dress bounced out of the passenger side of the truck. Cody put his arm around her shoulders, said something, and they laughed together through the back door. Waves of anger and jealousy broke on her. *You can't count on anyone.* She tried again to deny Jody's words, but Cody and the girl made it difficult. Determined this time to confront the problem, rather than run away, she marched to the back entrance. A large man in uniform stood at the door. *Rent-a-cop.* He stiffened and ordered her coldly, "No one gets in here. Go stand in line with the rest."

Another authority figure determined to block progress. *Play the respect game.* Jill smiled and backed away a step to reassure him she was not a threat.

"But, sir, I am a good friend of Cody's."

The hulking man was not a fool, not about to be tricked into losing this moonlighting pay that would buy a new camper, just because of some drooling broad.

"Sure, lady. That's what they all say. You groupies are always good friends. . . . Now just go around front like a nice little girl and pay the cover at the door."

He was going to be tough. "Please, sir. I know you are just doing your job. But would you go in and tell Cody that Jill is out here?"

While his face remained a blank, she could sense the battle taking place within. Maybe she did know Cody? That could be a problem too. Maybe not. Evidently her politeness tipped the scale in her direction.

"Ok, Ok. You stay out here." He disappeared inside. She held her breath, listened to the pulse pound in her ears. It seemed an eternity before he came back, his face angry now.

"Cody says he don't know no one named Jill. So do like I say. Give it up and go around in front." He shook his head in disgust and sat down on his stool, no longer intimidated by the need for decision making. Just another pain-in-the-ass groupie. He was going to go fishing in the Sierras as soon as he got that new rig, forget about all of these weridos.

Aware now that the problem was really serious, Jill did as she was told. Stood in line like a robot among happy, joking fans for more than twenty minutes. After she paid her admission, she froze in the doorway of the crowded room, uncertain of where to go. The couple behind jostled past. "Move it, lady."

Another voice behind her was familiar, "Told ya so." She turned, and her face must have been an open account-book because the waitress softened immediately. Janice grabbed her arm and propelled her to an empty seat at the bar next to her service area.

"I'm sorry, honey. About the phone call the other night, and what I said. And I did tell Cody exactly what you said. . . . He was worried all evening and as soon as they finished playing, he and B.J. went down to the pier to find you. . . . But . . . well, he just went wild when he found out you were with that other dude. He dropped Billy Joe off at my place and left in a fuckin' mope."

Jill tried, between Janice's table serving duties, to explain the innocence of her last two days.

"I believe you, honey. But convincing Cody is another thing. . . . You know . . ." She started to go on, probably about Marcia again, then must have thought better of it.

"Janice, who was that girl with him?"

The waitress looked puzzled, then laughed, "Oh, her. That's just some shirt tale relative . . . a cousin, I think . . . imagines she can sing. Cody's nice, lets her do a song with him, now and then. . . . She's nothin' to worry about." Jill laughed

171

too, with relief.

A roar went up then, followed by clapping and whistles, as Cody and the band came onto the stage. When he took the mike to make his introduction, Jill realized how much she'd missed that drawl in just a day. The band began one of their hit songs and she stared at Cody's face, hoping for some eye contact, but he never looked in her direction. As they finished, a long-haired customer yelled out a request for 'I Can Wait,' the song he wrote for her. Cody smiled and said, "Naw, we dont do that one no more." Then without hesitation, he began another that brought cheers from the crowd. The capsule of fear she'd been carrying since morning exploded letting its poison flow to every one of her body's nerve endings. She understood now that Janice was not being over-dramatic. The music and words were blotted out, replaced with only the pounding of the beat in her chest and the soles of her feet. At the end of the set Cody left he stage quickly and she hurried to intercept him. But another burly guard stopped her entrance to the back room. Janice walked up as she was pleading.

"I'll go in and try to talk to him." She was back in a minute. "No way, Jill. I'm sorry. He's fuckin' stubborn."

Over the protests of the muscle man, Jill planted herself by the door to wait for him to emerge again. Conspicuous by herself, she attracted the attention of the majority of stags at the bar. They came one after another, a mixture of hippie and cowboy types, to ask her to dance. The tiny, almost imperceptible, flicker of hurt at each rejection heightened her need to make Cody understand. Ron came out first, then Cody with Billy Joe beside him. She stepped in his path.

"I have to talk to you."

The blue eyes registered no recognition. He turned to the guard. "Ya'll better tighten up on your security." Then he stepped around her to smile and shake hands with someone at an adjacent table. The room and faces blurred as she heard him say, "Sure, man. I'll play that one for you. One of my favorites, too." He continued to the bandstand as if she didn't exist. Billie Joe looked back once, then quickly away again.

The big man in the uniform was gentle, "Don't take it so hard, honey. He's a big star, and he just doesn't have time for all the girls who have a crush on him. You'll find someone else better for you anyway. . . . As a matter of fact, I get off at . . ."

She wound her way through the crowd of tables and out the door. A warm breeze had cleared the smog and haze away, revealing the ever-present but usually invisible starlit sky. She looked up on her way across the parking lot. Tonight even the man in the moon seemed to sneer back at her. As she fumbled with the key, she realized she hadn't locked the car when an ears-splitting roar attacked from behind. Jumping as the electric shocks of fear pulsed through her, she turned and recognized the man from the other night, Neal.

He leaned back on his chopper-style motorcycle and grinned, "Scare hell out of you, did I?"

Her fear changed to anger as she shouted over

the motor noise, "I hate those things."

He turned the key and the gleaming machine was silent. "Oh, come on. Don't be mad. Just a little joke. . . . Are you going in or coming out?"

"I'm leaving."

"If you want to go back in with me, I'll buy you a beer?"

Her anger subsided, she sighed, "I'm afraid it would take more than a beer to make me go back in there." This Neal wasn't at all what she thought a Fiend would be like, too handsome and clean.

He scratched at his scalp and asked, "Trouble with your boyfriend? . . . That Cody can be a hard one to get along with sometimes." She started to defend him, but Neal continued, "Well, his loss is my gain. You smoke weed? I got some good stuff on me. . . . We could take a spin up the road and turn on a little?"

She shook her head. "No, I don't. . . . No, thanks. . . . I better go." Neal lounged back against the roll bar of his bike, a man well aware of his good looks.

"That's cool. Just an idea, but to each his own. Want a cup of coffee instead? I'm a good listener and perfectly safe."

She wanted to believe him. Maybe because she needed someone, anyone, to talk to. Maybe it was a way of getting back at Cody. Then Mara flickered through her mind and she accepted his invitation.

He turned the key and shouted over the din, "Hop on behind me. We'll run down to Denny's." He showed her where to put her feet and told her to hang on around his waist. They backed up, peeled out of the parking lot and down the street. The front fork of the bike gleamed far out in front and the ride was amazingly smooth. When she commented, he yelled back, "Sure thing. Rides like a baby buggy." The narrow seat felt strange but as the speedometer registered 70 and the wind whipped her anxiety away, she began to understand why these men took to their bikes.

Those infernal machines, her father called them. And she had always agreed, incensed as she was earlier, by the instant of fright and anger they caused so unexpectedly. But aboard was different. The sound added—was necessary. Deafness must be terrible, she thought. An Indy turn without the roar, jackpots without bells, coffee without the perk.

She turned her head right, then left, to let the stinging air hit one ear, then the other. The wind lifted her hair, turned it to a magic carpet following behind. Stores and cars and neon signs were a fast forward parade. The pavement, a gray velvet ribbon, to anywhere.

Neal geared down. She leaned with him, their bodies a necessary part of the machine as they rounded a corner at a high speed heel. Once more and they were in the parking lot. *No wonder Fiends were Fiends!*

Only when a departing couple stared, then hurried to their car, was she aware of how ominous her companion looked. Besides the vest with its eagle claw and gang name embroidered on the back, a huge jangling set of keys hung from his left hip, a long knife sheath from his right. His boots clanked the pavement as they walked to the coffee shop entrance. She was embarrassed at the hostess' rude greeting and could feel her face burn as they passed numerous booths to be seated by the kitchen door. She wondered now, why she ever accepted the invitation.

Neal flopped into the booth opposite her, leaned back against the wall with his feet extended into the aisle. The waitress, an older woman with a probable thirty-year service award, came over with two cups and a pot of coffee. She glared down at Neal's chained insteps and snapped, "Get those feet down. They're in everyone's way."

Neal grinned without moving, "I have a pain in this here knee from an old injury. Got to keep it up."

The coffee pot tipped dangerously above his legs. "I said, put your feet down . . . or get out. We don't need your kind in here making trouble."

Heads turned in their direction. Jill kept her eyes pinned to the carefully folded floral handkerchief fanning from the woman's uniform pocket. Neal stared first at the waitress, then the coffee pot, while Jill held her breath, frightened for the gutsy lady who had the nerve to challenge him.

Finally, he slowly withdrew his legs and with exaggerated politeness turned and sat up very straight, at the same time asking, "Is this all right, ma'am? Would you be so kind as to serve us coffee now?" The waitress slammed the cups on the table, poured them full and left. Neal looked at Jill and winked, "You're redder than a monkey's ass.

Don't you know biker chicks can't get embarrassed. This is the way we're treated everywhere we go. Nobody likes us poor innocent Fiends."

"Could it be the way you act?" She realized immediately that her sarcasm was a mistake. He retaliated in a loud voice.

"Well, now, aren't we the big shit." His volume increased. "Listen, lady, this is a free country. Just because we ride bikes and belong to a club, we're still Americans. . . . And I have just as much right to come in here as those niggers over there do."

Her eyes met those of the young mother in the booth across the aisle. The woman looked away and spoke rapidly to the two small boys with her. They protested as she insisted they leave their half-eaten hamburgers and follow her out.

"Oh, Neal, how could you?" She wanted to melt into the seat. She took a large swallow of coffee and burned her tongue. The Fiend was enjoying himself and not to be stopped. His lips parted into a sneer as he continued.

"Should have known to look at you, you was a nigger lover. . . . Listen, Miss Rich Bitch, the courts say every Jew and Spic and Nigger in this country can do anything they damn well please. Have any job, go to school in Beverly Hills. Bullshit! You white women are all the same. Fascinated with those big, black cocks. . . . Don't you know all niggers are inferior. It's true. Their brains are smaller. Even God cursed them. . . . Hitler was right, you know. That's why I wear this." He lifted the flap of his pocket to show a swastica. "We Fiends work hand in hand with the Nazi party. We're gonna get rid of all those cocksuckers." Her stomach churned. Yet she felt glued to the seat, listening to the ignorant and frightening indignities spew from his mouth. Basking in her discomfort, his intent from the beginning, she now realized, he dramatically scratched his crotch.

"I have to leave." Before she could stand up, he caught her wrist and pushed it hard against the table top, increasing the pressure until she stopped resisting.

The evil grin appeared again. "Oh, I'm so sorry. I forgot we came here so you could tell ol' Neal your troubles.'. . . Is that bastard Cody giving poor baby a hard time?" He flicked the snap on his hip sheath and laid a glimmering butcher knife-sized blade on the table next to her hand. "Want me to put a little scare into him for you? Maybe give those guitar pickin' fingers a slice just to make him sorry?" She tried to pull away but he held her wrist tight while the cold steel threatened. She glanced around for help, but all eyes were downcast, unwilling to interfere. How could this be happening in a crowded restaurant? Under thousands of watts of light?

"Don't be in no hurry now. Drink your coffee. I got lots of good stories to tell you."

The elderly couple in the booth behind him lowered their heads, concentrating on their eggs over easy. His eyes had a dangerous glaze as he continued. "You know, you can hire us to do your dirty work. We'll break that singing son of a bitch's arms if you want. Fiends will do anything.

. . . Want to hear a great story? Fuckin' best job we pulled ever?"

She didn't answer, determined she won't cry which is what he wants.

"Well," he continued, "we had us a camp up north one summer. Near this little burg of a town. One day, this old dude, one of the town's big deals. A banker he was in his tie and shiny pointed shoes. He drove out in his big fuckin' Continental and said he wanted to hire us. . . . There was this pack of wild dogs, see, that was causin' them folks a lot of aggravation. They was runnin' around, bitin' kids, shittin' on their grass . . . and the town folks didn't like it. So the pres or whatever he was, said he would pay us to get rid of them. Well, Trigger— he was president of the northern Fiends then, a real crazy—well, he said, 'Sure, man. We'll do it for you.'

"So that night we cruised around until we had them mongrels all rounded up. . . . What a trip! Lassoing dogs on choppers. . . . We tied them all together and took 'em back to camp. Then Trigger, he had a great idea." His voice rose in volume as his eyes scanned the other booths. "Can everybody hear me?"

A young couple across the aisle signaled each other and rose to leave. The long knife flashed and held steady, its tip pointed in their direction. Neal let his grin spread to a wide toothy smile.

The mustached man cleared his throat, then attempted a show of bravery, but his voice came out high, exposing his fright. "Come on, man. We're finished. We just want to mind our own business and leave."

Neal continued to smile, his eyes steady, the knife-handle firm in his hand. "Hey, come on, college boy. You'll want to hear this. And your sweet lady there, she'll like my story. Just sit still for a minute. Let ol' Neal finish."

The girl cried silently and her nose ran, but she didn't move to wipe it.

Neal glanced back to Jill. "OK, now, as I said, we got twelve of those mongrels rounded up. They was all kinds, part boxer, shepherds, some kind of huntin' hound. . . . And we was gonna have a line-up and shoot 'em—when Trigger he got this brain storm. The next night was Friday and 'the people of the town, they was gonna have a big barbeque at the firehouse. . . . So we decided to go. . . . We waited until six o'clock when everyone got there. . . . See it was right in the middle of that hick town and the old folks and families they was all gathered, eating and talking. We sneaked up to the end of the street, real quiet. . . . Had all them dogs roped together—and a dynamite cap tied to each of their middles. We lit them suckers then and they took off down the street." He began to laugh, punctuating the next words with swings of the glistening blade. "Just when they got to the party, them caps started going off. . . . Blowin' dog all over the street . . . chunks of bloody dog flying on the kids and old ladies. . . . And those crazy bastard mongrels, they tried to keep running, guts hangin' out, slipping in their own slime. . . . One bit black sucker with his insides wipin' up the street just kept going, dragging the others along with

180

him." Neal stopped, grinned at the girl across the aisle who was now shaking and sobbing silently. "Hey," he said to the man, "your chick don't seem to like my story. . . . Anyway, everybody was screamin' and yellin', even that old mother fucker that hired us. When the street was good and slippery, we started our choppers and cruised real slow like, through it all and out of town." He wiped tears from his eyes and continued, serious now, "Served the old bastard right. . . . I love dogs. . . . Killin' dogs ain't right. . . . Man's best friend and all that. God will get 'em back for it, you can bet on it. Jesus will make them suffer for their sins." He laughed again. "May even tie dynamite around their righteous, mother fuckin' middles and send 'em through the purly gates with *their* shit eatin' guts hanging out."

Jill put a hand over her mouth to try and hold back the rising bile, jerked away and ran for the restroom. His laughter followed her.

"What's the matter, pretty lady? Don't you like my story? . . . Hurry back now, hear?"

As she fled the length of the restaurant and around the corner of the counter, no one seemed to be aware of the scene at the other end of the room. Customers sipped coffee andd read papers, buttered pancakes, and stuffed sausages into their mouths. Once inside the ladies' room, she fell against the door, shaking. When her heavy breathing subsided, she listened for following footsteps, then opened the door a crack. Neal was nowhere in sight in the narrow hallway, and he couldn't see this area from the booth. But he could see the front door. A pay phone, her possible salvation, hung on the wall to her right. *Who can I call?* Cody won't come to the phone. The directory, attached to its steel rod to prevent theft, flopped closed twice as she alternately glanced behind her and searched through the S's. There it was—Santa Monica Sportfishing. She found a dime in her purse, dialed and prayed. She knew the phone was ringing in the dark baitshop. Afraid she had misdialed, she hung up and tried again. Just as she was about to give up, the familiar voice answered with an annoyed, "Yes?"

"Rick, don't ask questions, just listen." She told him where she was and what happened.

"Stay in the restroom. I'll be right there."

Back in the questionable safety of the small room, she sank onto the small stool at the make-up counter. Her knees began a dance, shaking to their own beat, ignoring an order to stop. When she looked up, the reflection in the mirror startled her. Ghostly, grey skin blotched with red. Eyes too big, about to pop from their sockets. She turned away and checked her watch, then jumped as the outer door opened—but it was only a mother with a girl about seven. The child stared solemnly throughout the handwashing process and as they left, the woman murmured "Sick!" After ten minutes, Jill could stand her prison no longer. She cracked the door. The hallway was empty. She walked its length and slid onto a stool at the counter just inside the restaurant, where she could observe, without being seen by the maniac at the other end of the room. The exit was in the never never land, halfway between.

Neal was still in the booth, leaning back again with both legs stretched out on the seat. The young couple was gone. A small oriental man in a suit, probably the manager, was standing at a table, apparently trying to convince the insolent man to leave.

Rick came through the door then, dressed in swim shorts and tee shirt. He glanced right and left, saw Neal and brushing by the protesting hostess, moved quickly to the booth. He spoke to the manager who retreated to the kitchen, obviously relieved. Rick slid into the booth where she had been sitting. Jill couldn't see Rick's face, but from Neal's expression it appeared to be the meeting of friends. When they started to get up from the table, she slipped back down the hallway to the restroom again, suspicious of the congeniality between Rick and the motorcycling paranoid. She leaned against the wall, bewildered, until she heard a soft tap on the door.

"Jill?" It was Rick. "It's all right now. He's gone. You can come out."

His arm around her shoulders felt strong and safe. As they walked to the door, the middle-aged waitress, carrying four plates of eggs, stopped in front of them. Her face and voice registered intense disgust as she looked at Jill, and muttered, "Your mother must be sick at heart. To produce a child . . . a pretty, little girl . . . and have her turn out like you . . . a slut that hangs around with trash." Rick's hand tightened on her shoulder, but he only said,

183

"Come on, let's get out of here."

Her legs felt like jelly as they walked to Rick's car. The woman reminded her of Mrs. Nelson. And she knew the kindly housekeeper would have the same opinion. She leaned back in the seat and closed her eyes. "I have to get my car. It's at The Ranch."

"What ever possessed you to go with him?"

"I don't know." *Yes, you do*. Mara. Well, you didn't find anything out about her. And Cody. His rejection. And Neil had seemed nice. She repeated again, "I don't know."

Rick drove into The Ranch parking lot and stopped behind her car. "I'll follow you to make sure you don't get in any more trouble." He sat stiff, looking straight ahead, both hands on the steering wheel. She touched his arm but he didn't move.

"Rick, thank you."

He didn't respond as she got out of the car and walked to hers. Cody's singing drifted from the club, reinforcing her need for him. The key turned easily in the lock, too easily. She hadn't locked the car. All of her camping gear—stove, sleeping bag, everything—was gone. She panicked, thinking about the package under the board. She wanted to look, but Rick had backed up and was waiting for her. So, she pulled out and started down the street. With one hand on the steering wheel, she lifted the plywood and scoured the area underneath. The compartment was empty. No car jack, no camera—no feather-light package of squid.

Jill gripped the wheel and tried to concentrate on

her driving, but the questions came non stop. What about Rick? She wanted to believe he was not involved. But what about the mysterious unloading of those packages? And why would he be friendly with someone like Neal? By the time she parked at the end of the pier, she was frightened—of the man in the car pulling in beside her. She decided not to mention the theft.

He stood waiting for her, a silhouette against the lights of the pier. She couldn't see his expression, but his voice sounded normal. No longer hurt or angry, he asked, "Feeling better now?"

She tried to appear relaxed, "All I need is a good night's sleep." But as they walked, even the pier added to her uncontrollable terror. Its welcoming daytime face had been replaced by a late night movie eeriness. The merry-go-round was locked in silence and the inky interiors of the closed shops and restaurants moaned quiet threats as she passed by. The fishermen scattered along the railing seemed somber and unfriendly. She glanced at Rick. He hadn't changed, grown horns or claws. He still looked like a carefree California surfer, oblivious to the cold or rough surface on the callouses of his bare feet. She flinched as his voice broke through her thoughts.

"Going to be a high tide tonight with that full moon. Bad fishing."

She looked up. The evil face still glared down at her. When they sent into the cabin of the baitboat and she looked forward, she could hear the fear in her own voice, "Where is Jody?"

"I sent her home with Irma."

Her mind raced. She couldn't think of a reasonable way to escape. Maybe when he went to sleep. "Well, you can have your bed back now, Rick. I'll sleep out here on the settee." *Closer to the door.* She reached for a folded blanket and began unrolling it. She could feel him behind her. He put his arms around her waist as he'd done that morning. This time she didn't dare shove him away. He turned her around and she marveled again at his good looks, the sensual attraction. Perhaps she was wrong.

He pulled her close and said, "I kind of thought, when you called me, instead of that cowboy friend of yours, that maybe you've made a choice." She willed her body not to withdraw as conflicting emotions waged an all-out battle within her. She couldn't deny the attraction but suspected it was a result of Cody's behavior. Yet Jody's words came back to her. *He's more your type.* She did love the sea and boats. And Cody had certainly been unreasonable with his jealousy. But the doubts about Rick kept creeping in. He saved her from Neal, yet frightened her. He knew about the drugs, had to be involved. Their lips met, and his kiss was so gentle and sincere she decided again she must be wrong.

"We could share Jody's place in the double up forward?"

It would have been so easy. To give in and forget for awhile about Cody and Mara and her suspicions about Rick. The temptation of warmth and closeness and security were almost more than she could bear. But an inner warning prodded her response.

"Rick, please." He backed away as if hit, but she continued. "I want you to understand. Too much has happened tonight. I'm confused and don't know how I feel . . . . I do care about you. But I can't make a commitment now, not when I'm exhausted. . . . Do you understand?" She knew her resistence was at a low ebb. If he had insisted, she would have ended up in his bed—to be sorry in the morning. To her relief, he only shrugged, his face giving no clue to his feeling. They climbed into separate bunks, she alone in the forward cabin—he insisted on the settee. She lay awake, long after his even breathing signaled his deep sleep, trying to clear her mind and stop the wild, disorganized thoughts from spinning out of order. She kept repeating one word over and over to herself, a technique she'd learned long ago was the only way to stop the mental chaos. As she drifted off to sleep, the choice of word announced her decision. Her earlier longings were misplaced. She was transported to the bed in the small trailer on top of the world. Cody . . . Cody . . . Cody . . .

She woke to voices and the k-thunk, k-thunk sound vibrating beneath her, curled in the warmth of the bed, then stretched, happy to be free of the night's tensions. Invigorated by her decision, she hurried into her clothes, no longer able to sleep.

Scott was at the wheel when she came into the pilothouse. The two of them were joking and seeing Rick like this reassured her again that she'd been wrong about him.

"Got ourselves a nice batch of those hard-to-find anchovies, tonight," he said, smiling like a little boy.

Scott showed his metallic grin. "Sure did. Rick's the best."

"Oh, look," she pointed. The sun's first rays crept slowly from behind the far-off mountains and buildings of the city. The haze changed from gold to grey as the sky lightened before them. Rick broke the silence first.

"Maybe we can arrange it so you can see this every morning."

Scott looked from one to the other of them, then decided he would go below and make coffee.

Rick took the wheel and unaware of her late night decision, continued, "You know, ever since I was Scott's age, I dreamed of owning this fishing operation. But I've never been able to put enough together to even make a dent in Ferguson's asking price. . . . Not until the last few years. But now I'm getting close." She knew what was coming and wanted to stop him, spare him the hurt. He continued to watch the water ahead as he finished. "And . . . I'd like you to be a part of it."

Jill stared through the windshield as the bow cut through a swell and sent irridescent spray over the rail. How could she tell him? She finally chose the coward's way by answering, "Rick, I still need some time, OK?"

His glance towards her, then back to the course ahead, was blank and non-commital again while his voice, although soft in volume, seemed to carry a threat, "All right. But don't take too long."

Her question popped out without any conscious

thought and surprised her. "Rick, did you ever know a girl named Mara?" Did she see a slight tightening of his jaw?

But as he turned, he only seemed puzzled, and answered, "No . . . I don't think so. Why? . . . Who is she and why would I know her?" His level gaze made her uncomfortable.

"I don't know what made me think of it. You know I like pottery. . . . Well, I bought a bowl with that name on it. The man said she was a local artist, maybe a girlfriend of the Fiends. . . . So I thought you might know of her."

"The Fiends are not friends of mine, Jill." Then he answered as almost everyone else had. "I think I'd remember that name if I had ever heard it."

Scott came with coffee and she decided for the thousandth time to forget about Mara and get on with her own life. She was anxious to get back to the pier.

Before the lines were secure, she stepped off the boat, in a hurry but wanting to find out first how Jody was. Irma was already in the restaurant and a young boy, her replacement in *Sea Maiden's* galley, was loading up the day's supplies. When he went to the back room, Irma asked, "Are you gonna take over again now?"

"I need a few days off right now," she responded, "then we'll see."

The woman put her hands on her massive hips and surveyed her, serious for once. "My girl, let me tell you. Rick is nuts about you." She lowered her voice, "He even told me. . . . And if I can give you any advise, it would be to grab him. Every gal in Southern California would like the chance. There's no one finer in the world than that lad."

Feeling like a traitor, she answered, "We'll see, Irma." Then, "But the reason I came over is to find out how Jody is?"

"Well, why don't you go out to *Sea Maiden* and see for yourself. She's back to work."

"You can't be serious?"

"Sure am. . . . That girl's made of rocks and nails, I think." The woman hesitated, then decided to get in one more pitch, "I don't usually say nothin', give advise, but I like you and I just think you should match up with Rick, that's all."

Jill ignored the last, a satisfactory response being impossible—and hurried to the fishing boat. When Jody turned around as she entered the salon, the girl's amazing recovery was apparent. The swelling on her face had gone done and the discolorations, although not gone, were fading fast.

"Jody," she said elated, "you look just great." The young face burst with pleasure and she bounded from behind the counter for a hug. Her body felt as strong and full of energy as ever.

"Oh Jill, I'm so happy. I'm healing so fast, I don't think I'll even have scars." She continued nonstop. "And all the pain is gone and Irma said I can decorate my room any way I want posters anything . . ." She took a breath and her face clouded, "But I feel bad about Mom. She didn't mean it, you know."

*How far we go.* We humans. A bird leaves the

nest never to return. But we will go to any length, fight the world, carry our roots to the grave. Mara made a fool of your father—and although he never knew it, you'll carry it on your back always. Jody may hate her mother but she can't stand for others to have the same opinion.

Jill hid her anger and replied smoothly, "Honey, we all know your Mom didn't mean it. . . . But for now, please stay with Irma. Maybe in a few years things will be different. . . . But Jody . . . I promised Dr. Adamson—that's how we got him to agree not to report it. . . . So you cannot go back there. . . . At all." She hated to use a threat but it seemed the only way to protect the girl from her own weakness and possibly another battering. It worked.

Jody agreed, then asked, "You gave up looking for that girl, didn't you?"

Jill looked around automatically to see if anyone else was in hearing distance before she answered in a low voice, "I thought we were going to keep that a secret?"

Jody avoided her eyes when she said, "I promised didn't I? I haven't told a soul. But I wish you would forget it. So no one gets hurt."

"What do you mean?" She was alert now to a nebulous something in the girl's words. "Do you know anything?"

Jody scraped at an imaginary spot on the floor with her toe, then began loading beer into the cooler before replying, "I just want you to be happy, that's all."

Jill was disappointed, sure now the girl was

giving her the same sales pitch as Irma's, just less direct. She said, "Don't worry, Jody. I'm going to be happy." She paused, "I have something to do now. Tell Rick for me will you?"

Jody's face lit up at the mention of his name and Jill could tell the girl was reading more into the message than there was.

"I sure will. Have a fun day . . . And get everything done fast so you can come back and work with me. You're a lot more fun than the dud they hired to take your place."

Jill passed the "dud" as she hurried off the boat and down the pier. It was a different place today. Three teenagers passed by with mustard-smeared corn dogs, too hot yet for the first bite. A Mexican couple stood arm in arm contemplating a ride on the bumper cars. The line of giant panda bears in the shooting gallery smiled in unison, as if giving encouragement for the encounter ahead. Even the theft of the night before refused to diminish her optimism. She did lift the board when she got in her car, and the package *was* gone. But she decided it was a blessing and hoped the thief would throw it away without knowing its contents. At least now she didn't have to make a decision about what to do with it.

The coastline had never looked so beautiful. The water was alive with surfers as she passed Malibu. She tried to watch the traffic and still catch a glimpse of their foamy rides but the waves weren't right yet. The black figures, wet suited against the chilly water, straddled their boards and bobbed in small swells, waiting for the perfect ride. If only we all had the expertise and patience of a good surfer, she thought. To recognize what's false and let it pass by without doing harm. To wait for the real exhilerating ride through the curl. Of course, there was always the chance of misjudging the strength of the wave, of being thrashed against the sand and rocks. But surfers picked themselves up, didn't they? To try again.

She drove almost past the road before she realized it, glanced in the rearview mirror and braked hard to make the turn. As the Pinto curved up the mountain, she wondered if smoothing out her life might be as difficult as straightening out the curves of this blacktop. She drove faster than usual, this time not from the fear of being followed but from fear of what was to come.

Cody's truck was parked behind the trailer and she was sure he would still be asleep. Dude barked when she tapped softly on the door and she could hear him sniffing at the bottom but there were no other sounds from inside. Jill hesitated, then tried the handle. The door opened a crack. What if someone, a female someone, was there with him? The thought paralyzed her and she was about to turn and go back the way she'd come—but Dude, overcome with joy at seeing her, shoved at the door and it flew back and hit the side of the trailer with a thud.

"Hey, Billy Joe? . . . Ya'll crazy? Comin' out here this early."

Her heart pounded at the sound of his voice.

"Cody, it's me."

Silence. It rang in her ears.

"Cody, I have to talk to you." Trembling, she stepped into the trailer, smoothed her hair. Why didn't I wash it, she thought, as she tripped her way over Dude the few steps to the bedroom. She stopped in the doorway. Cody lay shirtless and flat on his back in the waist high covers, his eyes closed. He didn't open them or move. The soft drawl had sharp edges that pierced her balloon of hope.

"I thought my message was clear. *Don't come back*! Now you're a smart girl. You should be able to understand those words."

Her throat tightened and all of the rehearsed speeches, the reasonable explanations, flew away. She answered meekly, "I don't believe you mean it."

His eyes remained closed, his body rigid, only his lips moved. "I don't want to see you. You were a bad dream. . . . One I've already forgotten."

Jill stood frozen, cursing silently the hot tears that refused to stay in place. When her words came they were equally uncontrolled, beginning with a whisper then increasing to a shrill hiss. "I'm glad I found out before I married you. How quick you are to doubt. . . . How incapable you are of trust. Cody Williams . . . Mr. Perfect . . . man of steel . . . . If everything doesn't go his way, he just forgets it . . . sits on his mountain top alone. And that's how you're going to be all your life, too. . . . Alone." Now depleted, she added, almost to herself, "And when the water sucks out you find there's nothing left but a sharp, rocky bottom."

The blue eyes opened for the first time; they

194

penetrated and accused.

"What's that supposed to mean?"

"Just something I was thinking about on the way up here that's all. Something you would never understand."

Dude nudged her hand with his nose and she reached to pet him. He nuzzled against her leg. Cody raised his arms, put his hands behind his head. The insolance of his grin was a warning of the words about to come.

"You're just back for the money. You had your little fling. . . . Fucking that sea captain with all the muscles. . . . Now you want to come back to good ol' Cody, where the livin' is easy. I had you pegged right that first day on the beach . . . you just had me fooled for a while, that's all."

Jill thought her head would split as rage stopped her tears and tightened every muscle in her body. Her voice continued out of control.

"You're sick, Cody. Sick, sick, sick. . . . My father was a millionaire. I've always had all the money in the world I ever wanted. And it never meant a thing. Never. . . . I'd have given it all to have him alive. . . . As far as the sea captain. . . . Yes, he has muscles . . . yes, he's beautiful . . . And yes . . . I could have gone to bed with him, in fact, he asked me . . . but I didn't because of you. . . . I had this strange foolish notion about trust between two people who loved each other. But I was wrong. . . . I don't love you, and you sure don't love me. . . . I should have gone to bed with Rick, at least he's human." She whirled and ran from the room and out the door of the trailer. Her lungs hyperventilated against the constriction of her chest and she leaned against the truck, too angry to move or cry. How could he think that? Accuse and degrade her? She leaned on the fender, willing her trembling to stop so she could leave, but it only increased.

She heard her name called through the open bedroom window.

"Jill, come in here again, please."

Why should I? She didn't answer, or move. The cool metal of the truck soothed her flushed face.

"Jill?"

His hands were on her shoulders and when he turned her around, his eyes were different, the ice gone. The muscles in his face contracted and relaxed, battling with each other.

"It's hard for me to say . . . I'm not much good at apologizing." He was having trouble not looking away. "But here goes. I'm sorry. I was wrong. I love you." He tried to smile. "There. How's that. I mean it."

She was in his arms then, unable to answer through the drowning sobs. He patted her back, smoothed her hair, kissed her neck, while she continued to cry uncontrollably. His voice was soft now, repeating over and over, "It's all right. We're gonna be all right."

They sank to the ground, let the tall grass engulf them. The stopper had been pulled letting all of the tensions of the last few days escape. She held his face and kissed him hard, her tongue searching for his. Her breasts swelled against his bare skin. They were both in a hurry, frantic to restore, reassure, reestablish. When they fell back exhausted and spent, he rubbed her thigh and said softly, "Ya'll can't fake that."

"I've never faked my feelings for you, Cody."

They went inside then and took a shower together, both silent, as if afraid conversation would somehow diminish the intensity of their emotions. They climbed into bed between the cool sheets and only then did he ask, "What about this millionaire stuff?"

Jill leaned in the crook of his arm and began. She told him everything, beginning with her grandfather's business. About her father. How much she missed having the mother that even Auntie Mil couldn't replace. As she talked about her father and Mara, his death and her disappearance, she suddenly felt the relief. None of it mattered anymore. Cody was the first person she had ever opened up to and by sharing the longstanding hurts and disallusionments they drifted away with the words. She felt at peace with herself for the first time that she could remember and finished her long story with, "It's over. Finally, over. I don't care anymore."

He fingered a wrinkle in the sheet without looking up. "You know, Babe, we all carry great big secrets around with us that make us act in the crazy ways no one else can understand. . . . I've never told anybody else this . . . but I'm gonna tell you . . . so you'll know why I acted the way I did. . . . Remember I told you about my mamma and daddy? Well, I left a lot out. . . . My mamma made a fool out of my daddy every chance she got.

. . . And he never knew it, least I don't think he did. He babied her, bought her everything . . . then he'd go out of town and she'd have some dude in his bed. I walked in on her and a magazine salesman one time. . . . You know, she wasn't even embarrassed. She just said stern like that it would kill my father if he found out . . . so it would be my fault if he died. . . . So I never said nothin'. After he did die, I asked her why. Why did she do that to him? She looked at me real honest like and just said she was different from most other women. . . . Said she loved Daddy but she had a big appetite. . . . That's what she said. . . . I left home that day and never went back." Jill heard the humiliation of the young boy. He continued softly, "That's why I didn't trust you, I guess. When I went down to the pier and you were out on that boat I just gave up. I couldn't ever take that. Being made a fool of."

*Maybe I'm lucky I never knew my mother.* Poor Jody and now this.

Cody threw the sheet off them, saying, "That's enough of the sob stories. We understand each other now and have great things coming up. Me and the band's got a big concert tour set up. Frisco, Jackson, all across the country. If we get a license, we can get hitched and make it a long honeymoon . . . When we get back we'll build us the biggest house these hills have ever seen. . . . With lots of bedrooms in case we want to raise a pack of kids. . . . What ya' think?"

"I think it's wonderful. . . . And we'll never make those kids suffer with their parents will we?"

198

"You got it." He pulled her out of bed. "Come on, let's go to City Hall."

Two couples were in front of them at the clerk's window but they didn't mind the wait, were content just to be near each other again. The young girl in front of Jill turned around at the sound of Cody's drawl.

Her face lit up. "Oh, you're Cody Williams aren't you?" she gushed.

He smiled politely and answered, "Yes, Ma'am," then turned back to their discussion of wedding plans.

"Oh, Cody, I have all your records." The girl poked her husband-to-be, who didn't appear as impressed as she was. He mumbled a greeting as she continued, "I talked Jim into taking me to The Ranch to see you. He doesn't like country music much." She caught her insult quickly with, "but he liked you. Didn't you, Jim?" The young man nodded embarrassed, but the girl didn't seem to notice.

"Would you give me an autograph?" Without waiting for an answer, she fumbled through her purse, found a small notepad and opened it to a blank page. She searched in vain for a pen. Jim, the disgust showing on his face, supplied one from his shirt pocket. Cody asked their names, then wrote, "For Sharon and Jim. Many years of happy marriage."

The girl grabbed Cody around the neck, kissed his ear, then stepped back and looked at him through lowered lashes saying, "You've made my day. You may not know it, but you've made my day."

Cody's eyes darkened dangerously as he pulled away but luckily the clerk said, "Next please," and the couple stepped to the counter. After their business, the girl continued another series of "Thank yous," and "You're terrifics," while Cody contained his rising anger. As the couple left, he whispered through clenched teeth, "I pity that poor sorry son-of-a-bitch."

"That was a preview, Cody. Of the concert tours. Girls hanging all over you." She laughed trying to relieve his tension. "That's the price you pay for fame."

But it didn't work, she saw, when he answered "Not if I can help it."

They decided to get married on top of their mountain. Cody wanted Billy Joe and Janice to be there, she decided to invite Jody and Scott, Irma and Hugo. "Let's have it at eight in the evening. We'll light up the garden area with hundreds of candles. Get married between the rose and cactus gardens."

He laughed, the incident with the girl forgotten, "That sounds like a thorny beginning to me."


"Holy catshit."

Jill rolled over in the empty bed, surprised to hear Janice's voice coming from the other room so early in the morning. She noted with amusement Janice's habit of using holy before her many expletives, perhaps as an unconscious attempt to soften their blow. But for Jill, it was now unnecessary. The girl, and the rest of the musicians, used the expressions with such regularity and ease, their impact dwindled and sounded no more vulgar than if they said Golly or Shucks. When she heard,

". . . a week in Vegas . . . I can't believe it," she pulled on a robe and hurried toward the voices.

B.J., Janice, and Cody looked up from their coffee cups.

"Morning, Jill," Janice smiled, "Sorry if I woke you but can you believe we're going to have a week of pulling handles and partying in the big town?"

Cody saw her puzzlement and explained, "Mornin', Babe. We just got word we're booked into the Golden Nugget in Vegas . . . kind of a shakedown for the bigger tour. We leave tomorrow."

She hesitated between disappointment, and excitement before asking, "Where will we be staying?"

"In style, man." Billy Joe slapped the table. "In real style. They're giving us all fuckin' free rooms in the hotel."

"Yep," Janice added, "And that's what you and me are gonna use that room for too. Lots of free fuckin'." The girl's thoughts changed quickly. "I gotta get some new sexy clothes."

"You won't need none," Billy Joe answered, "None at all. I'm gonna keep you chained to the bed of that free room."

Their little caravan left the next morning: Jill and Cody in their pickup; Janice and B.J. in his, Ron, John, Medic, and the instruments in Ron's van.

"Kevin's flying over tonight with a friend," Cody told her as they finally cleared the San Fernando Valley and turned onto the freeway towards Barstow. "Our first show is 10:30."

"Tonight? How late do you play?"

"Til four in the morning."

"My gawd, when do we sleep?"

He patted her knee. "Who said we was gonna sleep? We're going to Vegas to have ourselves a good time."

This was a side of Cody she'd never seen but she was as excited as he was and sleep seemed unimportant. Especially when they dropped off the freeway and turned onto Fremont, the main downtown strip. As barkers on the sidewalk passed out coupons to tourists in plaid bermuda shorts and the sound of nickels dropped into the hundreds of slot machines, bells, sirens, and conversation clattered from every doorway. Jill's thrill increased.

"There it is, Cody," she grabbed his arm and pointed, "There's the Golden Nugget." It was the largest club on the street. "Look, your name is on the marquee. Look, Cody Country."

He laughed, "I think you're gonna make a good groupie, Babe."

They turned the corner and pulled up to the entrance. An attendant in a short red jacket stepped up to open Jill's door.

In seconds they had turned the quiet lobby into a

jumble of instruments, luggage, and jokes. Other guests stared as they followed two bellmen and their rolling carts toward the elevators.

B.J. slapped Medic on the shoulder, "This is some pad, huh, Doc?"

The slight drummer flinched, "Yes, I think it should be very nice."

"Fuckin' A right!" B.J. answered.

They were led to side by side rooms on the fourth floor and when their door was opened, Jill and Cody gasped in unison. The combination of flocked wallpaper, heavy red velvet, a needlepoint settee, and black carpet covered with huge red roses, transported them back in time—to the gay 90's.

Cody handed their young luggage carrier a dollar, closed the door and whirled Jill around in the room. They rolled on the velvet bedspread, laughing like two preschoolers.

"Shit, I feel like we should be out pannin' for gold. See, I told you, woman, stick with me and I'll show you the world."

"Ain't nothin' like this in Ohio, Cowboy."

He laughed again, "Man, you're even gettin' to talk like a shitkicker."

Then their mutual passion stopped the silliness. Jill lay back motionless as Cody traced her brows, eyelids, the curve of her cheeks, with a whispered touch.

"God, I love you, Babe," he said quietly.

They explored each other in silence, taking their clue from the gentle caress of velvet beneath them. Jill ignored the repetitious ring of the phone beside the bed, listened instead to the crescendo of her own inner symphony.

When they finally lay back exhausted, Cody brushed her ear with his lips and whispered, "Know somethin', Babe?"

She asked, lazily, "What?"

"You're a fuckin' good lay."

They laughed any Victorian ghosts out of the room.

"Come on," he said standing up then and pulling her to him, "let's take a shower and hit the town." He stopped in the doorway of the bathroom. "Good Christ, Jill, we almost missed the best part." A magnum of champagne sat on the counter in its nest of ice, beside two crystal goblets. "Would you look at that fuckin' tub?"

"That's what it looks like to me," she answered, surprised at how much she sounded like Janice.

"I'll pour the vino, you run us some nice warm water."

The bath tub was large and square, a twentieth century addition to the nineteenth century room. Jill poured shampoo under the rushing water and in a few minutes they were settled in the warm foam, sipping the icy, bubbly wine.

"I tell everybody you're a nice girl," he said, "and here you are in Vegas having an orgy with a broken down guitar picker."

Jill was amazed herself at her lack of inhabitions since she'd met him. She'd been released from her self-imposed solitary confinement. The champagne numbed the tip of her nose but bared every other nerve in her body. She set her glass down carefully and shoved Cody under the water. "You got more than you bargained for, Cowboy."

They thrashed and splashed until both fell back panting.

A pounding began on the door then and B.J. shouted, "Come on, you sex fiends, we got to go get setup . . . then we're all going to some first class retaurant."

"Okay," Cody yelled back. "Be right there."


They saw the wide-brimmed black hats immediately when they walked into the casino. The four musicians were bent in concentration, as Janice slid silver dollars into one of the hefty slot machines near the front entrance.

"Are you guys nuts?" Cody asked, as they walked up.

"Hell, no," B.J. answered. "We each threw in a twenty. Gonna break the bank at this fuckin' place. They won't have enough money to pay us by the time we get through."

Jill noticed that Ron seemed to be included in the camaraderie and hoped silently that he wouldn't cause any more tensions.

A cocktail waitress came by with a tray of beer which they quickly confiscated with a five dollar tip.

B.J. pulled Jill up to the machine and said, "Come on, girl, take your first shot at a Las Vegas bandit. Janice ain't been worth a shit so far." He handed her a stack of silver. She followed their boisterous directions, slid three coins into the slot and pulled the handle. Two bars stopped in the center row while the third reed continued to spin. Then as if directed by a hand from above, the missing link fell into place and the bells and sirens started.

"Holy shit, holy shit, we won." B.J. grabbed Medic and swung him around. "We fuckin' won three hundred bucks."

The others pounded each other's backs, jumped up and down and shouted while a momentary fear immobilized Jill. *I'm not lucky. I've never been lucky. This can't be real.* The thoughts were shouted away as quickly as they'd come when the change girl brought three racks of silver dollars.

"We better cash those in and go get set up," Cody suggested.

"Hell, no," B.J. answered. "We already got everything organized while you two was messin' around . . . and we're in Vegas so we're gonna spend this silver like it is. Here . . ." He started pulling the coins out of the racks and handing them around. They walked out of the casino with the pockets of their jeans bulging.

As they stepped through the curtain of cool air in the doorway, the warm desert evening bathed their skin with its soothing freshness.

Billy Joe guided them to the corner. "Kevin's meeting us across the street at the Top of the Mint. Said he'd pop for dinner. . . . First time that cheap son of a bitch ever bought us a thing so I'm gonna have me the biggest mother fuckin' steak they got," he said as they stepped into the glass elevator that traveled up the outside of the building to the roof top restaurant.

Jill noticed another couple decided to wait for the next trip. It amused her when she realized it was the appearance of her companions that had made their decision. With the long hair, beards, and black hats they could have been a gang of outlaws.

She glanced at Cody, and for an instant her earlier fear returned, but then the city's lights spreading out beneath them, overpowered the nameless apprehension with their merry glitter.

The maitre d' took a step backward as they emerged from the elevator, then regained his composure and came forward with a practiced smile.

"Dinner folks?" He glanced nervously from one face to the other.

"Naw," Billy Joe answered for all of them, "we got to do some serious drinking first."

Janice, strangely quiet until then, added, "Right . . . Man, I need a shooter. All this nice shit is too much for me."

Kevin walked up, polished as always, and said to the nervous host, "These are my guests. We'll have a drink in the cocktail lounge before we go in to dinner."

"Very well, sir." The tuxedo retreated, obviously relieved to be rid of the grisly group, at least for the moment.

Kevin led them to a table where a young man, looking no more than sixteen, was already seated.

"I want you to meet my friend, Brian."

Long pale fingers toyed with a wine glass and an intimate smile passed between the two as Kevin sat down next to him. His eyebrows arched and the full lips parted in shock when Ron said, "Can you believe they call that shit music?"

He was referring to the piano player who was rippling out a cocktail hour version of "I Left My Heart in San Francisco."

The young man recovered enough to ask, "Don't you like piano music? It's always been my favorite in this type of setting. Good background for conversation."

Janice laughed and answered, just as the waiter came up to take their order, "Honey, we ain't much on conversation, just good hard drinking, that's what these assholes go to a bar for."

The marginal case of acne turned towards Kevin, who slipped into his usual fatherly role, "Now I hope you guys are going to behave yourselves tonight," he said. "Remember you are my guests."

Billy Joe stood up and began dumping the silver dollars form his pockets out onto the table. Heads at neighboring seats turned at the clatter and the waiter glanced toward the dining room then asked quickly, "May I take your order?"

"I'm gonna get this first round with my winnings," B.J. answered. "Shooters and beers all the way around. How's that? . . . And make sure it's Cuervo Gold, too. Don't try passin' that cheap shit from the well off on us."

Medic interrupted, "No, no shooter for me. I'll just have a Perrier with a twist, please."

"What the hell is that, Medic?" Janice asked, "Somethin' to cure the trots?"

"No," the drummer pushed at the bridge of his

glasses, "Perrier water comes from a spring in France. It's naturally carbonated."

"You mean all you're going to drink is a fuckin' glass of water?"

"Everyone should drink at least eight glasses of water a day," he replied. "And natural spring water is very high in essential minerals."

"Christ, Medic," John shook his head and laughed, "between all that bran you eat and all the water, you must be a hollow tube from your mouth clean through to your asshole."

Brian stared in disbelief.

Kevin patted his hand, "I told you when you wanted to come over here with me that you weren't going to believe these guys."

"It is very interesting," he answered. "I'll certainly have stories to tell my mother when I get home." Then to Kevin, he added, "Oh, before I forget, we'll have to go shopping tomorrow. I promised mother I'd bring her something nice from here."

The following silence was broken with the arrival of the drinks.

Ron said, "Cheers"; the four musicians and Janice emptied their shots of tequila. "Better bring us five more right now," he told the waiter before he'd left the table. "We got to produce some hot music tonight and since I'm going straight, man, I need some alcoholic fortification."

The piano player began the first notes of "Stardust" and several middleaged couples moved onto the small floor. The women were in long dresses, the man in suits and ties. Ron glanced up, then leaned around Kevin, looked directly into Brian's eyes and asked, "May I have this dance?" The boy fidgeted.

Cody's voice was steely as he said, "Knock it off, Ron."

Ron turned his gaze on Cody, smirked, then poked B.J. "Shit," he said, "Everyone else is dancing. Come on buddy, if Kevin's friend don't want to dance, how about you?"

B.J. stood up. "Hell, why not." They all laughed and the tension was broken as the two of them waltzed cheek to cheek, until their hats dropped to the floor. B.J. went into a hat dance then, his boot heels clacking the other couples off the floor. He fell laughing back into his chair.

The maitred' appeared then, went directly to Kevin and said, "Your table is ready sir, but I'd like to remind you that this is a subdued restaurant."

"We understand." Kevin grabbed for his mustache, "Don't we fellows." Then he looked at Janice and added, "and ladies."

"Sure, sure," Billy Joe said as he stood up. They all joined in to reassure the slick man in the bow tie, then marched silently behind him through the dining room to a large round table in the corner. Las Vegas twinkled below them through the large windows and to Kevin's obvious relief they appeared restrained by the dim, plush surroundings.

Until the waiter with the French accent came to take their drink order:

"Jill?" Cody questioned.

"A glass of burgundy, please."

"Hey, good idea," B.J. said. He looked up at the waiter, smiled, and in a serious voice asked, "How about bringin' us the biggest jug of cheap wine you got back there?"

The fake Frenchman struggled to keep the disgust out of his voice as he replied, "I'm sorry sir, we have no jug wine. I'll be happy to bring the wine list though so you can make a selection."

"Yea, Okay, sure."

He was back in a second with the velour-covered menu. Billy Joe opened it and whistled.

"Shit, look at this. I can't read one fuckin' thing on here and they're all . . . christ . . . fourteen dollars a bottle? Man, that buys a lot of Coors."

The conversation over the drinks was reasonably calm; until Ron asked suddenly, "You a musician, Brian?"

The young man set his glass down and his voice wavered. "No, I'm not. I'm a student, in theater arts."

"That must be interesting," Ron said. Then he turned to Kevin, "Kind of robbing the cradle aren't you, man? Makin' it with students."

Kevin's blonde complexion turned ruby, he half stood, looked around, then sat back again. "You're a rude son of a bitch, Ron, you know that. I think I liked you better when you were strung out and couldn't form your words. . . . Brian and I are just . . . friends."

Ron let a slow, lazy grin spread over his face, "Whoa, man, I was just joking. Shit, if you want to stay in the closet it's okay with me, man. Shit, we don't care, do we gang?"

Jill caught the glimmer of tears in the corner of Brian's eyes and prayed to herself that they wouldn't lose their grip and tumble down for everyone to see.

Cody stopped it. "Look, we're all friends at this table. So let's stop this badmouthin' shit and get on with our fun. We got us one important gig tonight." He lifted his glass. "Peace."

They took his advice and the rest of the meal was pleasant as they all ate, in Billy Joe's words, "the biggest mother fuckin' steak they got."

It was ten fifteen by the time they got back to the Nugget. Jill and Janice went to a front table in the lounge while the rest went backstage to tune up. They were both keyed up and excited for their men, especially Janice who talked nonstop as the guitar sounds drifted through the heavy curtain.

"I gotta tell you what I did as a special surprise for Billy Joe," Janice leaned closer. "You know what waxing is?"

Jill didn't.

"Well, you know like when someone has hair on their upper lip? Well, beauticians take warm wax and put it on and then when it gets cold they pull it off and the hair comes with it."

Jill looked at Janice. She'd never noticed any unwanted hair on the pretty blond's face.

"No, no," Janice laughed. "Not on my face. . . . I had a design done . . . to show B.J. how much I loved him."

Jill was confused but not for long.

"I had a heart done on the front of my snatch."

Jill burst out laughing. "You're kidding."

"No, I'm telling you the truth. Cost me twenty dollars for this gal I know to come to the house and do it. . . . Man, what a kick. Now I got my heart where it belongs . . . on my pussy."

Jill thought first of the pain, then B.J.'s reaction. She didn't plan to ask, but Janice answered both of her silent questions.

"Hardly hurts at all. I'm saving it for B.J. until tonight. Can't wait to see his face."

"Janice you're too much."

The lounge had filled by now and they stopped the conversation as the curtains opened to an uproar of applause and whistles. The band charged into their first song and Jill felt a swell of pride when she overheard the man at the next table tell his date, "They are so good I can't believe it. That Cody's wicked, man."

The audience fell into two general categories. Bouffant hairdos escorted by men who refused to give up their 32-inch waist jeans and still wore them under 40-inch middles; and the younger, hairy, braless set. The former preferred the old favorites and cheered boisterously for any Merle Haggard tune; the latter preferred the originals, especially if the song referred in any way to getting high.

Cody started a new tune, one she'd never heard, "It's a Saturday night, alcohol love affair." It told the story of a dissatisfied husband who waits all week to meet his lover at the corner bar. Both factions of the audience loved it and Jill shared Janice's pride when Cody announced that B.J. had written it.

The band's momentum built through each set, and by four o'clock, when the last tune had been played, they were all wide eyed and running on the steady stream of adrenolin the audience had showered on them.

"Come on, everybody," John told the small group backstage, "We'll all hit our room for some tequila and food. I'll call room service." He threw his arm around a leggy girl in a tight teeshirt and her plumper, stringy-haired companion. "You gals, been waitin' all evening to rub butts with us stars haven't you?"

"Miss Plump giggled and snuggled closer but John's attention was definitely on the gum chewing beauty on his right. She answered for them both, her eyes traveling towards Cody. "Wow, like really."

When they reached their floor, Medic begged off. "Sorry men, but I need my sleep. You know I don't drink and eating right before you go to bed is very bad for you. Makes your body work hard when it should be at rest."

"Shit, Medic," Billy Joe said, "my body feels the best when it goes to bed but doesn't rest. . . . Ain't that right, Janice?"

Janice looked at Jill and winked, "That's right, honey, and just wait until you see the surprise I got for you tonight. That old body of yours won't be doing no resting. Right Jill?"

John unlocked the door to the room he was sharing with Ron and in a few minutes they were washing tequila down with beer, gobbling cheeseburgers and frenchfries, and praising themselves

214

for a successful evening. Jill felt as estatic as Cody, like she had been on stage too, had performed to everyone's satisfaction. She was silently amused as the "Wow, really," girl planted herself on the settee next to him and began a flirtatious assault. He ignored it and went on with his music talk.

"Man, B.J. they liked your tune. We'll record it." He looked around. "Hey, where's Kevin?"

Ron got up from the floor, saying, "Kevin retired early. You know, he had to get his young friend to bed. . . . Come on, honey, let's get us some air." He pulled a hairy-legged girl in her thrift store outfit to her feet and towards the door.

When they left John said, "Man, that cat sure don't like fags. Maybe he's got somethin' to hide. Of course, if he'd pick up better looking women, instead of those hippie broads, maybe he'd be more turned on."

He passed the tequila and the chubby girl, identified as Pam, tipped the bottle and stopped the conversation as all eyes watched the amber liquid disappear.

"Shit," B.J. laughed, "we can't afford groupies like you."

John said, "Sure we can, B.J. Tequila makes you crazy and that's what we want is crazy ladies following us around."

Pam giggled, then staggered to her feet, "Well, she said, "If that's what you want, that's what you're gonna get." She turned up the volume of the FM and, as a disco song blasted through the room, began an obscene undulating dance. Not to be outdone, Patsy, the girl next to Cody, joined her.

Janice voiced her opinion that "Groupies suck," but the girls ignored her, concentrated on their gyrations. Patsy turned her talents toward Cody, rubbing her hands up and down her thighs as her pelvis drew imaginary circles a few inches from his face. Then in a quick movement she stripped her teeshirt over her head and stopped dead still with a triumphant smile. He stood up, and for an instant Jill felt a jab of jealousy as a slow grin spread across his face. But his voice was flat, "My daddy always said there was things that was best left covered." He crossed the room, pulled Jill to her feet and said, " 'night, gang." As they left, Ron and his girl were just coming back. Cody took one look at the musician's dilated pupils and said, "At it again, huh?," then without waiting for an answer, unlocked the room next door and stomped in.

Jill felt sick. Cody slumped on a chair and began tugging at his boots. "Shit, I knew it couldn't last. A great evening and Ron and that slut have to ruin it." He pulled back the heavy velvet drape and harsh daylight streamed in. "Why did I ever think I wanted this life? Go to bed when everyone else is getting up. Have to put up with a bunch of crazy people."

They climbed into the giant bed, too exhausted for any more discussion.

The stuffy chill of airconditioning, plus the artificial darkness, kept Jill—and Cody, too, if his tossing was any indication—from her usual deep slumber. Cody reached across her for the phone.

"Time, please." He hung up and swore under his breath, "Damn, it's 4:10 already. Day's almost gone and time to go back to work."

They dressed quickly, anxious for a breath of fresh air, but when they stepped outside the hotel the 100 plus temperature of the Las Vegas afternoon was a scorching disappointment. They stood looking at each other, neither knowing what they should do until 10:00 at night. They'd already discovered the truth about the town. If you weren't gambling, there wasn't much else—except food and drink.

Cody grinned, "Well, let's get us some breakfast . . . or dinnner . . . whatever the hell you'd call it. I can't decide." So back in they went, more thankful this time for the relief from the summer desert. They met the others, except for Ron, in the coffee shop but no one would have guessed this was the same highspirited group from the night before. Everyone moped over their meal in near silence, even B.J., whose humor seemed also to have been stunted by the afternoon which should have been morning. Cody and Jill escaped back to the room that had somehow lost much of its charm in less than 24 hours. They watched the evening news on TV and changed clothes without enthusiasm.

But when the curtain parted in the lounge, Jill saw the first of the miracles that was to be repeated all week. The entertainers came alive under the lights; their disagreements, disorders, and disappointments vanished in their genuine, hard driving need to please—and to be rewarded with applause. She marveled that Medic could give a flailing, sweating performance one minute and be moaning in the coffee shop the next. As the week dragged on his health, mental at least, declined until he was on a diet of boiled rice and hot tea.

Ron became more surly when he was without his artificial high, from whatever source; and Cody assumed the role when Ron got himself mellow. John and B.J.'s fluctuations were more subtle yet they all became a cohesive family, as close and closed as the Mafia, when they began their music.

The crowds increased for every show; by mid week the lines outside the lounge were routine. And with them came the hangers on, touchers, and clingers. Jill and Cody began ordering room service instead of suffering through meals downstairs with interruptions and stares. The Dr. Jeckyl/Mr. Hyde atmosphere was making its mark on Jill. She had an unexpected attack from her secret thunderbolt, the first since she'd met Cody. It left her shortcircuited with an unidentifiable fear. If we can just get home to our mountain, she started telling herself. If we can just get home to our mountain. She was packing Saturday afternoon, they would leave the next day. A tap sounded on the door.

Kevin raced into the room, his excitement obvious on his flushed face.

"Cody, you're going to Lake Tahoe tomorrow."

"Tahoe?"

Jill stopped folding a blouse and sat down on the bed.

"That's what I said. I just had a call. The opening act with Jim Nabors got in some sort of squabble and walked out. He likes a country group for a warm-up so they called and want you to finish out the week. It's only two nights but, hell, it's Harrah's in the main room . . . and next time, you're going to be the headliner."

The anticipation of ocean sunsets vanished into desert sand as Jill felt the lump of disappointment in her throat. She was immediately ashamed, especially when she looked at Cody. His grin spread as he said quietly, "No shit? That is a big deal. The main room huh?" Then his face clouded, "Kevin, do you really think we're good enough, that we can carry it?"

Kevin marched to the window and whirled around. "Christ, Cody, you know you're good enough. You're another Waylon Jennings . . . better, even. . . . You have the voice, great backup . . . and besides that, you know every goddamned broad in the place thinks you're singing just to them."

Jill hadn't thought of that beofre. She always felt he was singing only to her. Illogically, the comment made her like Kevin slightly less than before. She made an effort to sound enthusiastic as she crossed the room and sat on the arm of Cody's chair.

"Well Cowboy, it looks like you've got it made. I'm proud of you."

He pulled her onto his lap and wrapped her in a

passionate embrace, half for his manager's benefit. Then he looked up and said, "Go on, get out of here, Kevin. We got us some serious celebratin' to do. Don't worry we'll be packed in plenty of time."

The door closed quietly but they didn't notice. They were too busy tangling their bodies and emotions, seeking the reassurance that their mountain could be anywhere, as long as they both stayed together on top.

Although bone tired from lack of sleep and the long drive, Jill's fatigue vanished when they started into the mountains. This was her first time in the Sierras and the majestic pines lining the highway seemed to welcome her escape from the parched sand. As they passed a thick stand of giant Ponderosas she asked,

"Cody do you think we could stop?"

He checked his watch. "No, we're runnin' tight, why?"

"I just wanted to walk in that beautiful dark shade. To look up and see if the sky even showed through."

He laughed, "Not now. But there are plenty of them tall guys in Tahoe too so you'll get your chance there."

When they pulled up to Harrah's, she belived him. The casinos were there, with their miles of neon but they were somehow dimmed by the dramatic show of nature on all sides. The entertainment manager of the hotel explained that they would be staying in one of the club's houses, and as they drove to a large rustic cabin overlooking the emerald lake, Jill decided the ups of this lifestyle were worth suffering through a few downs.

Cody was distracted with the business of the evening show. He climbed into the van with the other musicians and they left Janice and Jill to inspect the lodging.

"We'll save you a table. First show's at eight."

The girls walked across the thick carpet of pine needles and into the house.

An elderly woman in a white uniform came forward to greet them.

"Welcome. My name is Martha. I'm the house-keeper and cook. I'll show you to your rooms."

They followed her past a two-story stone fire-place flanked by floor to ceiling views of the lake and down a long hallway.

"We have six guestrooms. All similar except some have twins. You can take your choice. I don't make the dinner meal because of the conflict with the show schedule, but I'll be happy to fix sandwiches or snacks and you'll find the bar in the living area fully stocked with everything you might want. Just ring this buzzer if I can be of any help. . . . Oh, I will serve breakfast and lunch anytime you like."

Janice threw herself onto the bed in the first room and bounced like a naughty child. "Aren't we the hot shit? Man, this is a long way from cocktail waitressing, isn't it?"

They hurried into the best clothes they had, anxious to get back to the club. The parking attendant didn't seem the least surprised to see two girls climb out of an old pickup truck in long skirts. Once inside the club they weren't sure how they would find their men. But the girl behind the reservation desk picked up the phone and in a second a man in a tuxedo was leading them through the kitchen, down one flight of stairs to a long hallway. He tapped on the first door and opened it without waiting. The familiar bodies were sprawled around the room, each with a glass in hand.

B.J. stood up and waved them in. "Look at this, girls, would ya'." He pointed to the far wall, a bank of chipped ice from one end to the other. Artfully laden platters of fresh fruits; vegetables, seafood, cheeses and meats competed for space with the liquors, wines and mixes.

Cody beckoned her to a seat beside him, saying, "Can you believe this? This is our fuckin' dressing room. Anything we want, the guy in the black suit said." He emptied his bourbon and stood up. "But we gotta sing for our supper first, so we better get upstairs. Rehearse with the sound and lights. Come with me Jill. I'll meet the rest of you guys up there in a minute."

As they climbed the steps he said, "I want to show you something." He spoke to the girl at the reservation desk and they went through the double doors to her right.

"I just want you to understand why I'm jumpy and hard to get along with sometimes."

In the dim light, the room filled with tightly meshed seating for hundreds frightened her also. The rows of empty chairs marching down the tiers toward the stage, were silent confirmation of the size of the audience.

"It will be different," she said as much to reassure herself as him, "when the room is full of your fans."

"That's what's scary. They're not gonna' be my fans. They belong to Jim Nabors . . . or worse yet, just highrollers who don't give one shit about the music, just come in here 'cause their ol' lady insists."

They could hear their friends behind the curtain, and started down the steps through the eerie cavern.

'You'll be great," she answered, "I know it."

She sat with Janice backstage as the musicians with help from the staff worked out the technicalities. Cody stopped several times to twist knobs on the mysterious banks of amplifiers.

"We'll never be ready." He shouted, cursed, and adjusted.

Jill could stand it no longer. She wished she could go to the room and miss witnessing the failure she was sure would occur. But she followed Janice's command go to out front. A few patrons had already been ushered into the big room but it seemed no less formidable. She mentioned her fears to Janice.

"Oh shit, Jill, don't worry. They'll have it together. They always get crazy nervous like that."

As the room filled quickly, and long-legged waitresses threaded their way through the teeming masses hurrying to get drinks served before the eight o'clock deadline, Jill analyzed the crowd.

223

Cody's highrollers were obvious in the front row seats and raised banquettes: paunchy men accompanied either by bejewelled matrons who were their wives, or flashy casino-hardened young ladies who were not. The next group in the pecking order were the rhinestone doctors and lawyers: men of obvious means, like Gene, who pretended with their expensive western suits to be ranchers from Susanville, not orthodontists from San Francisco. The tourists were at the back of the bus and seemed to be having the most fun. Overweight secretaries from Omaha laughed and joked while the front rows stirred with impatience.

The curtain parted, and Jill said a silent prayer— but it was unnecessary. Janice was right. Cody Country, enhanced by professional stage lighting and an expensive sound system, launched their act with a raucous first number that caught and held the crowd. They stayed with hushed attention through Cody's quiet solos, whistles and cheers when the beat increased. They opened the valve and let the pressure off, allowing Jill and Cody to enjoy their days at the lake *and* the evening shows. Word came down, through Kevin, that Mr. Harrah was pleased and Cody Country would be welcomed back.

Two mornings later they were packed once more and on their way home.

"It's been an exhausting, idyllic time," she said.

"Christ, yes," he answered as they drove back down the mountain, "But The Ranch is gonna be a piece of cake after this. We'll go home and hybernate."

224

When they finally dropped off the Santa Monica freeway onto Coast Highway, Jill glanced at the pier and thought guiltily for the first time in days about her friends there. She would call Jody tomorrow. The white package and its importance surfaced for a moment, but the impatience to get home overpowered the anxiety. The past, all of it, should be forgotten.

*Love is everything*. Each day was better than the last. Her body and mind, at last released from the self imposed prison, soared from one euphoric hour to the next. She avoided going to the pier because of Rick; declined evenings at The Ranch and the possibility of running into Neal. They took Dude for runs in the hills. Set up a table between the flowerbeds and ate dinner by candlelight overlooking the ocean. They spread a blanket and made love under the stars. Even the evenings alone, after Cody went to work, were free of their prior torment. He would hurry back to wake her at two. Her only fear was that it would end. Tha she would wake up and find she'd been dreaming. No, not this time.

Jill recognized Kevin's silver Mercedes when she came back from the supermarket, and resented the intrusion into their privacy, especially by him. She'd told Cody she didn't like or trust his manager, but Cody insisted the small man was responsible for his success.

"You don't understand, Jill. In the music business you can be great—but without someone to make things happen, you end up playing dives the rest of your life. Now we're damned good, the best, but without Kevin we would still be in Pico Rivera."

Remembering his words, she opened the door and made a sincere effort to be pleasant.

Kevin stopped talking to Cody and rose when he saw her. "Here's Jill now." He gave her a peck on the cheek. "We have a surprise for you." He handed her a large white box. She looked at Cody who was smiling like an excited little boy. He nodded his head.

"Go ahead, Babe. Open it."

She sat down and removed the lid as the two men stood over her, waiting. The tissue fell away, exposing folds of white jersey, silky, thin, yet opaque. She lifted the fabric from the box and stood up. The dress was strapless except for two narrow bands, dotted with rhinestones, that she could tell were meant to cross behind the neck and travel across a bare back to the waist. The material hung gracefully to the floor. She looked from one face to the other.

Cody grabbed her and gave her a shove towards the bedroom, saying, "Go try it on."

"But I don't understand. Where would I ever wear a dress like this?" A seed of doubt began. Lovely as it appeared this was not what she had in mind for her wedding. She wanted gauze and lace.

"It's a surprise," he said, "Just go put it on."

Kevin twisted his mustache. "Yes . . . and be

sure you take everything else off first. That creation was not designed with underwear in mind."

Jill sat down, the doubt changing to anger.

Cody stared at her, puzzled, "What's the matter, don't you like it?"

She glared at him, unable to comprehend what was going on and why Cody was a part of whatever it was. She tried unsuccessfully to stop the tremor in her voice as she asked "What . . . what makes your manager think he can tell me what to wear? You better explain."

Kevin turned his back and studied the pictures on the wall as Cody sat down beside her, put his arm around her shoulder.

"Lord, Babe . . . I'm sorry. We both are, aren't we, Kevin?" The manager didn't answer. "There's a big party tomorrow night at the home of the president of Country Records. Lots of my buddies and the big shots will be there. Kevin bought this dress as a special surprise for you."

She jerked away from him. "I see. . . . And did he pick your outfit out for you too? . . . Are we Kevin's Barbie and Ken dolls? He dresses us up just right and we make his 10% bigger? Is that it Kevin?"

Cody stood up, his voice icy now, "Forget it. You don't have to go to the party. In fact, your invitation has just been withdrawn."

Kevin still stood with his back to them, toying with some papers on the table. She was blind with fury at him, at Cody, at the disruption of their happiness.

"Why doesn't Kevin speak for himself. He's the

one with the silver tongue. Can you hear me high and might manager? Why don't you answer?"

Cody clenched his fists. "I said forget it."

Kevin turned then and for the first time since she'd met him, his eyes looked directly into hers without shifting immediately. He said quietly, "Look Jill, I'm sorry. I had no idea you would take it this way. . . . But . . . But I can see now why you did. . . . It was a mistake. I was coming by I. Magnin's today. The dress was on a model in the window. The mannikin looked so much like you I just went in on a whim and bought it. I guess it was intended as a thank you for making Cody so happy. . . . You do, you know. . . . I sure didn't want it to cause a problem. . . . To answer your other question, no, I didn't pick out anything for that old bastard to wear . . . he can go in his underwear for all I care. . . . Here, give me that damned dress, I'll take it back."

For the first time since she'd met him, she suspected Kevin was sincere—and she felt like a fool. Swallowing her pride, she hung onto the box as he reached for it.

"No," she said, "I'm the one who is sorry. I haven't been fair to you. Cody says you are a good friend and I believe him." She looked at Cody and asked, "Can I still go to the party?"

Still angry, he didn't answer.

"Are we going to have a battle over a stupid dress?" she asked, putting an arm around each of them. "As Janice would say, Fuck it." Then all three of them were laughing and it was over. How easy it was, to give a little. They walked Kevin to his car and instead of the obligatory peck on the cheek, she hugged him and he returned it. As he backed out, she realized what a hard job he really had. Selling personalities must be harder than selling tractors.

She spent the rest of the day between panic and excitement. Her first Hollywood party! Cody told her the names of the country western stars who would probably be there. He used first names—Willie, Waylon and Jesse, Dollie and Emmy Lou—as if they were old friends she should know. But only Jimmie Likely and his wife and singing partner of twenty some years, Melody Jones, were familiar to her. Cody had never met them but they were two of the wealthiest and most influential names in Nashville music. They had their own weekly TV show and donated their talents to innumerable charity concerts. Jill was impressed. Although Jimmie Likely's singing voice couldn't compare to Cody's, he did have a magnetism that forced millions to like him and watch his show. He was an entertainer not a singer; a personality not a talent. The Dinah Shore of the shit kickers, Cody said.


When the first blade of sunshine sliced across the down comforter, Jill slipped out of bed and went to the living room. The box was still in the chair where she'd dropped it and, taking Kevin's advice, she removed the dress from its nest of tissue and slipped it over her head, sans underwear. The soft fabric caressed her bare skin, teasing the sensuality sleeping beneath it. She tiptoed into the bedroom to look at herself in the full length mirror. Although glitter was alien to her tastes, the quality of the rhinestones on the thin spaghetti straps combined with the liquid flow of the white jersey to create perfection. While surprised by her unaccustomed vanity, she was still thankful for her slim body, even tan, and long neck—and ashamed of yesterday's anger at Cody's manager. Kevin had seemed sincere when he said the dress was a gift—not another manipulation of their life as she'd first suspected.

"Good Christ, Jill!" Cody sat up in bed. "You're one fine lookin' filly in that getup."

Her reflection smiled back at him and she struck an exaggerated model's pose as she answered, "They do say clothes make the woman."

"Oh no, you're wrong. As Confusius say, *'Man* make the woman.' " He grabbed her hand and pulled her onto the bed. "Now take that thing off . . . carefully . . . and climb back in here with me."

Their lovemaking was only a temporary relief from the nervousness she knew Cody was feeling as much as she. After breakfast he announced he and Dude needed a run and was out the door with the big dog at his heels, leaving her to fret alone. Kevin's call in the afternoon didn't help. He insisted he would pick them up, adding, "Country's newest star can't arrive at a Hollywood party in an old pickup truck."

Each hour tightened the knot in her stomach, until it was finally five, time to get ready. She closed herself in the bathroom and prolonged the hour by fooling with her hair, tying it up, combing it down. Then impatient, she hurriedly shoved a sprig of Baby's Breath into a casual twisted knot on the back of her head and decided the dress required no jewelry. When she came out, Cody's and Kevin's expressions made it obvious she was presentable. She thanked Kevin again for the dress, this time in all sincerity.

Now it was her turn to stop and stare. While she had been fussing with herself, the man she'd never seen in anything but jeans had transformed himself into a star. Thin bands of white leather outlined the pockets of his slim, black, western-cut pants and vest; his white ruffled shirt with full sleeves was open at the neck, adding a subtle sensuality. And when he grinned she saw the excitement of a child. No dull protective curtains hid the intense blue of his eyes tonight.

"Cowboy, you're gorgeous!"

He glanced down, obviously pleased, "Yea, well . . . I never been comfortable in damned Sunday go-to-meetin' clothes, though." He opened a drawer and pulled out a Polaroid camera, "Here, Kevin, take our picture."

The manager argued, "Come on, Cody. We're going to be late. You'll get enough pictures taken tonight."

"Bullshit. I don't want theirs, I want my own. Of me and Jill. . . . Just do it, Buddy." He made adjustments and handed the impatient man the camera. "Okay, now wait, we'll get over here between the chairs."

He put his arm around her shoulder and they froze their smiles. Kevin clicked the shutter and the strobe flashed. The photo ground out. Cody held it as they waited for the developing process to take place in his hand. Her dress emerged first, then Cody's shirt. They looked stiff and unnatural.

"No good, too dark." He readjusted. "Here, Kevin do it again."

"Damn you, Cody!"

He hugged her and Kevin pushed the button, caught them laughing into each other's faces.

"Great, great. Now . . . I'll take one of you and Jill."

"Shit, Cody. We'll never get to the party." Kevin rubbed his hands nervously down the satin lapels of his custom made tux.

A little boy with a toy, she thought, amused. Playing but also delaying. The gallery grew on the table top.

". . . one of me and Dude, he never seen me so pretty."

Kevin finally commanded, "That's enough, God damn it. You're not going to get dog hair all over that black suit. Now get your ass out in the car."

They sat in the back seat with Kevin acting as chauffeur. Quiet now, Cody clasped her clammy hand with his, seeking her nonexistant assurance. Finally, as they wound through a strange canyon where lighted houses seemed to grasp for toeholds on the steep cliffs, he asked with unconcealed nervousness, "Where does this big shot live anyway?"

Kevin answered without looking back, "Trousdale Estates. I think that's where Nixon built his house the time he lost the election."

"Crooks hang together, huh?"

"I wouldn't call someone who's going to make you a millionaire a crook."

"Now, I guess not. . . . What's this guy's name again? Mayer?"

"Richard C. Moyer. *Mr.* Moyer to you."

"Okay, teach, okay. Don't worry, I'll be on my best behavior." He squeezed her hand. "Won't we, babe? We won't do anything to embarrass ol' straight and narrow up there in the front seat, will we?"

"I'm not worried about Jill. It's you, you ornery bastard that gives me ulcers," Kevin muttered, blond hair had been carefully combed tonight. The bald spot on the back of his head had vanished. She was tempted to ask his hair stylist's secret then was immediately ashamed at her continued distain for the small, nervous man. He tried.

The street straightened out but continued to climb. Homes, only slightly smaller than the Taj Mahal, lined both sides. Colored floods lighted palms and shrubbery, cast eerie shadows against monstrous stucco walls. Wide terrazzo stairs and expansive courtyards, overflowing with masses of flowering annuals, gave the impression of public buildings—libraries, art museums—not homes. As the car stopped, a highschool-age boy in a short red jacket jogged up to open their doors and take the Mercedes to a resting place.

"Christ, Kevin!" Cody whistled. "Who would

want to live in a place like this?"

"A Richard Nixon," she said.

"Or a Richard C. Moyer," Kevin whispered as they began their awkward ascent of the two-foot wide steps.

She changed her mind. The architecture was definitely more Marriott Hotel. No one greeted them as they passed through the story-high double doors and she could not resist whispering, "Let's build a house like this, Cody."

He frowned for an instant, taking her seriously, then laughed, "Sure. We could exercise our horses every morning in the living room."

They stopped in the foyer, stunned by the immensity of the room in front of them. Guests clustered together in small tight groups, like passengers clinging to lifeboats, afraid they'd sink into the sea of thick blue shag carpeting. White coated stewards sailed from one refuge area to another bearing life sustaining champagne and hot hors d'oeuvres. Their travel was unhindered by furniture. Except for several large lucite cubes ladened with platters of food, the decorating relied on greenery. Giant Boston ferns hung from the ceiling on heavy iron chains, and islands of chrome urns scattered along the shoreline overflowed with leaves and vines.

"Man, this would be an easy place to clean," Cody said. "Just rake up the beer caps and cigarette butts in the morning."

"Shhh," Kevin warned.

The bear-like body of the man coming towards them was not at home in its black tuxedo; the upper half, at least, seemed to strain against the restrictions of cummerbund and tie—and the grey hair and beard had been at sea too long. "Well, well. Here he is. Our guest of honor!" The voice was deep and boisterous, no surprise.

Captain Schweppes of the Trousdale, she thought.

Cody smiled uncertainly, "Howdy, Mr. Moyer. . . . Nice place you got here." He eased her closer, his hand cold on her bare arm. "I want you to meet my wife to be . . . Jill."

Their host pumped his hand. "Cody, you old hillbilly son of a bitch, how do you do it? Find such a beauty." He grabbed her hand next and shook it with the same enthusiasm, "Glad to know you, young lady. And you can call me Rich." He hit Cody on the arm with his massive fist, "But I'm still Mr. Moyer to you . . . you're not pretty enough."

*Big man, big house. Big heart too*?

"Oh, Mr. Moyer," Kevin stepped forward and reached to smooth his hair, then thought better of it, letting his hand come to rest on the top button of his jacket before he continued, "Cody is thrilled . . . aren't you Cody? . . . with the new contract."

The company president stared down at the manager, disgust obvious in the set of his mouth. His words boomed out and Kevin's eyes darted furiously to see if anyone else was within earshot.

"Thrilled?" he roared, "Damn right he'd be 'thrilled' as you call it. More like happy as a priest at a nun's tit, wouldn't you say, Cody? . . . Course you got this little alter boy following you around waiting to suck up his 10% though, haven't you?'' His laughter rumbled until he glanced at Jill and mumbled, "Sorry."

A boy of about ten walked up then and stopped a few feet outside their circle. Actually, Jill looked closely to determine that the small figure was a child and not a miniature man. He was dressed in a midnight-blue velvet tuxedo, as professionally styled as his thick black hair. Although she smiled at him, the mahogany eyes stared steadily at her without any change of expression.

Rich threw a heavy arm around his shoulders and ignoring the child's slight withdrawal said, "Hey, want you all to meet my son. This here is Richard the second."

The boy shook hands all around, still without altering his solemn face. The father's identical dark eyes caught hers then as he said, "Will you excuse us for a minute, pretty lady? I have something to talk over with this boyfriend of yours and some people I want him to meet." Without waiting for a response he gathered Cody, who reminded her of a colt, first time in halter—and with Kevin trailing behind, took off across the wild blue sea.

"I guess he stuck you with me. . . . May I get you a drink?" the boy asked.

"In a minute, thank you. . . . Do you like parties, Rich?" She remembered her own discomfort as the only child at adult gatherings and felt sorry for the small figure beside her.

"Please don't call me that. Unlike my father, I much prefer Richard."

"Oh, I'm sorry . . . I . . . I just thought . . ."

"In answer to your question, no, I hate his disgusting parties . . . I don't live here with *him*. . . . I'm just visiting." A sigh escaped from the full, yet still expressionless mouth as he continued, "It's the typical child custody game, you know. Father pays the bills so he must get his money's worth in visitation rights. . . . Why I'll never know since we can't stand each other. . . . I live with Geraldine."

Jill didn't think she should be hearing this but she could see no immediate escape.

"Geraldine?"

"Yes. She is my mother. We live in Nashville."

"Oh, I see." *Nashville*. An opening for less personal conversation. "Then you must be a real expert on country music, coming from there?"

The steady eyes never left her face as he answered, "I can't stand that briarhopper shit."

The bottled up tension of the day rolled out with her laughter and she fought to control a threatened attack of giggles.

The boy's lips attempted but failed to smile. The slight curl of his mouth seemed condescending, even more so when he said, "You seem to find that funny. . . . But I prefer classical music. . ." He glanced at the wall and her eyes followed his to what was certainly an original Picasso. "I am also a serious artist. I have studied with the best water colorists in the world. . . . Country music falls into the same catagory as that crap." He pointed at the painting and finished, "Some people have no taste."

She searched the room, desperate for a way to

end this conversation, but Cody was nowhere in sight, nor anyone else she knew. "I think I will have that drink now." Richard stopped a passing tray, handed her a glass and took one for himself. He took a sip of champagne and said, "I'm sure you've been aware of my stares. It's your coloring. I would like very much to paint you. . . . To see if I could capture the burnished copper color of your hair . . . perhaps against a background of greenery. . . . You know, you are a lovely lady."

"Well, thank you, Richard. Maybe we can arrange it." *Thank heavens*! She saw Billy Joe and Janice, standing alone, looking as lost as she felt. "Will you excuse me now. I want to go speak to some friends."

The nod of his head had the formality of a bow as he said, "Of course. It was most pleasant meeting and talking with you." And then he smiled, but it was without warmth or any trace of childishness and she felt a sharp sadness for the little man who had somehow learned to walk without ever crawling.

She wound her way through the milling humanity, relieved to escape the aspiring intellectual. Her lips were dry and stuck to her teeth.

"Would ya' look at what the cat drug in?" *Good old Billy Joe*! Cody's bass player and best friend greeted her with a low shrill whistle from between his teeth then continued in his best West Virginia accent, "Jill, ol' gal, you sure are a vision tonight." B.J. was always the same, no Hollywood party would change him. He wore his usual faded Levis and trademark black hat with the wide brim and pheasant feather in the band.

Jill smiled and curtsied. "Thank you, sir," she answered, then turned to Janice adding, "and I think your lady is a lovely sight too."

Pink chiffon ruffled across the cocktail waitress's pale shoulders; she had gathered her blond hair into a bouquet of curls on the nape of her neck. The delicate, angelic face was always a mismatch with the words that rolled so easily from the girl's tiny mouth.

"Shit!" Janice fingered the satin bow on the front of her dress. "Took me all day to get ready. . . . Can you believe this place, Jill? They could put the whole Ranch in here and never find it. . . . Holy fuck . . . I'd hate to have to serve the drinks. Would take an hour to get to the bar and back."

Jill laughed and drained her glass. A delicate strawberry souffle, topped with chili powder, that's Janice. *Where is Cody?*

Billy Joe hailed a waiter and handed them all another glass of champagne. He downed his and reached for another before the tray moved away. "Not as good as Coors but it's free." He poked Janice. "See, these big shots don't use no cocktail waitresses. Just queers. Did you see the way that turkey glided up here? His feet don't even touch the ground."

Janice poked him back. "I saw him . . . and he wasn't a fag. He was cute . . . cuter than a certain asshole guitar player I know." They traded elbow nudges as Jill continued to search the room.

The number of guests had grown into a confusing muddle of tuxedos, silks, satins, denim

239

and cowboy hats. She finally spotted Cody standing next to one of the latter with an older Hollywood type female looking on.

"Come on you two. Let's go round up your buddy. He looks like he could use a friend."

The snatches of conversation that reached her as she led the way confirmed the curious mixture of people in the room.

"est teaches us that we're all assholes. . ." Polyester print and large tinted glasses.

"Ronstadt copped out . . . singin' that middle of the road crap for that Governor boyfriend. . ." Reddish mustache drooping into an unruly black beard.

". . . the ones from San Salvador are far better live-ins and you don't have to pay them as much." Gold chains and no bra.

". . . yea . . . sure . . . I'd like to hear some of your tunes . . . we . . ." Cody stopped, his relief obvious. He grabbed Billy Joe and pumped his hand, hugged Janice and started to make the introductions. "This is a buddy from Texas, Jed Turner . . ." then he hesitated, "and Mrs. . . I'm sorry . . . yes, Mrs. Irving."

The woman's eyes roamed over Billy Joe and Janice, rested a second on Jill, then dismissed them all. Mrs. Irving, a woman of fifty or more, turned her suspiciously unlined face and violet eyeshadow back to Cody. Her feline purr failed to hide extended claws as she said, "I was about to say. . . . You know, frankly . . . I have never cared for your kind of music. The closets I ever got to . . . how would you say it? . . . Down home? . . . was maybe Steinbeck's *Grapes of Wrath*. And that was certainly depressing, don't you think?'' She fingered the gold chains imprisoning her decolletage—one bangle was appropriately engraved with the words 'Super Bitch' . . . and continued without waiting for a response, ''But those songs of yours . . . all about drinking and poverty and jail . . . about no good shiftless people. Why in the first place the lyrics and melodies are so simple they sound like they've been written by a sixth grader.'' False lashes fluttered and the thin lips parted into a tight smile. ''I do get a kick out of the songs about affairs, cheating, I think you call it . . . but the rest . . . I just don't understand how you can like it . . . . Depressing really.''

Cody had stood silent and attentive through the lengthy commentary, but now Jill felt his fingers tighten on her arm and recognized the danger signals. His eyes darkened to slate grey and the slow grin brought an answering response from the woman but failed to hide the twitch beginning in the hollow of his cheek. Jill held her breath and waited as he nodded his head in agreement and said, ''Ya' know ma'am, you're right.'' His exaggerated accent thickened more, ''Ah'd give anything if ah could play better . . . write purtier songs . . . maybe like Mancini . . . or Sinatra. But ma'am you'll have to understand . . . ah'm gist a country boy . . . ain't never had no schoolin' to speak of . . . my daddy run off when I was just a baby and left mamma with twelve kids to raise . . . my sisters they all got pregnant when they was twelve, thirteen . . . three of my brothers is in prison right now . . . so to be real honest, ah jus' sing that trash for the money. . . . Jus' for the money, that's all. . . . Ain't that right, Billy Joe?"

"Sure is true, Cody. We was jus' talkin' about that the other evening, Ma'am," B.J. answered straight-faced.

Mrs. Irving was silent for a moment then began, "Oh, I do understand there are vast cultural differences in . . ."

"Lady," Janice looked from one to the other of them, missing the sarcasm, "Lady, you got your head stuck up your ass . . . you know that? . . . Fuck Sinatra. Ol' Blue Eyes is a cocksuckin' has been. . . . The greatest ever was Elvis, and Cody's next . . . not that scrawny wop prick that runs around with jews and niggers. . . . And as far as cheatin' . . . forget it, Lady, unless it would be your ol' man cheatin' on you." She took a breath and finished, "Holy shit, Sinatra sucks."

Heads turned in their direction, the woman's face tightened in disgust as she looked from one of them to the other, then the sculptured bottom swam for safer shores.

Cody and Billy Joe slapped each other's hands and doubled over in silent hilarity. She joined them while Janice stared after the retreating rear. "Stupid cunt!" she added.

Kevin materialized from a nearby gathering of tuxedos. "Do you realize . . . ," his face turned pink as his voice grew more shrill, "Do you realize . . . that was Sylvia Irving . . . the wife of the head of production." He grabbed for the security blanket of his mustache, watching helplessly as his reprimand only increased their volume. "He can make or break you," he hissed. But like children confined too long in church, once started they couldn't stop. They wiped at their eyes and held their sides while the laughter rolled between them.

Finally, Cody threw an arm around Kevin and drew him into the circle. "Don't worry, ol' buddy. I know Sam Irving. . . . He's a hell of a good Joe. . . . And he probably wishes every morning he could tell old Sylvia just what Janice did."

"What's so damned funny?" Rich walked up then and turned to Jill without waiting for an answer. "Well, I see you escaped from that prick son of mine. . . . Sorry I stuck you with him." He didn't sound sorry at all and she felt sympathy for the boy in spite of his eccentric ways. His father continued, "That kid walks around like he's got a cork stuck up you know where . . . I swear they got the babies mixed up at the hospital." He must never have looked at Richard's eyes or his own in the mirror, she thought.

The room grew suddenly quiet and they turned with the others toward the door. Rich excused himself.

Hail to the chief! His Majesty had arrived—with his queen. A gasp, followed again by reverent silence settled over the waiting audience.

Jimmie Likely dazzled the eyes. He stood immobile at the railing of the raised foyer, a blaze of blinding light. His long, tight western coat, the flared pants, the highheeled boots were all a Clorox white, and covered with thousands—no millions—of sequins and rhinestones. Teeth to match caught the light and clashed with the rough weathered face. Jill could see the scar that had become a trademark, cutting through his right eyebrow.

His partner was a study in contrasts. She posed with one knee slightly forward. It tightened the clinging black metallic cloth of her dress and successfully revealed every contour of bone and flesh underneath. The raven hair fell from a center part, straight and thick to below the waist. Graceful, slender fingers ended in burgundy talons. Her lips parted in the slightly bucktoothed smile typical of most country women singers.

Richard C. Moyer walked to their center stage position, hugged them both, then turned to the room full of record industry serfs. They waited, producer and musician alike, ready to hang on every word.

"I just want to say, first of all, I'm happy to have all of you here in my home tonight. . . . We're one big family at Country records. It's more fun that way. . . . And we're thrilled with our beautiful new sound studios out here on the coast. . . . But I want you all to remember . . ." The crowd waited in silence through a long pause, meant to add importance to the words which followed.

"You can take Country out of Nashville. . . . But you can't take Nashville out of the Country."

The room vibrated with cheers and applause. Rich smiled and nodded. "So here to prove it, our company's back bone and my dear friends . . . Jimmie Likely and Melody Jones . . . Jimmie . . .

Melody." He hugged them both again and stepped back.

Jimmie waited for the applause to die down. "Thanks, Rich. He's the greatest, isn't he?" The noise erupted again. "And what he says is true. We are one big happy family. . . . Ain't that true, Melody?"

She spread her arms, giving silent benediction to her congregation.

Jimmie continued, "and we're happy to be here tonight, even if it was a damned long airplane ride. . . . But right now, I want to get one of my oldest, newest, and most talented members of our family up here. . . . I say oldest because he's been recording with Country Records a long time. . . . I say newest . . . 'cause he's had a couple of big hits lately and is finally getting the recognition he deserves . . . and the money." A titter went through the crowd and B.J. whispered "Amen, brother," under his breath. Jimmie continued, "Now the talent part . . . well, that speaks for itself . . . Cody Williams! Cody, come on up here."

He squeezed her hand and made his way through the smiling crowd.

"Well, thank you Jimmie." His grin was relaxed now as the performer in him took over. "Y'll know I'm not a man of many words. . . . Maybe I should sing this. . ." Everyone laughed. "but I want to thank you, Mr. Moyer. . . . And Jimmie and Melody for coming so far. . . . And I just want to say I'm one lucky dude . . . I can make a living doing something I love. . . . All of this is wonderful. And I'm not going to turn down all that money. But I'll never stop playin' those honky tonk bars. . . . Never . . . 'cause that's where it's at, man. My songwriting would end if I ever quit that. . . . Right, band? . . . Got the greatest guys in the world working with me, too. Come on up here all you bad dudes and take a bow. . . . Here they are. Give 'em a hand. They make it all possible."

He was back at her side then, shy again. His eyes sought hers, telling her silently that he wished they were home now, just the two of them alone on their mountaintop. But bodies of wellwishers crowded between them.

She excused herself and seeing a hallway off the foyer decided it must be the way to the powder room. The champagne made her glide across the carpet. She turned the corner to quiet doorways, five or six, open on each side.

"We kind of match don't we?" The familiar voice started her. Jimmie Likely was sitting alone in a small library. The books that covered two walls floor to ceiling appeared new and untouched, like the rest of the house. "Come in." The teeth were even whiter closeup, the scar deeper. "You're Cody's girl, aren't you? Saw you together out there. . . . Don't you think we make quite a pair, you and me?" He must have caught the surprise in her eyes for he added quickly, "Hell, I didn't mean nothin' by it . . . just both of us in white, with the rhinestones, that's all."

She relaxed. "Yes, you're right to both. I am Cody's girl and it does look like we picked our clothes from the same rack."

The famous lazy grin appeared as he said, "Well, I don't know about that dress of yours coming off a rack but Nudie socked me fifteen hundred bucks for this damned ridiculous monkey suit. . . . Sit down." It was a gentle command and she slid gratefully into a chair, happy to get off her feet, while he continued, "Had to get out of there for a while. Too many people, too much talk. . . . Would you like a drink?" He crossed to a bar in the corner and poured two glasses of bourbon without waiting for an answer. The familiarity of his face on television made her feel she knew him.

"Are you happy for Cody?" he asked, handing her a glass.

"Well, of course I am." The question surprised her.

"Oh, I don't mean the money. We all like that. What I'm talking about is how things are gonna change for the two of you. You know don't you that he'll quit playing his beloved bars. . . . We all do. 'Cause concerts is where the money's at . . . and his stable of bosses—Moyer, agents, managers, accountants—they're gonna take over. Tell him when he can take a . . . oh, excuse me. Anyway, them bars and clubs just won't be the same. He won't be able to relax without getting mobbed. . ." She remembered the girl at the license bureau, Patsy in Vegas, as he continued, "Everywhere you go, people want to talk, to touch. Gals will climb all over him . . . try to get him in the sack just so they can say they made it with Cody Williams."

"You make it sound awful."

He drained his glass and returned to the bar for a refill. "It is," he said quietly, and when he turned back the lines in his face made him look eighty years old. "Girl, do you know why we're here in Los Angeles instead of home with our children?" The dimple in his cheek deepened then disappeared. "You think we're here for a party? To say something nice about that cowboy of yours? . . . Shit no! . . . You heard the speeches out there, one big happy family . . . well, you might say that's true . . . we're here . . . we're here so our old and *dear* friend, Rich Moyer . . . so he can go to bed with Melody again, that's why."

Jill sat frozen, the dark eyes, unreadable pools, gazed steadily into hers, making it impossible to look away. She felt her face flush as he continued with a hoarse rasp that added to the harshness of the next words. "She's a good lay too. He misses it since he moved out here . . . she misses it too."

"But why?" Her voice broke.

"Why do I put up with it? . . . Simple. We got kids. Because I love her. And she loves me. And she loves Rich. The eternal triangle. . . . The only catch to the whole thing is, Richard C. Moyer don't love nobody." Jimmie was silent for a moment, ran his finger around the rim of his glass. "Richard C. Moyer is one of them men that don't know the difference between makin' out and makin' love. . . . And those dudes are dangerous. . . . He'll end up breaking her heart."

He stood up then and she followed suit, unable to think of a response.

"What's your name? . . . Jill? . . . Well, you seem like a nice girl. And Cody seems nice, too. . . . I'd hate for things to go bad for you. So just be careful. If you see it start to happen, whatever it is—a bad gig for him, another broad—Hell, I don't know what to tell you. . . . Maybe just pull the walls in around the two of you and don't come out 'til summer."

He smiled, the dimple there again, and took her hand. The fear for herself and the desire to comfort him overcame her embarrassment. She threw her arms around his neck, saying, "I'm so sorry . . . you're a nice man." Then she surprised herself by repeating Mara's words, "Someone told me once that love is everything . . . I hope it will be true for you."

He stepped back and grinned the familiar TV grin, "Shit! Right now, honey, love ain't worth a bag of beans."

Back in the main room, the islands of humanity had swelled and melted together to form a solid mass. Melody and Rich were nowhere in sight. The female iceberg was probably defrosting under her massive boss in some virginal, white-carpeted upstairs bedroom, she thought. Jill waved to Cody but he was still occupied and made no attempt to come to her. Is this what Jimmie Likely meant? A hand glided up her spine and came to rest at the crook of her neck. She pulled away and turned to see Gene. His grey, Prince Valiant haircut looked more ridiculous than ever with the western-cut tuxedo he was wearing.

"Don't do that." She took a step back, anxious

to put space between them. "Where is Marian?" She wanted to remind him he had a wife but he sluffed over the question.

"She couldn't make it." Then he smirked, "What's the matter pretty lady? Your boyfriend too busy for you again? Was the last time I saw you, too." He handed her another glass when her head was already swimming from the unaccustomed alcohol. "You know, these cowboys are very macho," he continued in his usual conspiratorial tone, "only want their women when they want them. Don't know how to treat a lady."

He continued to confirm the distaste she'd felt for him the first time they met.

"Not like you, I suppose," she answered.

He ignored her sarcasm. "Right . . . I made you an attractive offer the other night. . . . Better think about it. Any weekend you say."

She started to walk but he grabbed her wrist. She glanced toward Cody but he was still deep in conversation—with a woman.

The evil cuspids smiled at her, "Jill, I want to ask you something. . . . Have you ever seen a duck fuck? . . . No, wait a minute. I'm serious. . . . This is just one of Gene's lessons of life, you might say. . . . Now just answer, have you ever seen a duck fuck?"

She clenched her teeth. The evening was taking a wrong turn. "No, I don't believe I ever have," she answered.

He eased the pressure on her wrist. "Well, just stand here and listen, maybe you'll learn something. . . . You see, the female duck, she goes

waack, waack, waack. . . . Loud . . . very loud
. . . and then she swims like hell. Now the old
drake he takes off after her . . . follows nose to
tail while she goes round in circles. Finally, he
mounts. Puts his bill on the top of her head and
shoves her under the water. . . . Holds her down
until you think she's going to drown. . . . Her
head finally comes up. Waaaa . . . down again.
Waaaa . . . down again. On and on. And you
know what?'' He rubbed his hand up her arm,
letting it come to rest under her chin. His face close
to hers, registered the obvious distain for women
his next words emphasized, ''When it's all over,
the lady preens . . . and can hardly wait for the
next time.''

Jill willed herself not to withdraw, even to laugh
with him as she answered, ''Auntie Mil and Mrs.
Nelson would never believe it.''

''What does that mean?''

She reached up and pulled his head down, his ear
next to her lips. ''It means. . . . It means, I wish
you and all the other old drakes of the world a limp
dick.'' She whirled away toward Cody with Gene's
laughter chasing her. *A man who doesn't know the
difference between making out and making love.*
Well, if nothing else, she thought with amusement,
Janice would be proud of her.

''Can we leave now?'' Cody frowned. The girl at
his side was young and beautiful. She looked up
and frowned too. ''Never mind.'' She wheeled and
raced toward the door.

A waiter stepped in front of her at the edge of
the foyer, ''Care for any, miss?'' He extended a

small silver tray in her direction. It appeared to have nothing on it but several streaks of white powder and a few straws.

"What is it?" Her head was pounding.

"Coke, miss."

"Coke?"

He smirked. "Cocaine, care to try a line?"

*So this was where those packages at the pier ended up?* She tipped the tray and the white powder talcumed the front of the surprised man's black pants. She stepped around him and went out the door.

The air was cold on her bare back and arms as she clattered down the ridiculous front steps.

"What kind of car, miss?" It was the same young attendant.

"No car. I'm walking."

He looked amused. "Whatever you say, ma'am."

She stopped at the end of the drive and slipped off her shoes. The pavement was smooth. Of course, new homes, new street. Everything slick and perfect—except the owner's lives. As she started left, back the way they'd come, so did the tears. Once traveled down its own canyon between nose and cheek. She let it go. *Jill, the joker.* Like the graffiti Cody told her he saw high on the wall behind a men's urinal. What are you looking up here for when the joke's in your hand? *Love is never having to be a joke.* She should have told Jimmie Likely that one.

She rushed on, the thoughts pummeling her brain, fighting for order. She would call first thing in the morning. At a decent hour for once. Not wake her in the middle of the night. Auntie Mil, I'm coming home. Put sheets on the bed. Get my box of treasures out of the attic. *I'm coming home*.

Most of the houses were dark now, except for the decorative lighting in the shrubs. Maybe no one actually lives in them, she thought, maybe they're just facades, movie sets. Or only opened for parties. She walked faster with no idea where she was. No moon tonight. At least *he* isn't sneering at me, she thought as she glanced up at the black, starless sky.

The car was quiet as it pulled up on the wrong side of the street next to her.

"Get in."

"No." She speeded her pace. The car idled along beside her but she refused to look at it.

"I said get in this damned car."

She stopped, no longer angry. "It's no good, Cody. It just won't work . . . we're from different worlds. I don't know you, and you don't know me." She finished, "Go back to your party. Enjoy your success. Be happy."

He stared at her, silent for a moment. The street light cut his face into angles as sharp as his next words, "You're right. We are from different worlds. And maybe you don't know me, but I sure as hell know you. . . . So Okay, I will go back. . . . And you go right ahead and walk out on me. . . . Run! . . . like you always have. Take off. Work up a good hate again. Take off on your wild goose chase. . . . Find your fuckin' Mara. . . . What you gonna do then? Spit in her ear for

Christ's sake?"

He stepped on the gas and wheeled the Mercedes into a drive, backed out and turned around. The tires screeched as he slammed on the brakes. The passenger door flew open at her elbow. "Get in, Jill. You're not gonna get away with it this time." He sounded tired, as fatigued as her body and mind. She obeyed his order, sinking numbly into the soft leather seat.

"Where is Kevin?"

"He'll get home." He turned the car around again and they went silently back the way they came. He concentrated on the road, both hands on the wheel, his jaw taut.

This is only transportation, she told herself. A way to get to my car, pack and go home. Back to the safety of the house on the river. I'll go to Ohio State and become a teacher. You always know with children, where you stand, what they're thinking. Like Rich's boy, poor child. He probably knows about his father and Melody. That's what I'll do. Be a teacher.

"Was that jealousy back there?" She was too washed out to respond. He didn't seem to expect it as he continued without looking in her direction. "Well, if it was, I'm flattered. . . . But I think you should know . . . that little gal I was talking to . . . she's Medic's wife. I would have introduced you if you'd stayed around long enough."

Medic's wife? Embarrassment washed through her, flushing classrooms and the lonely house in Ohio out the window. She wanted to explain. But she couldn't tell him about Jimmie. About Melody and Rich. She would never tell anyone. Or how Gene could make life so smutty, created jealousy when there was no reason.

Cody glanced at her, the hurt on his face deepening every line, reminding her again of Jimmie Likely. No, she thought, we're not going to let it happen to us. She reached for his hand.

"Cowboy, I love you . . . I'm sorry."

He didn't answer, her hand fell back in her lap, and the silent barrier widened between them as they rode up the winding road to their retreat.

Dude thumped his tail on the floor, but never opened his eyes when they walked in the door. Jill froze in the center of the room. What was it? A scent, a indistinct feeling. The fear slithered up her spine, then raced down her arms; she shivered.

"What's the matter? You cold?

"No." Her feet wouldn't move. "Someone's been here."

Cody was tired. He sighed and looked around the small room. "Naw," he said. "My guitar, that's worth twenty-five hundred bucks. It's still right there . . . and the TV and radio. . . . Besides, Dude ain't gonna let no one come in here. . . . You're just tired."

"I know it, Cody," she insisted, "someone has been here." She glanced toward the bedroom.

"Okay, come on, we'll look the place over." He flicked the light on in the kitchen. Their glasses were where they'd left them on the counter. Nothing was different in the bathroom. He walked into the bedroom, peeked under the bed. "See, no boogie man in here." When they came back out he pointed to the camera on the table. "Now if some-body was gonna rob us, they sure would have taken that."

That was it! The photos weren't spread out on the table like they'd left them; they were in a neat stack beside the camera. She picked them up and went through them.

"Where is the one of you and me?" Her voice rose hysterically, "The one we liked best? Where is it?"

Cody took the stack from her hand, went through them and said, "I don't know . . . maybe Kevin took it. Sure, I bet he did."

"Kevin?" she wailed, "why would Kevin take it?"

"Jill, for God's sake . . . maybe . . . I don't know . . . maybe to get it framed, to surprise us. I bet that's what he's going to do.

Reasonable. Yes. He sneaked it into his pocket as they were going out the door. Cody was right. Dude wouldn't let anyone in here. And no one would break in just to steal a picture. She tried to relax but a minuscule remnant of fear remained.

"Come on, let's go to bed."

With the small lamp in the living room switched off, the stars outside the window seemed close enough to touch. Their mountain was above the pollution of the city; if only it would save them from the pollution of the city.

Their party clothes made a pile of black and white in the corner of the bedroom. Just like Jimmie and Melody's. She shivered again. Was anything in life black and white?

256

Their bodies touched, tentatively at first, then curved together. Cody was a man who knew the difference between making out and making love. Tonight they were used up, wanted only to be close, to feel the security of each other.

He finally responded to her earlier apology. "I love you too, babe." In a moment his even breathing told her he was asleep.

The missing picture. Stiff in his arms, holding her breath, listening until the silence hurt her ears, she finally fell asleep—but not before hearing Jimmie Likely's warning. Pull the walls in around the two of you.

The sun brought safety. Its light swarmed the paneled walls of the bedroom, chased away the demons of the night. It gilded Cody's hair and smoothed the lines of his face. The sun was a friend.

"Cody, wake up."

He groaned and turned over, then at up, startled.

"What? What's the matter?"

Jill pulled him back down and rolled on top of him. "Nothing's the matter. I just want to talk about our house. . . . I think we should use solar heating."

"Yea?" He rubbed at his eyes. "What time is it anyway? Solar heating? You woke me up to tell me that?" He squeezed her in a bear hug. "Last night you were leaving. This morning you're building a house."

"Last night was black, this morning is white."

He smiled, the slow lazy smile, she remembered

from their first meeting on the beach. "You know, Babe. Sometimes I think you're crazy. But I guess I'm stuck with you. . . . So OK, let's talk about our house. . . . What kind of house do you want?"

"What kind of house do you want?" She climbed off of him and lay back down, flat on her back, waiting.

"Well," he said, "it's up to you of course, but I've always kind of liked the houses they build up in Big Sur. You ever been there?"

"No."

"They're modern. . . . Not like that stucco barn last night. But all wood, the walls go every which way, all different levels so you get lost, don't know which room is which. Like some giant puzzle."

"With lots of glass? And windows where they shouldn't be? A house where children can crawl around and not get hurt-or hurt anything?"

He opened his eyes. "Yep. You got it."

With no real sofas and chairs, just piles of down cushions . . . and a huge fireplace in every room." She was soaring. She could see them, making love and candy apples, playing with their children, popping popcorn.

Cody caught the ride. "And we'll have ponies. All the kids will have their own pony."

"How many? Kids, that is."

"Oh, seven or eight at least."

"Cowboy, I think you plan to keep me home, barefoot and pregnant."

He sat up, serious. "No, Jill. I want us to have some time together first. I want you to travel with me. . . . I'm gonna need you, to help me through it. . . . That party last night scared me."

She answered quietly, "It frightened me too, Cody." She rested her head on his back, her arms around his chest. They sat motionless, each lost in their own thoughts. Finally, she said, "But the sun is shining today. And we have it all to ourselves. So let's not waste time thinking about all that Hollywood garbage. We're going to be fine."

"I'll give it three years," he answered, "Then we'll spend all our time here . . . with solar heating . . . whatever in the hell that is."

They sunbathed after breakfast, speaking little, as if words would destroy the magic. Only their fingers touched as their bodies lay prone and still, the perspiration beading on their foreheads.

"I'll drive you in tonight. I want to go shopping for a wedding dress."

"Great! We'll go early. I'll take you out to dinner."

The booth in the corner was snug and private, worth waiting for. They basked in the candlelight, sending silent messages across the table. The Galley's steaks were huge and Jill ate every bite, plus the homemade bread *and* the baked potato with sour cream *and* butter. As if she couldn't satisfy her appetite for pleasure.

When it was time, she dropped him off at The Ranch. "I'll be back later, probably around ten after the shopping center closes. . . . Although I might stop by Irma's house for awhile. I don't want Jody to think I've forgotten her."

"Pick out a pretty dress." He kissed her quickly

and disappeared inside.

Jill drove away so lightheaded she felt sure her tires weren't touching the road.

She slowed to a stop as an elderly couple stepped off the curb into the pedestrian crosswalk. The woman walked with the aid of a cane, and her arthritic body, although extremely thin, seemed to put too much strain on the feet inside the old run-over shoes. Each step was a slow, methodical effort but her companion didn't appear impatient. Their gnarled fingers were entwined and they looked neither right nor left as they made their determined journey to the other curb. When the woman was safely on the side walk, the small gnome of a man turned, gave a toothless grin, and waved the traffic onward.

Jill started up again, touched by the unspoken affection of the scene. No man *is* an island, she thought. I've been wrong for so long. I hated my mother for dying without giving me a chance to know her. And then my father left me too when I needed him so much. And Mara. She though back through all her bitterness. And all of the wasted years since.

She remembered again her feelings about, Chuck, her first boyfriend and the night after her father's funeral when he had taken her for a drive. They had parked along the river, sat silent, staring at the frozen water. He had been shy and uncomfortable at first. Then his words came in a torrent. He said he would always be there, he loved her, wanted to marry her when they were old enough. It was freezing without the heater on, and her teeth began to chatter and would not stop. He started the car and drove to his house. His parents were in Florida. He built a fire in the den fireplace and they took off their coats and mittens. Hers were white angora. The fur left its mark on everything she touched but she wouldn't give them up since they'd been a gift from her father.

They sat on the oriental rug absorbing the heat, then he reached for her. But she had lain numb as he fumbled with her clothes, then his. When he touched the magic buttons her body responded while her mind seemed to watch from afar.

Later, in her own bedroom, she had stared in the mirror at her thin, adolescent body—decided it was a tomb that had her trapped inside.

As the traffic light turned red, she wondered how she could have been so wrong. To have made herself suffer with the bitter, resentful loneliness. Maybe Chuck did love her? She sighed. Well, Cody *does*, she knew that.


The passenger door of her car flew open and she recognized the knife. But this time it was not laying on a coffee shop table. It was pointed at her ribs.

Neal slid into the seat beside her. "Well hello there little girl. . . . You know, ol' Neal's kind of put out at you. . . . Seeing as how you forgot to say goodbye to me the other night." She could feel the tip of the blade through her teeshirt. "Now how about turning, easy like, right into that supermarket parking lot."

She did as she was told. She had to stay alive.

For Cody. Neal directed her to park in the back row. An old green Chevrolet pulled in next to them. She could see three men, more Fiends, two in the back seat, one behind the wheel.

"Now turn off your lights. . . . That's good. . . . Now you're gonna slide over here nice and easy and get out." Jill calculated her chance of jumping and running but Neal counteracted the idea by saying, "Don't think I won't cut you. . . . I've left more than one dude wishing his pink guts wasn't hangin' all over the pavement." She remembered his dog story and eased out, the knife in her side, and into the back seat as he directed her, between the two men. One had his dirty blond hair caught in a red bandana headband, the other wore his trademark Fiend vest without a shirt. They both had on filthy, grease-smeared jeans.

Neal got in the front seat and gave the orders. "Get her blindfolded and on the floor."

Jill whispered, afraid her normal voice would set them off, "Oh, Neal, please. Rick will be after you again." The two men shoved her to the floor between their feet as they all laughed.

The one on the driver side said, "Rick . . . oh sure, man. . . . You're livin' in a dream world." He jerked her head up and tied a dirty rag over her eyes. She could feel the cold blade under her chin. She forced herself to hold still. His voice was high-pitched and excited, "Now keep down, whore, and don't move." The car eased out of the parking lot. The pulse pounded in her ears as she tried to listen and think. It was only a joy ride she told herself. Neal just getting even for his bruised ego.

She flinched at the sound above her head, then recognized it as the rattle of a paper bag. High Voice spoke again, "Here, Axle, have a brew." She could hear tops being popped and smell the beer. He leaned to hand the cans forward then reached around her back and gave her breast a hard pinch, at the same time saying, "Sorry, woman. I'd offer you a sip but I don't think you could drink it in that position." They all laughed again. "Maybe later." Axle, the driver, said, "Cool it, man." He sounded angry.

Her legs were already cramping, her right foot was asleep and her face was smashed against the other man's boot but she willed herself not to move—clenched her fists to keep from screaming. *It was just a joy ride.* The car turned off the main street and went around corners, reversing its path until she had lost all sense of direction. She heard a siren in the distance but it dimmed, then disappeared.

The second man, the one with the headband, put his hand on her back. "Awful quiet down there. Ain't you having a good time?" He leaned over, his foul breath hot in her ear as he whispered, "Sorry, you ain't gettin' any." She jumped at the shock of cold liquid seeping through her shirt. He was emptying his can on her back. "Take it easy, take it easy," he said. Then, "Shall we give her the wet teeshirt award?"

The brakes slammed and the car came to an abrupt halt.

"What the fuck you doing, Axle?" The voice was Neal's.

"Stop it, back there . . . I . . . I can't think."
The one named Axle sounded nervous, near
hysteria. "This ain't my bag."

From her left, "Oh poor baby."

Then bare chest said, "Axle, I always knew you
was a pussy."

"Shut up. Just shut the fuck up." His voice
rose. "I ain't driving this car no further."

The slap resounded in her ears. A hand shoved
hard on her head, pushing her face tighter against
the leather boot. The voice was Neal's again.

"Sorry to do that, man. But Axle, you gotta
grow up. Now, come on, let's get goin.'"

The motor started and the car moved slowly
now. She could hear the driver's heavy breathing.
High Voice whispered "Pussy" under his breath.

Jill tried counting to herself, to keep track of
where they were going, but the numbers jumbled,
until the minutes could have been seconds, or
hours, or days. They finally stopped. *They were
going to let her go now.*

Neal said, "Get her out."

High Voice grabbed her by the back of the hair
and said, "OK, broad. If you want to go on living,
keep quiet."

She tried to move her numb body but before she
could make her legs cooperate, she was jerked up
and out of the back seat. She felt the skin on her
right arm tear on the door latch. It burned while
thousands of needles pricked her feet as she tried to
stand.

"Walk."

She stumbled on an uneven surface—then felt

concrete or blacktop beneath her feet. Her back-seat companions dragged her along, then in front of her she heard a door open, and she was shoved through it. The room, wherever she was, erupted in an excited mixture of voices.

"Right on, man."

"Good work, troops."

"Cool."

Finally, a female, "Oh shit, not another one."

She recognized Neal's voice, close to her ear, "Shut up, Lucy. You're just jealous."

The voice answered, "Jealous, my ass. Shit, this one looks so high and mighty, she probably don't even have a pussy."

Neal jerked the blindfold off and twisted Jill's face close to his as he said, "Oh, yea, Lucy. They all got pussies. Don't they honey?" Now she knew this was not just a joyride. She threw her head back and screamed. The volume of her own voice frightened her even more and stopped all conversation. Neal's eyes flashed, then he hit her hard across the side of her face.

"You're gonna break my fuckin' eardrums."

She fell to her knees in the center of the huge room. Her breath came in hunks, threatened to choke her as she tried to swallow it. She attempted to focus her eyes to the cold light from large flourescent fixtures overhead.

They were in a large warehouse or garage. Ten or so Fiends and four girls were lounging against two walls on old mattresses and sleeping bags. Their chopper bikes lined a third, one torn apart in the corner. Behind the cycles, an arsenal of pistols, rifles, and shotguns hung on nails from the studding.

Neal pulled her to her feet again and said, "Don't bother with that noise again. There ain't nobody around here to hear you."

Jill tried to appeal to some shred of decency that must be buried in him somewhere.

"Oh, Neal, please. Let me go. I'll never tell anyone."

He only laughed.

She looked around frantic, caught the eye of the one who must be Axle. He was thin, with acne scars. She tried appealing to him. "Please, help me." He concentrated on the floor, his hands shaking at his sides.

Her voice was a wail as she asked Neal, "Why? Why are you doing this to me?"

"For Pappy Mac." They all turned then to look at the heavy man in the corner as Neal continued, "Pappy Mac there, he's our senior citizen. . . . And poor, ol' Pappy, he ain't had any for awhile. . . . Leaseways, nothin' clean." Everyone laughed and Jill took a step backwards before she was stopped by the two men at her sides. They each grabbed an arm and bent them back and high up until she was immobilized by the pain.

The heavy man struggled to get his three hundred or more pounds up from the mattress on the floor. As he lumbered toward her, she swallowed the bile in her mouth. He looked about fifty. His head was shaved and he had a filthy, grey beard. A gold earring dangled from his left earlobe. His bare chest protruding from the Fiend vest was a tangle of black hair, like repulsive graffiti on a wall. A cyclops navel stared at her from the mass of flesh hanging over his low slung jeans. He reached in one pocket as he said, "You're sure pretty as a picture. Been hard all day, just thinkin' about it."

Jill stared at the Poloroid print in his hand. *They were there last night in the trailer*! I'd rather die. No, I have to stay alive for Cody. Try to hypnotize yourself. She fixed her eyes on a spot on the floor until the obese man flicked the blade of his switchblade knife open a few inches from her nose. The pressure on her arms increased as she tried to back away. Her eyes focused unwillingly on the blackheads dotting his nose and cheeks.

His voice gurgled as he said, "Hi, Honey." Jill squeezed her eyes shut. "Oh, come on now. You and me, we gonna have some fun. You like to get it on with ol' Pappy?" He touched the tip of the blade to her mouth. "Nice lips you got there. You like kissin'? Huh? . . . Like kissin' older men?" He shoved his mouth hard against hers, his breath a mixture of halitosis, beer, and cigarettes. As the men pulled her arms tighter, she gagged and Pappy backed off. "What's the matter? I thought you'd love me like you love that fuckin' cowboy of yours." He surveyed the room. The others were lounged back watching the show. He smiled at his audience and asked, "What say we see the merchandise?" They all answered in the affirmative. Jill gasped as he grabbed the hem of her shirt and with one swipe of the knife slit it straight up the middle. His audience clapped and yelled.

Jill recognized the dirty blonde's voice from before.

"Good Christ, look at those little titties. Not worth your effort, Pappy."

He ignored the comment. "Let's get a better view, boys." The two men dropped her arms and pulled the remains of her shirt off, then increased the pressure again. The pain seared and she prayed she would faint.

"Not so bad," Pappy continued. He drew imaginary circles around her nipples with the knife tip. To her horror, they popped out hard and erect.

"Well, would you look at that? She likes me."

Jill spit and screamed, "My God, what are you?" She couldn't control the waves of hysteria and tried to struggle free, even as the pain blinded her.

Grease-encrusted fingers swiped at the man's face, smearing the trickle of her saliva through his grey beard. He snarled now, "We're animals, bitch. Just like you. With a need to breed. . . . So give us a chance. Maybe you'll like it."

Jill tried to concentrate on this morning. The sun, the ocean breeze, the birds, Cody. Oh God, I told him I might go to Irma's, she thought. He won't even be worried about me. She searched the faces in the room for a glimmer of help but they all stared back solemn, waiting. Only Axle refused to meet her eye. His hand still trembled as he took a deep drag from a marijuana cigarette and passed it on.

A red-haired man with a pony tail, to his right,

268

yelled, "Come on, Pappy. Quit keeping us waiting."

The fat man whirled and pointed the knife in the direction of the voice. "Shut up, Carrot. I'm the boss." He turned back to her, "And I like to take my time." He reached for the snap on her jeans and pulled. The zipper rasped open, then popped off its track. She gasped again and screamed.

"You are animals. All of you. Why don't you get it over with. Like the pig you are." Her long hair fell over her face, blotting out the room. But the fat legs moved closer. A hand gathered her hair together in the back of her head and jerked, snapping her neck. The voice was low and mockingly gentle.

"Now honey, that's the fun. Ain't you never been with a real man? . . . A real man, he take his time . . . so you enjoy it." She turned her head away from his acrid breath. He jerked again on her hair to bring it back inches from his face. She was startled by the pale blue of his eyes. My God, they're the same as Cody's.

"I don't like all this long hair. . . . It kinda gets in my way." The room was silent, the audience caught up in the drama of the scene. Pappy noticed it too. "What about the rest of you dudes? Think we should get rid of it?"

Jill struggled to pull away but he held on and brought the knife up under her chin.

"Easy there, easy. . . . This here blade is sharp. . . . I wouldn't want to slip and cut that pretty neck."

Everyone cheered as he pulled a handful of hair

out tight. She could feel the cold metal flat against her right ear. With a quick slice, he cut, then opened his fingers and watched the locks tumble to the floor. He continued hacking until he held the last handful in front of her face. Then as if to remove her last trace of dignity, he rubbed the ends across her nose and cheeks, saying, "There now, that's better isn't it?"

Her tears started and wouldn't stop, tickling and burning the welt where Neal had slapped her.

"Oh pretty lady, don't carry on so." The filthy man wiped at the tears with the wad of hair.

"We can all see that pretty face better now. Can't we?" The crowd laughed.

Then he pulled at her jeans. "Now be a nice girl and just step out of those duds for us."

Jill ran the heel of her shoe down High Voice's shin and kicked helplessly.

"You fuckin' bitch!" The wounded man tightened the pressure on her arm until she was sure it would snap. She hoped again that it would break and send her into unconsciousness.

"Lift your foot now. That's a good girl. Now the other one." Pappy threw the pants to one side and she slumped naked except for her panties. Her guards jerked her upright.

"Well, would you look at the cute lace bikini." She gasped as the cold steel slid under her pants next to the hipbone. The material snapped and the pants fell around her ankles. Naked, terrified, and embarrassed, she started to shake as the crowd erupted with excited conversation. The blonde shouted, "Well, look at that. I'll bet she dyes her hair. Buys a double batch so she can have a snatch to match."

The tip of the knife ran down her midline.

"Oh, I don't know," Pappy said, "Looks gen-u-ine to me. And sweet, baby. . . . Sweet and clean."

The men released her arms and let her slide to the floor. She remembered trying to crawl; her arms heavy weights that collapsed under her. She tried again to crawl, first one way and then the other, a naked caged animal. The room rocked with laughter and catcalls.

"Man, Pappy look at that white ass."

"No freckles on her butt either."

They let her flounder on the cold cement through dirt and metal shavings and her own hair.

Her brain snapped like a lens shutter, open, closed. Armpits reeking with month-old sweat, tattoos, sharp belt buckles. As each of the men took their turn, invading her orifices with vicious indignity, as their secretions smeared and dried on her skin, she tried but couldn't conjure up the memory of Cody, or his gentle love. When Axle whispered, "Sorry. Got to prove myself," her mind cut out, refusing to register anymore.

"Okay, girls, get her cleaned up. Man, she's a sick mess."

The blonde, Lucy, slowly pulled herself up from one of the mattresses and with a black-haired girl came to the center of the room and dragged Jill into a small filthy bathroom. They dropped her on the concrete floor next to a urine-spattered toilet. The dark girl reached for a handle and icy water sprayed from a shower head coming off the wall directly into the room.

"That should wake you up, sweetie."

She thrashed away as the freezing water pummeled her back to life, then she slipped and fell again on the floor. Suddenly the water turned warm and when Jill looked up the two girls were taking off their clothes.

"Pappy said we could have our turn now, Honey. Just as soon as we get you cleaned up." Her eyes burned as they soaped her hair and body. White scum traveled across the floor and into a drain by the toilet. She watched it, numb and unable to fight; a beaten, defiled organism, too soiled for soap and water to ever successfully cleanse.

The blonde grabbed her right breast, at the same time plunging her hand between her legs. "Now us."

The door burst open and Rick was standing there, his face contorted. He jerked the brunette from under the water and said with the same viciousness he'd used with Jody's mother, "Stop it, you dumb cunts. Get her dressed."

Jill found the strength to stand up and fall into his arms. "Oh, Rick. Thank God, thank God."

He shoved her away and left the room.

The girls turned off the water and took turns drying themselves with one grimy towel. When they finished, the blonde tossed it to her and said, "Do the best you can." She went out and came back with a man's undershirt and a pair of ragged cutoff jeans, ordering, "Put these on."

With Jill's will to survive restored by the icy water, she followed the girls, as directed, back into the room, confident now that Rick had arrived to save her. The reassurance when she heard him say to Pappy, "You're a bunch of pigs," changed to terror when the fat man laughed sarcastically and answered, "Well, listen to the beach boy. Killin's OK, but fuckin's not."

Jill opened her eyes to the strong smell of whiskey. Rick, in his usual after-work attire of swim shorts and bare feet, lounged opposite her in the pilot seat of *Sea Maiden*. Only the gun in his hand was alien to his skipper role. The grey metal glowed in the dim light and mesmerized her as effectively as a hypnotist's swinging watch.

"Not a sound out of you, understand?"

Jill realized she was no longer gagged as he continued in a low voice,

"It really doesn't matter though. The fishermen on the dock saw us laughing and joking as we carried an obviously drunk young lady down the pier and onto the boat. . . . So even if you yell now they'll pay no attention. . . . Just think you're coming out of your drunken stupor."

She finally found her voice, asked, "But why, Rick? How could you let those animals do that to me? . . . Why?"

"Because you know about the drugs. They found the package in your car." He paused, his face a handsome blank, then asked, "Are you an undercover narc?" She weighed the possibility that they would be afraid to kill her if she were, then decided no, she better be honest.

"Oh Rick, I'm not. I had even decided you were an innocent bystander. . . . That it was Mr. Ferguson's operation. And I didn't care. I came here to find the girl, Mara, the one I asked you about. . . . And someone called J.D."

His voice was sharp with sudden interest, "Why?"

When she told him about the letter his body sagged and she contemplated and rejected going for the gun.

"My God, Jill, why didn't you explain before? I thought when you asked about Mara you were on to her connection with the Fiends . . . that it had to do with the dope . . . I'm J.D."

"No one else ever called me that. . . . It was a joke with Mara. . . . You know . . . like that rich dude . . . J.D., like J.D. Rockefeller. . . . I loved Mara. But she wanted the world and fast. Couldn't wait for me to get the money together to get this boat business. That's why I got into this drug shit. . . . To get ahead faster. I should have known that once in, I couldn't get out. Then Mara just took off one day. With your father. She wrote me, and I answered, hoping she'd come back. But the last I heard from her she said she had it made, had all the money she needed. Was somewhere in Arizona . . . said something about indians."

Jill tried to keep her voice soft as she pleaded, "Rick, I'll never tell a soul. If you'll just let me go. Please . . . I promise . . . I swear."

His jaw muscles worked and she had an instant

274

of hope before he spoke again, "You know, I really cared for you and I thought if we got together . . . and you weren't a narc . . . everything would work out. But when you went back to that cowboy, there was no other way. The Fiends said you couldn't live. . . . As they say in the flicks, you know too much. . . . So as soon as Neal comes back, we have to take you for a ride."

He spoke of her approaching death without emotion. As if he were telling her the latest weather report. Although terror roared through her, she knew it was hopeless to plead. He had already found it necessary to kill the poor teenage cook before her, and for the same reason. It was incongruous then, for him to apologize for his motorcycle friend's earlier behavior. The repulsive fat man's words rang in her ears. Murder's okay, fuckin's not.

Neither of them expected it. Spotlights blinded them and a voice from a bullhorn blasted into the pilothouse, "This is the police, we have you surrounded."

Jill threw herself down the steps into the main cabin and crawled behind the counter of the galley. The voice continued, "Throw your gun out and come out yourself with your hands behind your head." She knew Rick was in plain view and had nowhere to go. She heard him say under his breath, "Damn you, Mara," and then to her relief the gun made a dull thud on the teak deck.

It was over. She lay sobbing with relief until an officer found her and helped her to her feet. Jill stepped off the boat, amazed that the phalanx of police cars barricading the pier could have come without their seeing or hearing them. Rick still looked like a clean-cut lifeguard, even as he was handcuffed and put into the back of one of the patrol cars. Its red light blinked a farewell.

She answered the lieutenant's questions; he put out an all points bulletin on Neal and sent another army to the Fiend's warehouse. Then she asked him,

"But how did you know to come here?"

"Your boyfriend called when you didn't show up. We checked the shopping center, his place. . . . Then one of our snitches called in . . . we've had this place under surveillance for quite awhile. . . . Anyway, that about wraps it up." He turned to the officer at his side. "The rest of us are going to get out of here. You guys stay and finish up your report . . . and just in case that chopper clown should show up."

"Oh, my God, Cody . . . I have to call him."

The officer reached in his pocket and handed her a dime. "Over there, ma'am." She ran for the phone booth as all but one car drove slowly off the pier.

She watched the denim tighten against one thigh and then the other as the figure emerged from the darkness into the grotesque green fluorescent light from above. Even as he sprinted closer the western boots made surprisingly little sound on the weathered planks of the pier.

"Cody!"

She ran too, ignoring the pain the rough surface inflicted on the soles of her bare feet. When she was near enough to hear his galloping breath and see the relief loosen the tightness of his jaws, when she was almost in his arms; the night exploded with a burst from behind, a sound made more strident by its effect.

His mouth had no time to even speak her name. Jill was sucked into the loud gasp, along with the rest of the unspoken words. The blue eyes registered surprise—then filled with a soul-seering fear; knees buckled and his body began a slow motion battle with gravity. The splash of red, like the beginning of an abstactionist's painting, grew bolder and more brilliant as if determined to eradicate the plaid pattern on the front of the shirt.

The instinct of self preservation threw her to the ground. Splinters grated into her cheeks and arms and knees as she crawled and clawed her way over the ten feet of separation. She gathered him to her, brushed a wayward lock of hair from his forehead.

The shouts and running softened to whispers as she held his head close in her lap like that first day he'd taken her to their mountaintop.

"Sing, Cowboy," she whimpered over and over, "please sing for me."

A hand tugged at her arm.

"Oh my God, why didn't he stop when I yelled, 'Halt'. I thought . . . I thought he was. . . . Please, Ma'am. Let go of him. I radioed for the paramedica but let me see what I can do."

The first wave of reverse peristalsis began and each successive contraction grew stronger, until the contents of her stomach—the undigested remnants of their candlelight dinner—spewed onto the dock, then oozed and dripped, along with her hope, through the cracks to the ocean below.

When she looked up, surprised to see moisture threatening to spill from the rookie cop's eyes, the blinding flash exploded in her face.

"I got it! I got it! This one will make the front page of every page in the country."

The scream began deep in a black, inner caldron and, like a bubbling witch's brew, increased in volume until it finally boiled over and died in the light of truth. The abrupt silence that followed was the most fearsome of all as it delivered its undeniable message.

*You're alone, Jill. You're alone again.*


The service was simple. The band played two of his favorite songs and Billy Joe said a few words before he broke down and couldn't go on. Jill remained dry-eyed through it all, even when an overzealous reporter jerked the scarf from her head so the shorn locks could be photographed for national T.V. The crowd outside, a mix of fans, newsmen, and curiosity seekers, pushed and shouted against the police lines as they exited to their cars. She saw the toothless fisherman among them and noticed he was crying. He waved but she didn't respond.

Everyone wanted her to stay. Billy Joe said he would take Dude and she could bed down at his house for as long as she wanted. Jody begged her to move in and share her room. Janice offered her a room of her own. But she asked B.J. to take her to her car.

She drove into Santa Monica to a sporting goods store and replaced her stolen camping gear. The cashier said "Have a good day," when she paid the bill.

A fog came in, and as Jill drove up Coast Highway she couldn't see much beyond the breakers, but as she turned and climbed higher, the sun came out again. She drove up the lane and parked behind the trailer. It looked lonely now on its concrete slab setting. She walked around to the front and picked up the rake. The gardens were neat and free of weeds but she smoothed them anyway. Clipped off a few faded roses. She sat down and thought about the first time they had made love—right here. Today she couldn't see the islands, just a sad, grey haze. A funeral shroud. Jill put the rake back in its place and left the way she'd come. As she turned onto the main road, she said goodby to Heartbreak Hill. It had never given anyone happiness for long. She stopped and looked at her map, then in a vacuum, found her way through the Los Angeles freeway system and oblivious to the chlorine smell and brown horizon passed through San Bernadino and Pomona and on into the Mohave desert. Scrub growth flashed by and the landscape continued to widen, making her feel more alone. The light traffic on the highway was invisible as the car motor repeated over and over, "You're alone again . . . you're alone again . . . you're . . . ." She drove until after dark, then pulled into a rest stop and unrolled the new sleeping bag. The motor of the huge truck parked beside her, kept running to preserve its refrigerated cargo, took up where the Pinto left off. Alone again, alone again. The hypnotic repetition granted her sleep.

The next morning she stopped in a small store, bought some food and asked directions to the Colorado River. The clerk, a young boy, said, "There's campgrounds down about a mile."

Remembering the night she'd left Cody, she said, "No."

"Well," he said, "If you want to camp alone, turn left at the power lines. There's a dirt road. Just follow it awhile and you'll see the water. But watch out if it looks like rain. We have flash floods sometimes and you could end up floatin' out in the middle."

Jill thanked him and followed his directions. She pulled the Pinto under a small tree and got out to look around. The sand was coarse and dry, nourishing enough for only the hardiest of vegetation. She took an apple from the icechest and walked to the edge of the water. Small rocks covered the shoreline and hurt her feet as she waded into the cold, ankle-deep water. Its temperature was a shocking contrast to the 100-plus desert air, but swimmable, she decided. She finished the apple and stripped off her clothes. The first dive reminded her of the Fiend's shower and she began to cry. The trance-like vacuum of the last two days split wide, spilling its collection of horrors as she swam far out into the river. Icy ripples nipped at her as she turned over onto her back and floated. Jet streams crossed the universe above her like a giant child's scribbling with a white crayon on blue paper. If I just lie back and quit paddling, she thought, I'll sink and be gone. No one will care. But as she tried it, as the cold water filled her mouth and then her nose, self preservation won out. She flipped over, thrashing and sputtering. She paddled furiously to keep her head up while she coughed the water from her lungs. Now panicked, she wondered if she could make it back to shore. Be calm, side stroke, rest.

After what seemed an eternity, she looked around but her car seemed no closer than before. Her nude body was chilled and each stroke was an effort. The sun was dropping at an alarming rate toward the hills behind her; now she knew she had to make it and willed herself to continue. Just one more, just one more. Finally, too drowsy to care anymore, she stopped her movements, content to sink into a hypothermic dream. Her foot kicked the rough bottom and she crawled onto the beach. She laid exhausted, her body numb to the sharp stones or evening chill, until a rebirth of terror vibrated through her and she raised her head.

At first she thought it was Dude standing by her car. But then she realized it was a coyote, a female, large and well fed. She froze and stared hard into Jill's eyes, then turned and unhurriedly trotted off into the bushes. She reappeared again, high on a bluff overlooking the cove, stopped for an instant and looked back then disappeared over the other side. Jill dragged herself to her feet, her body icy and covered with goosebumps. As she walked to the car for a towel and some clothes she began to laugh. It became hysterical, making her sides and stomach hurt. "I'm not alone," she said aloud. As she reached into the back seat, she realized the coyote had tried to rob her. The plastic latch on her new ice chest was covered with teeth marks. A few more minutes and it would have been open. Jill dressed quickly and gathered driftwood, made a fire ring of boulders and started a fire. She stood close to the flame until her jeans were too hot to touch. Then she heated a can of beans and ate the first meal she'd had in two days. She poured a small amount back into the can and carried it up the dry wash just out of the light from the fire. She had a great urge to share her meal with her solitary visitor. She dragged her sleeping bag out of the back seat and spread it next to the fire with her feet closest since they were still cold. The night was dark, without a moon, but the milky way stroked a path overhead and the larger planets reflected in the mirror smooth water of the cove. She slept without dreaming and woke to the still grey dawn. The fire smoked weakly but rose quickly to devour added tinder and then a larger log. She hurried up the wash and was delighted to see the tin can had disappeared. She peered in all directions at the cliffs around her but there was no sign of the coyote.

Jill stayed three days, with one twenty-four hour period drifting into the next as she sorted out her thoughts. She longed for Cody, felt guilty for their fights, remembered every word he'd said to her, she to him. Every touch, every smile, his voice, his songs.

She caught a fish on the rod her father had given her. It was under the front seat and had been overlooked by the thief. As she brought the small trout in over the rocks, it rolled panicked eyes and made a soft croaking sound. She wet her hand, like her father had taught her and took it gently off the hook, then put her hand in the water and released it. The fish lay still for just an instant, then flicked its tail and disappeared into the depth of the river. Its eyes had looked too much like Jody's that morning on the boat.

Jill cleaned her stove and put it away. She opened the ice chest and took out what remained of her food supplies. A piece of cheese, some salami, two eggs. She carried them to the same spot where she'd left the beans. She wished she would see her hostess again. After all, this was the coyote's home, she was only a guest.

With that in mind, she packed everything into her car, scattered the rocks from the fire ring, and scooped sand and pebbles over the ashes. The cove looked the same as the day she'd come. Jill drove out to the main highway and turned left. She knew where she was going. The burning intensity was back and growing stronger. She would start with Flagstaff. To find Mara and her indians.

# ASTROLOGY
# FOR THE WÖRKING GIRL
## By Paige McKenzie

PRICE: $1.95 BT51467
CATEGORY: Non-fiction

In this practical guide, Paige McKenzie combines her extensive business experience, her knowledge of astrology and her good humor to help the career woman understand relationships between recognized Sun Signs and a host of personal and career problems. And she offers specific ways for dealing with conflicts, and such specific problems as: When is the best time to make a job switch?

# DESTINY'S DAUGHTER
## By Frances Noble

PRICE: $2.25 BT 51462
CATEGORY: Historical Romance (original)

Esmee d'Espey is the illegitimate daughter of Queen Catherine de Medici. Beautiful, spirited, and unaware of the royal blood that flows in her veins, Esmee comes to the court of Queen Catherine to seek her fortune. Both Princess Charlotte and Esmee fall in love with the rugged Henri de Conde, leader of the Huguenot forces. Amid the opulence and intrigue of the French court, Esmee is plunged into a life of luxury, excitement, disappointment and heartache as she struggles to win the love of the one man who will never be hers alone!

# CHOICES
## Corinne Gerson

PRICE: $1.75 BT51476
CATEGORY: Novel (original)

On a business trip to London with her physician husband, Nancy Loomis meets a handsome Englishman and suddenly finds herself swept up in a passionate love affair. Nothing could be more surprising—more exciting—nor more frightening. Then, when it seems all the decisions of her life have been made, Nancy is faced with a whole new world of possibilities—and the eternal question: Does it take more courage to go on or to turn back?

**SEND TO:** **TOWER PUBLICATIONS**
**P.O. BOX 270**
**NORWALK, CONN. 06852**

## PLEASE SEND ME THE FOLLOWING TITLES:

| Quantity | Book Number | Price |
|----------|-------------|-------|
|          |             |       |
|          |             |       |
|          |             |       |
|          |             |       |
|          |             |       |

### IN THE EVENT THAT WE ARE OUT OF STOCK ON ANY OF YOUR SELECTIONS, PLEASE LIST ALTERNATE TITLES BELOW:

|   |   |   |
|---|---|---|
|   |   |   |
|   |   |   |
|   |   |   |

Postage/Handling

I enclose...

**FOR U.S. ORDERS,** add 50c for the first book and 10c for each additional book to cover cost of postage and handling. Buy five or more copies and we will pay for shipping. Sorry, no C.O.D.'s.

**FOR ORDERS SENT OUTSIDE THE U.S.A.,** add $1.00 for the first book and 25c for each additional book. PAY BY foreign draft or money order drawn on a U.S. bank, payable in U.S. ($) dollars.

☐ **PLEASE SEND ME A FREE CATALOG.**

**NAME**_____
(Please print)

**ADDRESS**_____

**CITY**_____ **STATE**_____ **ZIP**_____

**Allow Four Weeks for Delivery**